The Carriage Rocked Twice...

※※※※※※※※※※※※※

then settled on its side. The horses were quiet; snow sprinkled into the carriage, and Emma dared not move. First, she could hear nothing but the pounding of her heart. Then she became aware of Mr. Wister.

"Miss Fraser, you're shaking like a leaf. Are you sure you're not injured?"

"Yes, quite certain. It is nothing more than a shock, I suppose," she managed, all the more discomposed by the feel of his hand moving about her arms and legs, checking for broken limbs.

"Here," he said, turning slightly and rearranging the blankets. "I believe it would be better if we shared a blanket."

"Share a blanket?" she barely got out, her trembling worse with each passing second.

"Yes. Under the circumstances, I'd be less a gentleman if I didn't do everything within my power to make you as comfortable as possible."

In the next second, he had slipped his arm beneath the blanket and wrapped it about her shoulder so that her head was cradled against him.

A comforting, woodsy male scent curled round her, and at length, Emma's quaking subsided.

"Ah, Emma."

"Yes?" she whispered.

In the next instant his lips were upon hers.

※※※※※※※※※※※※※

Also by Nancy Richards-Akers

The Mayfair Season
Philadelphia Folly

Published by
WARNER BOOKS

ATTENTION: SCHOOLS AND CORPORATIONS

WARNER books are available at quantity discounts with bulk purchase for educational, business, or sales promotional use. For information, please write to: SPECIAL SALES DEPARTMENT, WARNER BOOKS, 666 FIFTH AVENUE, NEW YORK, N.Y. 10103.

**ARE THERE WARNER BOOKS
YOU WANT BUT CANNOT FIND IN YOUR LOCAL STORES?**

You can get any WARNER BOOKS title in print. Simply send title and retail price, plus 50¢ per order and 50¢ per copy to cover mailing and handling costs for each book desired. New York State and California residents add applicable sales tax. Enclose check or money order only, no cash please, to: WARNER BOOKS, P.O. BOX 690, NEW YORK, N.Y. 10019.

A Season Abroad

NANCY RICHARDS-AKERS

WARNER BOOKS

A Warner Communications Company

WARNER BOOKS EDITION

Copyright © 1988 by Nancy Richards-Akers
All rights reserved.

Warner Books, Inc.
666 Fifth Avenue
New York, N.Y. 10103

A Warner Communications Company

Printed in the United States of America

First Printing: October, 1988

10 9 8 7 6 5 4 3 2 1

For all those who have ever faced the dilemma:
What does one do when the heart says one thing
and common sense says another?

CHAPTER
ONE

July 1817, England
"Slow your 'orses!" Jem Hawley hollered from his perch atop the coachman's box.

But the driver of an oncoming curricle, singing a raucous ditty with his foppish companions, did not hear the frantic coachman.

Jem Hawley tugged sharply on the reins, turning the stately barouche-and-four from the path of the recklessly driven vehicle. A glistening sheen of sweat broke out across his face as he comprehended the true extent of the wild goings-on in the narrow byways of Brickhill. Literally hundreds of carriages, carts, and wagons had converged on the village for the event that the London odds-makers had dubbed the Wager of the Decade. Rumor claimed that more than two hundred thousand pounds was at stake; fortunes could be won or lost in a matter of minutes. Here, social rank held no sway, and sporting men of every ilk, from the toniest dandies to the lowliest denizens of dismal factory townships, were crushed cheek to jowl, behaving in an excessively boisterous fashion. Jem pushed back his hat to swipe at the moisture on his brow and cast a nervous backward glance at the young mistress.

A slender young lady in a green walking gown ornamented with black braid and gilt buttons, a matching parasol furled and resting by her side, was sedately poised on the velvet-covered passenger seat. Sitting erect as a school matron, she appeared unruffled by the scene that grew less civil with each passing moment.

The coachman shook his head as he tried to maneuver four frightened horses through the crowd. 'Twas a good thing someone could remain calm in the midst of this pandemonium, he thought as another bout of fisticuffs erupted to the right-hand side of the vehicle. Deftly, Jem veered away from the rowdy clutch of bosky dandies.

Hadn't he been telling Miss Emma it was only Bedlamites who'd venture to Brickhill on an afternoon when Bill Neate was scheduled to fight the Belcher? And wouldn't the earl be raking Jem over the coals for driving Miss Emma out when he knew well and good that a boxing match was no place for a proper bred lady of Quality? But Jem Hawley did not have fingers and toes enough to count the number of times he had overheard the earl lecture Miss Emma to stop, think twice, and look before she leaped. It was not that the young miss was headstrong or defiant, 'twas merely a case of an overly forthright nature and not enough common sense. This venture into Brickhill was one of those leaps without a look, and the only good thing for it was that the earl himself had come to Brickhill earlier in the day. Now if only that tiger would find the earl and fetch him to the carriage before there was an accident, or worse, one of them bucks recognized Miss Emma. The earl would never forgive Jem if there were any scandalous whisperings about the young miss.

The object of the coachman's concern, although presenting an implacable facade of tranquility, was more than slightly discomposed by the surrounding fracas. Miss Emma Fraser of Upper Brook Street, Mayfair, and Heather House, Argyll, had never seen worse, not even the time Uncle Torquil had permitted her to ride along to a cockfight on the Isle of Dogs. Then she had not had to suffer lewd stares, for Uncle Torquil had disguised her in a great cape and set a boyish cap upon her head of coppery curls; then she had not had to turn a deaf ear on language she knew was suited only to a brothel, for one hard stare from her uncle and the boldest of men would toe the line of propriety; then she had not felt in the least bit of danger, for Uncle Torquil had kept her a secure distance from the riffraff milling about that musty warehouse.

This immediate situation was vastly different; Emma's apprehension was not unfounded. Crude sorts were all about her, jostling the carriage and making every manner of outrageous remark as they passed.

" 'Ows about a wee bit of the ol' in-an'-out?'' cajoled a man, who appeared not to have the vaguest familiarity with soap and water. He leered at Emma revealing a row of jagged yellow teeth, and Emma, having the distinct impression that he had made a very improper and equally personal proposition, blushed to the roots of her coppery curls and raised her pretty chin in ladylike disdain. The man emitted a drunken guffaw and passed on, but the worst of Emma's trials and tribulations was yet to come.

Of a sudden, a well-dressed gentleman of more than ordinary dimensions, his intricately arranged cravat sadly wilted, stumbled out of the crowd and fell against the barouche. Endeavoring to regain his balance, the portly personage groped about Emma's ankle.

One whiff told Emma he was extremely foxed. "Heavens!" she exclaimed in outrage, placing the fringed willow green parasol between the offending hand and her ankle.

"Your pardon, m'lady," the gentlemen slurred as he raised his head. Blinking twice, his eyes narrowed and then widened at the sight of the green-eyed female seated in the expensive barouche. He fixed a look of blatant admiration on Emma and regarded her like a starving hound about to pounce on a juicy bone. On a hiccough he retracted his previous words, "M'lady, indeed. Ain't no lady b'fore m'eyes. 'Tis a lady... *bird*. And who might y'be, m'lovely ladybird?"

Repulsed, Emma pressed against the back of the seat. Ladybird, indeed! She knew what the man meant and barely resisted the overwhelming urge to thwack him with her parasol.

" 'Ere now," barked Jem with a flick of his whip. "Off wiv you! Don't be botherin' the young miss."

But the stout gentleman did not heed the coachman; instead, he attempted to climb into the seat beside Emma. Puffing and panting, his face taking on a hue of the brightest carmine, he managed to land himself on the floor of the carriage, his short legs dangling over the side, his head lolling against the opposite seat.

Emma was conscious of a heightening of color in her face. She stiffened and lifted her chin even higher. This was beyond the bounds of all mortification. Emma had never been so offended, and she knew her uncle would be livid with rage if he witnessed this. She glanced desperately at the portly gentleman and then toward the clamorous throng that was beginning to center its attention on Emma and the uninvited occupant in her carriage.

"Please, sir, remove your person from my carriage this instant! We wish to pass," she stated with the hauteur of a grand duchess. Despite an unsettling nervous twinge in the region of her stomach, she managed to pin him with a wholly indignant eye.

Still the gentleman did not budge. Truth to tell, he appeared on the verge of a fit of some sort.

"Is my uncle anywhere in sight?" Emma asked Jem, a touch of panic creeping into her voice.

The coachman scanned the crowd and shook his head. "Don't see hide nor hair of the earl, Miss Emma."

With no previous warning, a deafening roar of cheers rose from the far end of the roadway. Instinctively, Emma's gloved hands clutched the parasol handle; she was beginning to regret sincerely her decision to come to Brickhill. The crowd pressed forward like a great army determined to annihilate whatever lay in its path. Terrified animals nickered as the rabble scrambled for a better view. Men of rank hung from the uppermost branches of trees alongside flash-house felons, they scaled dangerously aged walls and even perched on the roof of a nearby cottage.

"What is it, Jem?" she asked, poking her parasol at the persistent gentleman whose left hand continued to stray toward her ankles. "Really, sir," she hissed determinedly, "you must leave this carriage at once!"

The crowd roared with renewed vigor.

Jem stood. "Appears the pugilists are arriving, Miss Emma. Bill Neate's the favored 'un, miss," he enthused, quite forgetting that his first duty was to the young mistress and the earl. Absorbed in the unfolding drama, he craned his neck to the left, then to the right. "Swathed in a great golden brown cloak, he be, and smilin' broad as a lad afore Twelfth Night. Just threw his hat in the ring, miss, all cheerful-loike, and he's takin' a bow."

At this spectacle, the crowd took up a chant. The precise meaning of the words was impossible to discern, but whatever was being said, Emma deduced the fight had commenced. To her horror, two rowdies hoisted themselves onto the carriage wheels of her barouche as the portly gentleman belched in a thoroughly revolting manner. Emma shuddered.

Would they ever leave this place in one piece? she wondered, her last shred of fortitude deserting her. *I'll never ever do anything again without asking Uncle Torquil. I promise. I'll always think twice, and I'll listen to Uncle Torquil and Jem and Lady Wheatley. I promise.*

In desperation, Emma prayed for one more chance to prove to her guardian that she could indeed be the proper young lady he wished her to be. If only they could depart from Brickhill without incident, she would, from this moment onward, do everything her uncle wished, including becoming betrothed before this Season was out and marrying the gentleman by Christmas. But how were they to escape this pandemonium before disaster befell them? She would never find a husband if she were maimed in a riot, for no man wanted a crippled wife. Oh, what was she to do?

As if in response to her silent plea, a smooth voice accented with the melody of a foreign drawl broke through the hubbub. "Might I be of some assistance, my lady?"

Emma swiveled, her straightforward gaze coming to rest on an exceedingly tall gentleman clothed in buckskin breeches and a mulberry coat. Despite his distinctly American drawl, his fine features were very British, and his authoritative bearing was undeniably aristocratic. Chiseled cheekbones, a high-bridged nose, and firm mouth gracing a lean, bronzed face gave him the unique distinction of possessing a rare and thoroughly masculine beauty. His hair, where it fell from beneath his tall hat to skim the collar of a blindingly white shirt, was a shimmering blue-black. But it was his eyes that captured Emma's notice, deep-set blue eyes placed squarely in the middle of that tanned face. She had never seen such unusual eyes. They reminded her of ink when the powder first mixes with water and the dark navy in the center of the inkwell fades to a paler blue about the edges. Tiny lines flared out from those eyes, an indication he spent a significant amount of time out-of-doors. Unable to prevent herself, Emma marveled at the handsome gentleman, while for his part, the young gentleman did not remove those fascinating eyes from Emma.

Jeremy Wister, Philadelphia born and bred, but recently the inheritor of the title Earl of Cadogan, had spied the slender auburn-haired beauty when her carriage negotiated past his bosky companions. That brief glimpse of her face, peeking from beneath a stylish hat of moss silk, left him wanting another. Creamy cheeks delicately flushed, full lips as pretty as ripe plums, and green cat's-eyes with auburn brows winging exotically above their engaging brightness were enough to entice any healthy male. None of the simpering misses who had paraded before him at Almack's held a candle to her beauty. There was natural spirit in the proud tilt of her head and in the way her eyes flashed defiantly at the drunken fop who dared to trespass in her carriage. Jeremy could not resist a closer look at so special a lady.

He repeated his offer of assistance and watched in amusement as she struggled to shake herself free of his speculative gaze.

Emma bent her head downward to disguise the girlish blush she could not prevent rising in her cheeks. She had spent nearly half her life in the company of gentlemen as she was a constant companion of her bachelor uncle and his friends; heretofore, she had never been uncomfortable in the presence of the opposite sex, and yet, she was unaccountably out of sorts in this stranger's presence. Indicating the unwanted passenger who had commenced moaning in a most ominous tenor, she replied forthrightly, "I believe this gentleman ought to join his friends posthaste."

The handsome man made a courtly bow after which he tipped his hat and smiled warmly at Emma. "Your wish is my command, my lady. But if that is the most you demand of me, my male pride has suffered a wounding blow, and I shall consider myself a poor man, indeed, for I would gladly perform any service you asked," he concluded gallantly.

Peeking up at him from beneath the brim of her bonnet, Emma caught her breath. The effect of his smile when coupled with his low, resonant drawl was devastating; it caused a most extraordinary and entirely unexpected thing to transpire. For the very first time in her eighteen years, Miss Emma Fraser's heart somersaulted with what could be naught but the pangs of romance. Confusion prevailed upon her, and again, she dipped her head until she was sheltered safely in the depths of her bonnet, feeling for the first time fully and unaccountably shy. She longed to return his friendly smile, but dared not, for suddenly, this man with ink-blue eyes and a friendly smile unsettled Miss Emma Fraser more than the motley crowd that surrounded her.

"Thank you, sir. Your timely intervention is most appreciated," she responded in a surprisingly sedate voice, offering him the demurest nod.

Obligingly, the gentleman hoisted the stout fellow off the floor of the carriage and propelled him toward his cronies. In the next instant, the barouche lurched forward, the rowdies tumbled off the wheels, and Emma lost sight of the blue-eyed gentleman. Without thinking, she raised her hand to wave farewell, and as he was swallowed up by the throng of spectators, Emma experienced a wholly unexpected disappointment that she had not learned his name.

A few yards down the teeming lane, Jem brought the vehicle to a halt. He yelled out, "There be the earl, miss, comin' this way roight now. Don't you worry none, we'll be 'eaded 'ome in the flick of a lamb's tail."

A scowling gentleman—whose fine tailored clothes and athletic posture heralded him a Corinthian of the first degree—was striding rapidly toward the gleaming black barouche. Emma saw her uncle and relief flooded her countenance.

"Holy ghost, Emma Margaret!" Torquil Hamilton, the Earl of Gairloch, bounded into the seat beside his niece and ward of eight years.

"Oh, Uncle Torquil—"

"I ought to ship you off to Botany Bay on a voyage of improvement!" he berated vehemently, severe scowl lines settling across his forehead.

"But—"

"Whatever maggot possessed you to venture forth to a boxing match?"

Emma disregarded this cranky question and flung her arms about her dear uncle's broad shoulders. "I'm so relieved you've found us!"

He extricated himself from Emma's hold, took off his beaver hat, and ran lanky fingers through raffishly full golden brown hair. "Well, yes, of course," he muttered as his initial wrath faded and he observed Emma's genuine distress.

"I was beginning to despair of ever seeing you again. What a splendid sight you are!" she declared with a charming smile.

Torquil Hamilton, not to be placated by his niece's artless display of contrition, visited a frown of displeasure upon her. "Speak up, Emma. Have you a plausible excuse for such untoward behavior?"

In her eagerness to set matters right, an explanation spilled out of Emma. "Oh, I know 'twas shockingly havey-cavey of me, but there was not a thing to do at the town house, and I was merely hoping for a wee bit of amusement. At the time, I didn't think it such a dreadful notion." She pursed her lips in a plaintive pout. "Coming to Brickhill seemed precisely the thing. I never imagined there would be such disorder. 'Tisn't a bit like the time you took me to Hungerford with Sir Nigel and Gentleman Jim."

At the reminder of that outing, remorse pinched the earl's handsome features. To think that he had once been insane enough to take a schoolgirl on an excursion to a prize fighting match was positively disgraceful! Torquil studied the exquisite young lady beside him and sighed. He adored his niece and deeply regretted such an asinine whim as deeply as he regretted the numerous other misguided decisions he had made about Emma's upbringing.

Soberly, he said, "How wrong I was, Emma, to believe I could take a child gallivanting with me from horse sales to sparring matches and all manner of games of chance. What I was thinking, I'll never know. Look at you! Quite the loveliest miss on Town this Season, but no more prepared for the marriage mart than I. Yet find you a husband we must, for I'll not countenance anyone saying Miss Emma Fraser of Heather House, Argyll, is on the shelf."

"Pray, dearest uncle, don't blame yourself. You've done nothing wrong." Affectionately, Emma took one of his hands in hers and stared at the man who had been her only living relative for more than eight years. In the summer of her ninth year, Emma's papa had died with her mama while boating on the loch, and it had seemed a miracle to the lonesome, grieving child when her dashing Uncle Torquil had come and fetched her. At first, Emma had found it strange to travel from one party to another by her uncle's side, but soon she came to adore Torquil Hamilton and his jovial friends. What child of ten would not adore a life of constant fox hunts and curricle races, visits to Vauxhall, the opera, and Astley's Circus, and several jaunts to the Continent? "You acted out of naught but love, dear uncle, and there's nothing wrong in that."

"Nothing wrong?" he asked, again threading lean fingers through a thick mane of sun-warmed brown hair. "Nothing wrong in dragging you off to Paris because I'd mortally wounded a man in a duel? Nothing wrong in forcing you to endure my years of exile? Or allowing you to dress as a lad and accompany me and some of the hardest rogues in the kingdom to Vauxhall? Nothing wrong in teaching you to ride astride like a hoyden, and to handle a pistol with more skill than half the crack shots at Manton's? I ought to have left you in Argyll in the keeping of a good strict nanny. Ought to have sent you off to a boarding school with girls your own age and ought to have given full and thoughtful consideration to your future long before this summer."

"You did what you thought best," she said, her Highland lilt ringing with conviction. Despite the years in the company of her uncle and his notorious friends, and despite the long list of untoward skills she had honed, Emma remained remarkably innocent. She never realized the true vocation of the ladies at Vauxhall, nor the unfortunate reason for their midnight sail across the Channel. Her uncle's friends were kind and honest and generous, and it did not occur to Emma that anything more than simple honesty and goodness of heart assayed the quality of a person's character. When Emma saw Torquil Hamilton, she did not see the dangerous rakehell so many women pursued, husbands feared, and mamas kept from their unspoiled daughters. She saw only the dear man who had made a place for her in his heart and life, the dear man who had kept his promise to a weeping child in a graveyard. "I'll never leave you, Emma," he had vowed, and she loved him fiercely for his devotion and caring. An unaffected laugh bubbled forth from Emma. "And what fun we had! You made those years positively glorious. I wouldn't trade my childhood for all the eligible beaux in Mayfair. For, I warrant, a gentleman wouldn't be worth the paper he might sign his name upon, if he let so small a thing as my unconventional childhood cloud his opinion of me."

A weary sadness clung to the earl's next words. "Emma, you must believe me when I tell you 'tis far too easy a thing for one's reputation to be tarnished beyond repair. Circumstances far less formidable than the color of a gown have been known to ruin a lassie's chances on the marriage mart. I am bound and determined to prevent that from happening to you. By the by, where is Lady Wheatley?" asked Torquil, referring to the widow who had fallen on reduced circumstances and whom the earl had engaged to tutor Emma in the finer points of being a lady.

"I've not been shirking my lessons, nor did I abandon the sweet lady to the mob. Fear not, Lady Wheatley is safely ensconced in her chambers at Upper Brook Street enjoying a well earned rest. She provided me an entire morning's worth of lessons in water coloring and flower arranging. Two attributes she vows shall guarantee that I rise above the commonplace on the marriage mart."

"Flower arranging, you say?" Torquil interjected on a chuckle.

"Pray don't laugh, for sadly, 'tis the only womanly skill at which I've the least bit of talent."

The earl stifled his amusement. "Lady Wheatley seems to think 'tis a wifely attribute, does she?"

"Yes, sir, which brings me in a rather roundabout fashion to the second reason why I thought 'twas a prodigiously clever notion to travel to Brickhill."

"It does? Does it?" he inquired cautiously.

Giving a nod, russet red curls bobbing about her heart-shaped face, Emma elaborated, "It seemed to make excellent sense that if you wish me to meet young gentlemen, there could be no more advantageous place than this. What better way to see a gentleman's true colors than where he can be at his leisure?"

A wry grin settled upon Torquil's countenance. Yes, Emma was a most uncommon female, and if it were not for the fact that no one save himself and his chums who had known Emma since she was a wee lassie could appreciate her startling tendency to approach matters in this thoroughly direct and unpretentious fashion, he would be excessively proud of the woman she was becoming. Torquil placed a high value on being straightforward and honest, but Lady Wheatley had assured him those were not attributes most men welcomed in a prospective bride. Apparently, an erect carriage and graceful walk, a sweet voice and amiable temperament, plus a modicum of skill at flower arranging were qualities that measured a lady's suitability.

"Of course, my logic was dreadfully flawed," Emma hastened to amend. "This was no place to look for a suitable husband. Why, I've never seen such a ramshackle lot. There's not a man in the entire district I'd call a gentleman save you and my rescuer."

"Your rescuer?" Every paternal instinct was manifest in the earl's suddenly anxious voice.

"Yes. He was a tall man, almost as tall as you, and speaking with the strangest drawl. Faith, I believe he was an American."

"An American?" The earl's gaze narrowed. The only Americans he knew were brash and randy adventurers. "Didn't offend you in any way, did he?"

Emma laughed. "Of course not. Truth to tell, he's the only one who hasn't since I embarked on this ill-fated excursion." Observing the tension in her uncle's face, Emma checked herself before relating the tale of the inebriated fop who had collapsed on the carriage floor. Her dear uncle's only fault was a fierce temper, and although she loathed doing so, some wiser instinct counseled her to merely state, "The gentleman helped to keep the rabble at bay."

"I'm grateful there was someone of sound mind to see to you. Hope you did your best to comport yourself as Lady Wheatley would have liked. Wouldn't want to hear your name bandied about at White's."

Emma patted his hand. "Let's not go over that again, Uncle Torquil. You worry overmuch."

"Worry overmuch, you say? Nay, Emma, a lady can never be too cautious when her reputation is involved, for once maligned, 'tis near impossible to prove the gossip ill-founded."

The raw emotion in his voice stunned Emma. She had never heard her uncle speak so reflectively. It was almost as if he were in pain. With a reassuring smile, she promised, "Fear not, Uncle Torquil. I'll make you proud of me."

"I'm already proud, puss." He dropped a brotherly kiss on the tip of her nose.

"Then why the lessons and the lectures?" she asked in bewilderment.

"Because I want you happy and wed to a proper gentleman."

She grimaced. "My happiness depends on marriage?"

"To a certain extent, yes. Marriage may not guarantee happiness, but without it what does one have but a lifetime of loneliness? I would not wish that for you, puss. You deserve the best." He paused and stared over Emma's shoulder, a faraway look in his eyes. At length, he concluded, "Ultimately, I wish you to be free from gossip. Marriage to a gentleman of rank and impeccable reputation should ensure that."

Following those astounding words, the earl fell silent, crossed his arms over his chest, and closed his eyes. Emma studied the lines about his eyes and mouth and wondered if he was lonely. Was that why he had sounded so maudlin? The thought had never occurred to her before, for Torquil Hamilton was always in the company of a gay group of ladies and gentleman, always on his way to another rout or hurrying home from an evening at Watier's or Boodle's with his friends.

She heaved a meaningful sigh. It did not seem possible that he was lonely. Or was it? Mayhap Uncle Torquil was talking about that strange hollow ache she had begun to feel of late. It had come upon her only twice, but it was a sensation she could not forget, sort of like being very hungry at the end of a long journey. The oddest thing was that Emma could not put her finger on what caused it to occur. All she knew was that it left her with the distinct feeling that something was missing in her life. But that was silly, wasn't it? She had Uncle Torquil and Lady Wheatley and a growing circle of acquaintances, and every moment of every day was replete with activities. Again she sighed. What did she really know about being grown-up? Nothing.

There was much she did not understand, and it seemed the more she did comprehend of the world, the more unanswered questions there were to perplex her. Leaving Uncle Torquil and getting married was one of those confusing things.

Until recently, Emma had always assumed she would never leave Uncle Torquil; now he wanted nothing more than to see her married. At first, the thought of separation from her uncle had been unimaginable, but if it would please him to see her wed, Emma decided she would do so. But whom she would marry, Emma could not fathom, for she had never met a gentleman suited to the task. Unlike other girls her age, she had never been in love, yet long ago Emma had made up her mind about the sort of gentleman she would like for her husband, and she would not settle for less. Of course, he would be like Uncle Torquil and her papa. He would be a Corinthian, an outdoorsman, a soldier, an honorable and loving man who did not judge others on pretense, but would, as Torquil had always taught Emma, search below the surface for the true person inside.

On the outskirts of Brickhill, Emma pivoted in the seat for one final glance at the mayhem. To her surprise, she discovered herself straining for a sight of the blue-eyed gentleman, and her thoughts wandered back to the moment when he had doffed his hat and smiled so warmly. That had been the strangest thing, she reflected, the way her heart had soared upward only to spiral downward like a Roman candle. Never before had she blushed like a schoolgirl in any gentleman's presence, nor had any gentleman made her feel as lightheaded and peculiar as the stranger had done. And never before had she given any gentleman a second thought. Strangely, she found herself wondering about that blue-eyed American. A thousand little questions came to mind, the foremost of which was: When would she see him again?

CHAPTER
TWO

Four mornings later found Torquil and Emma strolling down South Audley Street bound for Mme de Rigny's exclusive ladies' millinery shop. A frivolous hat with velvet ribands and a cluster of silk flowers never failed to make Emma smile, and Torquil had suggested this shopping excursion in the hopes of perking up her spirits.

It was not that Emma was depressed; rather, she had been such a pattern card of decorum since Brickhill that Torquil scarcely knew the reserved young person at his side. Gone was the animation he appreciated in Emma. Gone were her unabashed reactions to the people and sights she encountered. Verily, one of the reasons Torquil had been unable to part with Emma all those years was her unaffected disposition; Emma made each day a pleasure, for she did not observe the world, she plunged in and enjoyed whatever was offered.

Over the course of the past days, Torquil had made the grim discovery that Emma's candid nature and the behavior acceptable for a proper lady were incompatible. He was loath to see Emma so subdued, but, as her guardian, Torquil knew it was for the best. He was determined to see her wed, and to that end, 'twas vital that Emma curb her forthright temperament lest she be dubbed indiscreet and thoroughly wanton. It was to be hoped that a bonnet or two would lessen the blow of becoming a model of propriety and restore a measure of her previous unfettered delight.

Several paces ahead, a high-sprung phaeton stopped to allow a young gentleman and an elderly lady to alight. The Honorable Quentin Sayre fussing over his mama, the Baroness de Guise, who could not locate one of her kid gloves, espied Emma on her uncle's arm. All too quickly, he turned away from his mama to click his heels in a ridiculously overeager greeting.

"Good afternoon, Miss Fraser. My lord." Sayre grinned at the lovely Miss Emma Fraser. She was, despite an unsettling habit of gazing directly into one's eyes while conversing, an undisputed incomparable. Only the other evening Sayre had been fortunate enough to stand up with her at Haverleigh's rout. Those few moments of her undivided attention were bliss and had done much to raise the young gentleman's status before his peers. "How delightful to see you, Miss Fraser. Mother, you have met Miss Fraser, I believe."

Emma executed a curtsy that would have launched Lady Wheatley into paroxysms of pleasure. " 'Tis a pleasure to see you again, Baroness."

An exceedingly sour expression dominated the baroness's angular face. Were it not for the chit's mother, God rest her soul, the baroness would not deign to acknowledge Emma. She focused a long-suffering gaze on the earl, then gave Emma a hasty nod that barely qualified as polite.

Sayre addressed the earl. "*On dit*, you shall be at Stanhope's in Essex this weekend, sir. Might I hope Miss Fraser will be in attendance?" Oblivious to his mama's displeasure, he fixated a gaze of unabashed adoration on Emma.

"Yes, we plan to be there," was Torquil's brisk reply, none too pleased that he would likely be spending his weekend keeping this puppy away from Emma.

"Splendid. Positively splendid," gushed Sayre. There was a flush upon his cheeks. "May I say, my lord, that I look forward to the weekend with great expectations?"

In the next instant, the baroness hustled her son away before he might make a proper farewell, and Torquil was heard to mutter beneath his breath, "Great expectations, indeed. We'll see about that."

A giggle escaped Emma. "What did you say, Uncle Torquil?"

"Sayre ain't for you. Not the right sort atall."

Silently, Emma agreed. Sayre was attentive and a pleasant conversationalist, but she would never settle for a boy still at the beck and call of his mama. He was not the man she would marry; he was not at all—the astonishing thought came unsummoned—like the handsome American in Brickhill. Emma almost lost her footing. *Oddsbodikins!* she thought crudely. What had gotten into her? 'Twas remarkable enough that she had wondered when she might see the blue-eyed stranger again, but to fancy marrying someone she did not know was preposterous. Such thoughts were evidence of that rash behavior Uncle Torquil cautioned her against, and they could lead to naught but calamity. Telling herself this did little good. She could not banish the mental image of those ink-blue eyes and that warm smile, nor the giddy sensation that rippled through her when her heart skipped a beat. Emma forced herself to think of something else.

"Will Lady Cressida be at the Stanhopes'?" she asked the earl while they waited as a pair of sweepers cleared the crossing at the corner of Hill Street.

"Gad, no! Why'd you ask a thing like that?" he retorted with thinly disguised aversion.

"Given the amount of time she's spent at your side this Season, it seemed natural." Emma tilted her head sideways to catch her uncle's reaction.

"Natural?" Torquil's expression revealed blatant disgust. "Nothing natural about her atall. The lady's been nothing but a pest. Feels like my shadow's become flesh and blood each time I find her hovering at my shoulder. Wouldn't have accepted Nigel's invitation if Lady Cressida was going to be there. She's the grabbingest female I've encountered in an age." With one hand he held Emma's elbow to guide her across Hill Street, while with the other he tossed a coin to one of the sweep boys. Extreme consternation showed upon his masculine features.

Emma giggled. "You make her sound like an octopus, but I thought Lady Cressida rather pleasant when she stopped to chat with us on Rotten Row. She was exceedingly gracious to invite me to ride in her new curricle, and you were horrible to say I couldn't. You hurt her feelings, you know, for she knew 'twas all a bam when you said I had a previous engagement."

"Hmm." The earl's stride lengthened. Lady Cressida Carlisle, née Lytton, was as beautiful as she was reckless. Nobody knew better than Torquil Hamilton how to make his way among the petticoat line. Yet no matter his years of experience, he had never encountered a more impulsive, more trying individual, and he cursed the foolishness that had led him to embark upon a flirtation with the lady.

Emma continued to sing the lady's praises, "And she's most pretty. Why, Lady Cowper says she's past forty, but I think she's fresh as a schoolgirl. And she's clever. Her conversation's not half so boring as the other ladies' I've met this Season. She talks about real things, not who's marrying whom and the color of the newest silk at the Exeter Exchange. She's done real things, too. Can you imagine a lady captaining her own sailing craft to Ireland?"

"Pray, don't set your cap to follow her example," implored Torquil in anxious tones. "She's twice widowed, and the gossip's quite on the mark. Lady Cressida's old enough to be your mother, Emma Margaret. And she's a loose screw into the bargain. Not atall the sort of lady you ought to be seen with." On a lighter tone, he added, "I'm trying to secure your reputation, not destroy it."

Following a somewhat frustrated sigh, Emma, who would have preferred talking about the unique Lady Cressida, inquired most sincerely, "If not Lady Cressida, then what lady is for you, Uncle Torquil? Here we are in London to secure a husband for me, but when I'm settled, won't you need a wife?"

This question stunned the earl. His jaw muscles clenched unconsciously as he stared straight ahead, maintaining a steady pace down the sidewalk. It had been eleven years since he had fancied himself in love with Lady Alicia Bellamy, and eleven years since he had vowed to remain free from any woman. He had met Lady Alicia during her first Season, and within a fortnight, their betrothal was published in the *Times*. It was shortly thereafter that the rumors began, every evil-tongued gossip in London claiming to know better than Torquil the most intimate details of his life. In the end, Lady Alicia had scorned the earl, choosing to place her faith in tattle rather than in the man she was pledged to marry. Most women, particularly ladies, he had long since discovered, were like the fickle Lady Alicia. Shallow, perfidious, and easily swayed by gossip. More than a decade later, it mattered little that he had not really loved Alicia, nor did it matter whether the stories about him and the Duke of Warwick's wife had been true or false. What mattered was the lesson gained. It was a bitter one about the value of reputation, and the earl was determined Emma should never have to learn it for herself. Responding to his niece's most unexpected query, he merely said, "I'm long past the marrying stage."

"Taradiddle. If you're so certain marriage shall bring me happiness, then I wish it for you for the same reason."

Torquil gave an uneasy laugh. "I am, dear puss, a confirmed bachelor. I'm quite content with my lot, and there ain't a lady in the realm capable of shaking me free of old habits. Of that I assure you."

In the next instant, they reached their destination, and the earl's hand tightened about the doorknob to Mme de Rigny's establishment. An overhead bell tinkled as the door opened, and madame hurried forward.

"Lord Hamilton, it is a pleasure to see you and your charming companion." The Frenchwoman focused an assessing eye on the tall, reed-thin, auburn-haired beauty who entered on the arm of her best customer. The earl often brought his *chère amies* to Mme de Rigny's, and he never spared any expense. The milliner grinned. It was a pleasure doing business with a man who knew how to spoil a woman.

Comprehending the course of Mme de Rigny's thoughts, a disapproving frown etched Torquil's brow. He corrected the Frenchwoman's mistake. "Allow me to introduce my niece and ward, Miss Fraser."

Mme de Rigny remained composed. She did not betray the slightest disbelief that the exotic creature with green eyes and ripe plum-colored lips was the dashing earl's ward. "*Enchanté*, mademoiselle. It shall be a pleasure to design a special creation for you." She ushered Emma to the counter where an abundant supply of ribands, plumes, and laces were displayed alongside numerous hats in every fabric from straw to crêpe to velvet. Removing Emma's bonnet, she backed up several paces to study the girl's coppery hair and alabaster complexion. "*Très bien. Très bien,*" she clucked, setting to work.

In fascination, Emma watched the hatmaker select a wide-brimmed bonnet of vibrant blue silk; she put it next to Emma's face to check the color and nodded her approval. Skillfully, Mme de Rigny wrapped a silver velvet riband about the crown and tucked into it a cluster of silver-and-blue striped Zebra feathers. Her work completed, she held the hat forth for inspection.

"Oh, madame, 'tis exquisite," enthused Emma.

Torquil observed his niece with satisfaction. It was a pleasure to see a bright smile return to her eyes. He grinned at the one person upon whom he had bestowed his every affection for so long.

"How do you like it, Uncle?" Emma inquired after Mme de Rigny set the hat upon her short curls at a daringly cocky angle.

"Isn't that a bit ornate for the country?" he asked, not wanting to disapprove but wishing that Lady Wheatley had been able to accompany them. Through no fault on her own, Emma's natural beauty tended to invite criticism; her unusual height, alluringly slanting eyes, and vibrant curls needed to be played down. The earl fervently wished that Emma present an impeccable vision of propriety when they arrived at Sir Nigel and Lady Stanhope's estate in Essex. His friend, Nigel Stanhope, had known Emma since she had become his ward, and the baronet's new bride had included several eligible bachelors on her guest list for the express purpose of meeting Emma. Hopefully, there would be at least one gentleman who was a cut above that pup, Sayre, and Emma might find it easier to form an attachment for an agreeable gentleman in a setting less stifling that the drawing rooms of Mayfair.

"Milord and his lovely relation will be visiting the country? *Je comprends*," stated the Frenchwoman, always eager to accommodate her customers' needs for special occasions.

"We've been invited to Stanton Hall," put forth Emma enthusiastically. She was immensely fond of Sir Nigel and could think of nothing better than to quit London for several days of riding and dining al fresco at his ancestral seat.

Mme de Rigny clucked. " 'Tis a pity, *mais votre oncle* is correct." In the next instant, she plucked the frothy creation of blue and silver from Emma's head and pushed it to the rear of the counter. She turned her skills to a chip bonnet onto which she fastened a nosegay of jonquil and pale peach silk blossoms with matching grosgrain streamers to tie beneath the chin. "*Regardez*, mademoiselle, monsieur. *Voilà!* You will be as pretty as springtime in Kent."

"Quite right," Torquil agreed, thinking that Emma did, indeed, look as unspoiled as a bright May morning. "Wrap it up, madame, and please prepare two more of similar design in shades of green and blue, and a riding cap in gold."

While the milliner was boxing up the hat, Emma reached for the discarded blue-and-silver bonnet. The striped feathers were soft as air, and Emma tweaked one, watching it bob merrily above the shimmering royal blue bonnet. Next she turned the bonnet around to view it from every angle, and then, never dreaming to resist the impulse, she picked it up and put it on. Quickly, she moved and stood before the mirror to study her reflection.

Catching sight of Emma, Torquil shot her a sideways glance. "I'm not certain Lady Wheatley would approve."

"Likely not," replied Emma on a wistful sigh. "But you must admit 'tis splendid."

"Indeed, and you look a veritable dasher," he said. Again, Torquil remarked to himself what an uncommon lady the teary-eyed little girl in the graveyard had become. In a world in which society placed a premium on sham and affectation, Emma's unpretentious spirit was like a pine-scented Highland wind. It was a shame to blunt it. None of the men Torquil knew deserved a lady as special as Emma, for she would be friend and companion as well as wife and mistress, and he could only pray that she would find someone who would not quash her unique charm.

Emma blew her uncle an audacious kiss, and he laughed as she pirouetted about the shop. Past mounds of pastel-dyed netting and vases of peacock plumes she whirled, the musical laugh which the earl loved filling the tiny shop. She waltzed to the end of the polished mahogany counter, executed a playful curtsy to her image in the pier glass, then spun toward the bay window where she came to an abrupt halt.

Her mouth formed a silent *O* of surprise.

There was the blue-eyed American! He was standing on the sidewalk and watching her in open amusement.

A trembling hand flew to still the pounding of her heart. Emma lowered her thick lashes, daring only to glance at him from beneath their protective mantle. What she saw caused a flaming blush to climb up her neck and fan across her cheeks.

On a broad grin, the gentleman distinctly mouthed the words, "Good day, my lady." Glancing first at the hat and then at the rapid rise and fall of Emma's chest, he offered her a nod of approval, his black brows quirking upward, a wolfish grin upon his lips.

Aghast at his brashness, Emma lowered her lashes again. Next she glanced over her shoulder, fearful that Uncle Torquil might have seen how boldly this man dared to treat her. The earl was confirming an order for several other hats that Mme. de Rigny promised to deliver to Upper Brook Street by tea time on the morrow; luckily, he had not seen the American's audacious gaze. Emma's heart raced. Heavens above, did the American think her a fallen woman out on a shopping spree with her benefactor? Emma cringed at the thought. Mustering every ounce of the loftiness she had observed in Almack's patronesses, she leveled a thoroughly ladylike and very reproachful stare at the bold American.

That the beautiful girl in the daring bonnet was every inch a lady was undeniable, and Jeremy Wister experienced the sting of regret that he had been so cavalier. His sole excuse was that she had been on his mind these past days. Since that afternoon in Brickhill, he had found himself scanning the private boxes at the opera for a sight of her, and searching the faces of the ladies on Rotten Row at the fashionable hour in the hopes of encountering her. It was remarkable, but true, and to have stumbled upon the engaging sight of her cavorting in a shop window was altogether tantalizing. She was as pretty and vivacious as he recalled, and when he caught the glimpse of recognition in her green cat's-eyes, he experienced a boyish moment of elation. It had been wrong to greet her so boldly. He would call out any man who dared to treat his sisters in such a disrespectful fashion, and he executed a penitent bow. This apology was rewarded by a softening of her haughty mask.

A smile broke across his handsome face. " 'Till we meet again, my lady," he mouthed. After a second and even more respectful bow, he turned on his heel and strode up South Audley Street.

For several moments, Emma stood stock still. She could do naught but gaze at the empty window. All that remained was a view across the street to a row of town houses, and a white-capped nanny in a gray cloak pushing a perambulator down the opposite sidewalk. Had she mistaken the meaning of his silent words? No, she did not think so, and once more her heart somersaulted. It was a glorious sensation. Intriguing and challenging. And miraculously, it no longer frightened Emma; indeed, she felt like flying. All logical thought fled her. She had seen her American again, and it was only a matter of time before they would be formally introduced, she vowed with the fanciful determination of a young lady smitten beyond reason.

That evening at Cadogan House, St. James's Square, three places were set at the formal dining table. Tapers flickered in sconces about the room, crystal goblets sparkled in the candlelight, and a centerpiece of ferns mingled with foxglove dominated the table. An ormulu timepiece resting in a mantel niche struck half past eight, and Jeremy Wister and his grandmother, the Dowager Countess of Cadogan, took their seats in carved Georgian side chairs. As usual, they would commence without the third party, Jeremy's aunt, a lady of the most unreliable character who had never been on time for anything in her entire life.

The countess gave a discreet nod in the direction of the majordomo standing by the service entrance. The servant moved away from the swinging door, and like clockwork footmen entered carrying silver trays laden with beef in a puff pastry, steaming roast duckling, and an assortment of vegetables smothered in creamy sauces. The dowager countess preferred the beef; the duckling glazed with marmalade was Jeremy's favorite. There was little point in preparing anything particular for the absent diner; when the lady was in attendance, she seldom did more than pick at her meal like a parakeet.

"I received a parcel in this morning's post, Grandmother. There was a gift for you from Melanie." Jeremy drew a package from his waistcoast pocket. He folded back a layer of tissue paper to reveal four oil miniatures. Smiling, he picked up one and stared at it for several ticks of the mantel clock before passing it to the elderly lady.

"What a thoughtful child. How ever did your sweet sister know I longed to see your family?" The dowager held up a mother-of-pearl lorgnette to better view the first of the tiny paintings. "Isn't this lovely. There's no denying it is a more than credible likeness of my own darling Amelia and your father," she said on a melancholy sigh, savoring the picture of her daughter, a delicate, dark-haired beauty, seated beside her handsome American husband. "Look at the love in their eyes, Jeremy. And how young the both of them are, hardly a day older than that autumn when they wed in Philadelphia. 'Tis hard to countenance my darling Amelia is a grandmama."

She set the portrait beside her water goblet. "And what other miracles hath the talented Melanie accomplished?"

Her grandson grinned. "I shan't tell you who's next. You must guess," he said, selecting the miniature of his sister, Louisa Catharine. And while his grandmother studied the picture, he enjoyed a taste of duckling washed down with a healthy dose of madeira.

"Ah, 'tis the culprit who made my lovely girl a grandmama and myself a great-grandmère. If Louisa Catharine didn't look so content, I'd be vastly put out by the chit," declared the silver-haired dowager countess. She let the lorgnette drop and held the tiny picture at arm's length to study Louisa Catharine, who was well rounded and blond as a cherub. The two little boys clinging to her skirt and the babe on her lap were as rosy-cheeked and fair-haired as their mother. Smiling, she set the portrait of Louisa Catharine and her children alongside that of her daughter and son-in-law.

The third miniature was of two lads standing behind a girl on the threshold of womanhood. At nine and eleven, Willie and Franklin were Amelia and Tony Wister's youngest children; Augusta was fourteen and the youngest of the girls. She was a lanky brunette, who since she was closer in age to the boys was at times a bit more rambunctious than was acceptable in Philadelphia for a young lady of fine birth.

Giving her coifed head a nod, the dowager remarked, "Afraid this miss reminds me of my own youngest gel." Her eyes lingered on the empty chair across from Jeremy. Momentarily, she returned her regard to the portrait, adding in a pensive voice, "Mayhap it is what led her astray. Being the youngest of the girls, that is. Like young Augusta, she was closer in age to her brothers than her sisters. Never will understand the chit. Old enough to have grown children and still unable to get to dinner on time. Augusta ain't a loose screw like her aunt, is she?" She stabbed a piece of beef wrapped in pastry.

"No, Grandmother. Augusta's quite a sensible girl. Possesses a keen interest in her studies and has never caused Mother or Father a moment's worry." In point of fact, Jeremy's fingers were crossed beneath the table. While he spoke the truth, he omitted telling his grandmother that like her aunt, Augusta had a definite predilection for situations that were often dangerous and definitely unladylike. Knowing how the older woman fretted about her daughter, Jeremy did not wish to further overset her with sorry news of her grandchild.

On a satisfied nod, the elderly lady ordered, "Let me see the last one."

"Believe you'll like this the best," responded Jeremy, taking one final look at the portrait of Melanie, the eldest of his three younger sisters. Melanie was the romantic, the artist, the dreamer, and it was Melanie, sensitive, modest, and shy, who was her brother's favorite.

"A self-portrait!" his grandmother exclaimed, staring fondly at the young lady with ink-black hair, enormous ice-blue eyes, and fragile, aristocratic features. " 'Tis true, the gel's by far the most exquisite of the Wister girls. And if I know Melanie, 'tis a vastly underrated interpretation of her beauty."

Jeremy agreed. "Melanie's beauty is surpassed only by her modesty."

"Was there a letter?" she asked, taking a final look at the exquisite young lady.

"Yes, Grandmother. Here it is."

Positioning the lorgnette several inches from the paper, the dowager countess perused the missive. "Hmm," she mumbled as she turned to the second page. "Says your parents are taking Augusta and the boys to visit the McKeans in Louisiana. But what about Melanie? Why ain't she going?"

"You know Melanie. She's far happier remaining at home and painting. But she won't be alone. I promised to return for Christmas," he said with brotherly concern.

On a distinctly disapproving nod, the dowager remarked, "Still prefers moping about, does she? If you ask my opinion, I say you're quite misguided to continue humoring the gel. Ought to put a halt to her reclusive behavior. Ain't atall healthy. What's it been? Nigh on four years since her beau died, I warrant. High time to circulate, else she'll remain on the shelf till her dying day."

Jeremy did not like his grandmother's tone. There was little of the sympathy he believed his sister deserved. Jeremy adored Melanie and had been thrilled when she became affianced to his best friend, Charles Biddle. But in 1814, war was raging, and their joy had lasted only three short months; it ended when Charles died on board the USS *Dover* during a naval skirmish.

"'Tis callous to force the mending of a broken heart, Grandmother. Only time can do that, Melanie says, and I believe she's correct. She's a delicate young lady. None of us wishes to push her too quickly."

"Fustian. The chit ain't witless, y'know. Nothing wrong with her other than that unfortunate stutter, and as long as you encourage such introverted behavior, she'll only become more withdrawn. The gel's a recluse, and she'll never find happiness nor shake that cursed stutter, if she don't get out more often."

Patiently, Jeremy said, "She will in her own good time."

"You indulge the chit, Jeremy, and though I know it is naught but well intended, allowing her to remain isolated from young ladies her own age or beaux ain't good. If she depends on anyone, it ought to be her husband, not her brother."

"Whether 'tis good or not, 'tis well I should indulge her," Jeremy retorted bitterly, recalling Charles's death and the pledge he made on the deck of the *Dover*. It should have been himself, not Charles, standing on the captain's bridge when the British six-pounder hit the deck. No matter what anyone said, he would always blame himself for Charles's death and Melanie's anguish. It was that simple. "Grandmother, Charles was my best friend, and I promised him I'd always look after Melanie. 'Twas a vow to a dying man, and one I shall never break."

"Harrumph. Letting her stay cooped up like an invalid ain't any help. Should have dragged her along on this trip to London like I suggested. A Season would have been precisely the thing to shake her out of her slump." The dowager stabbed the air with her lorgnette. "Melanie's blessed with the famed Lytton looks. Would have had every buck in Town dangling after her. And I wager the stutter would have vanished once she realized the wealth of her merits. Splendid match, I could have made for her this summer. Splendid match."

"Be that as it may, Grandmother, I intend to be home in time for Christmas. Melanie and I will celebrate the holidays together. Won't you come with me?"

For a brief moment the lines in the elderly woman's face seemed to fade away and her eyes brightened considerably, but her answer was in the negative. "'Tisn't possible. I'm no sailor. Nearly perished the last time your grandfather took me to Philadelphia. Couldn't possibly survive another voyage at my age. But I do have one request." She picked up the miniature of young Augusta with her brothers, a frown creased her regal brow, and her eyes shimmered with emotion.

"What's that?"

"I'd like you to take your aunt back to Philadelphia with you."

"Take Aunt Cressy to America?" Jeremy fairly gasped at the prospect of escorting his flighty aunt as far as Hyde Park. It was a daunting notion. The lady was a thoroughly ramshackle creature, and he did not wish to be responsible for her. Certainly not halfway round the world. Good God, the lady would have Society Hill on its ear in no time!

"Yes, I'd like you to take her to America," the dowager confirmed.

"Dare I ask why?"

"Gel's formed an unseemly attachment for Torquil Hamilton, Earl of Gairloch."

"Don't know the man."

Suddenly, the dining room door burst open. "La! My nose has been twitching these past minutes, Mama. Have you been saying dreadful things about me to Jeremy?" trilled the very lady in question as she floated past the dowager countess. The musky scent of an exotic Eastern perfume clung to the air in her wake. Wearing a pale blue muslin creation of shockingly thin fabric, ebony ringlets trailing down her bare back, Lady Cressida gave the impression of a female who had dared to defy the passage of time and had triumphed.

"Evening, Aunt Cressy." Jeremy stood as a footman seated his beautiful and unrestrained relative. A second footman was close behind with a dinner plate, which he set before the lady.

Discreetly, the dowager countess raised her linen napkin to fan away the cloying perfume her daughter had so liberally applied. "No, m'dear. We were discussing Torquil Hamilton."

"My Fatal Earl," Cressida said affecting a thoroughly unrestrained swoon, nearly knocking a breast of duckling to the floor. "La, Jeremy, you would adore Torquil. Not atall your average London fop. Quite the outdoorsman. And though he claims no interest in politics, he's a republican at heart. Verily, he quite reminds me of you. You'd quite approve of him, I vow."

"Poppycock!" her mother exclaimed and turned to Jeremy. "Hamilton's a rakehell and a thoroughly immoral lecher. No better than Cressy's two husbands. A libertine and wastrel like the both of them with a reputation so blackened Cressy'd never survive a liaison with the gentleman. Name's been associated with naught but the most infamous females, and besides, he's significantly younger than she is! What man with decent intentions would pursue a woman old enough to be his mother?"

"Mama!" cried Cressida in mortification. "I'm not *that* old, nor is Torquil so young. He'll be thirty come the New Year."

Frustration seized the dowager countess. Cressida had always been too headstong for her own good; talking to the girl was like reasoning with a dancing bear. Despairingly, she said, "Jeremy, you must agree to take her away. Though I'm reluctant to admit it, Cressida can't take care of herself, and I won't see my daughter bamboozled and heartbroken again."

"Oh, Mama, I'm a grown woman," she retorted, her words at odds with a distinctly childish pout. "Twice widowed as you must remind me and hardly of an age to be bamboozled."

Suppressing a grin, Jeremy prompted, "Tell me about this Fatal Earl." He was curious to know more about Cressy's latest victim, for Jeremy, knowing his aunt, did not doubt she could spin circles about any man, including the devil himself.

Before Cressida could speak the countess said, in sober tones, "It is positively sinful what Hamilton's done to stain the honor of an old family name. Knew his mother, lovely gel, a Ranleigh from Sussex. Father, the ninth earl, was a fine gentleman. But their progeny were nothing but a disgrace. Only had two children. A daughter who ran off with a curate's lad, and the heir, Torquil."

Ignoring her mother, Cressida, who seldom listened to

her own words, put forth unthinkingly, "He's a dashing Corinthian, Jeremy. Handsome as a schoolgirl's dream of a Highland laird who would sweep out of the hills to kidnap a bride. Actually, devastating is an apter description. Takes one's breath away with a single glance. And knows precisely how to please a woman."

"Cressida!" The dowager countess paled visibly. "The man's a villain. Wherever he goes, scandal follows. Why when he was but seventeen, he killed the Duke of Warwick, and that was only the first husband who met an untimely demise by his hand!"

Jeremy sat bolt upright, his grip tightened dangerously about the stem of his wine goblet. There was but one thing he was willing to hold against any man. Adultery. A man who preyed on married women was the one variety of scoundrel that Jeremy disdained beyond reason. He could not tolerate, nor forgive under any circumstance, anyone who might be unfaithful to one's spouse or any man who might be a party to marital infidelity. Jeremy placed great store in the sanctity of matrimony; his parents had set a loving and sterling example that he intended to follow and uphold.

Having caught her grandson's attention, the dowager concluded, "As if his numerous affairs and dueling history weren't wicked enough, he's perpetually in the company of a young girl. Claims she's his ward—daughter of his sister and the curate's son—though they say the gel's really his natural daughter."

"Egad, Aunt Cressy, you don't fancy yourself in love with this man?"

The lady gave her ebony curls a willful toss. "Course not. Mama's making mountains out of molehills as usual. He's enormous fun, and I do wish I might see more of him," she mused wishingly. "Truth to tell, I've the unsettling impression he's getting ready to throw me over."

"Discard you, m'dear? Oh, this is bleaker than I imagined!" cried the older lady. "Cressy dearest, you must escape. You will take her to Philadelphia, won't you, Jeremy?"

"How can I refuse you, Grandmother?" he teased, though inside he knew a strong conviction that he must remove his aunt from the attentions of a confirmed rakehell, a man who likely knew nothing of honor or loyalty. "Aunt Cressy, will you come willingly to Philadelphia?"

Before she might reply, her mother threatened, "If you don't, m'dear, I'll find a way. Doesn't matter how old you are." Again she jabbed the air with her lorgnette. "Sent your sister, Amelia, off to America. Did wonders for her, and before I die, I'll see you there as well."

"Oh, fiddlesticks, Mama, you're not about to die! Really, I can't bother with this now. I'm off to a masked garden party at the Marquis of Atholl's," she trilled as she rose from her seat, her fork never having been lifted. Discerning the anxiety etched darkly upon her mother's countenance, Cressida circled the table to plant a kiss on her forehead. Impulsively, she added, "I shall consider America, if it pleases you, Mama."

"Course you will, m'dear." The dowager waved a bony hand at her daughter as she left the dining room. After the door closed, she turned to Jeremy. "And what of you, m'dear? High time for you to be settling down. Young man has a duty to secure the line, y'know."

Jeremy set his wine goblet on the table and sighed. Ever since his arrival in England, the dowager countess had harped on the importance of assuring the succession. It was a touchy subject; Jeremy did not share her aristocratic attitude about marriage to preserve ancestral lines and family posterity. Finding himself in possession of a title neither pleased nor impressed Jeremy, and he certainly was not going to turn his life topsy-turvy because of it. He was perfectly content with his life; he enjoyed working in the family shipping business and bank, and he was surrounded by family love, comfort, and companionship.

"Could make a splendid match, if you'd only give me the nod," she added.

Displaying an infinite measure of tact, Jeremy stated, "Grandmother, I've no desire for a splendid match. 'Tis my intention to select my own wife in my own good time, not to settle for one of the *haut ton*'s incomparable misses merely to guarantee the title. I desire a wife I might love and who might love me in return." He did not wish to offend his grandmother, but neither did he intend to leg-shackle himself to a woman who knew nothing about love. He yearned for a woman who understood what it meant to be friend and partner and lover to her husband.

"Love, you say? Well, my boy, I can't quibble with that," conceded the older woman. "But what's holding you up? Surely between the ranks of young ladies in Philadelphia and London there's been at least one special lady who might claim your heart."

Automatically, Jeremy shrugged his shoulders as if to say "No," especially not since his calamitous courtship of Sophie Hingham. Then, of a sudden, the image of the young lady in the shop window flashed through his mind. Astonishing though it might be, he could not help wondering if the vivid beauty he had rescued in Brickhill was a lady to be taken seriously in that regard. Was she different from the vapid damsels he had thus far encountered in ballrooms on both sides of the Atlantic? Was she a lady who might gallop across the Pennsylvania meadows at his side without complaining of the megrims? A lady who might converse in a forthright fashion at the dinner table rather than plead ignorance of topics outside the realm of the gentle sex? And, of the utmost importance, was she a lady he could trust? A lady, unlike Miss Highham, who would want him for himself, not his family fortune or newly acquired lands and British title? A smile curled up at the edges of his mouth, as Jeremy Wister decided that, indeed, he would like to possess the answers to those questions.

Catching sight of her grandson's expression, the dowager countess could not help speculating who might have caused that enigmatic grin to cross his face. Mayhap something was afoot after all. She would have liked to pursue the issue, but knew that too much meddling could do more harm than good. Instead, she inquired conversationally, "By the by, have you any weekend plans?"

"Matter of fact, I've an invitation to the country—from Sir Nigel Stanhope and his bride."

"Excellent, m'dear. Exceedingly nice family—the Stanhopes—and some of the best fishing on the coast is to be found at Stanton Hall." She nodded at the footman to clear the table for the next course, then concluded, "You're in for a special weekend, I'm certain."

CHAPTER
THREE

"You must think me an abominable hostess," Lady Stanhope said to Emma and Lady Wheatley as they entered the small drawing room at Stanton Hall. Although she was no green girl, being more than five-and-twenty, Lady Stanhope was anxious to secure only the best impression in her new role as mistress of her husband's establishment. "No sooner do you arrive than Nigel imposes upon your uncle to accompany him to the farthest reaches of the estate. How my husband might ask a guest to assist in overseeing the repair of a dyke, I hardly fathom. 'Tis not my notion of a weekend of rustication."

"Men will be men," said Lady Wheatley loftily as she settled her generous figure into a well-worn Queen Anne chair by a casement window that faced out upon lawns shrouded in a rainy mist. At length, she added, "And as there's nothing our frailer sex can do to turn matters otherwise, 'tis fruitless to worry, m'dear."

Emma also sat before the row of leaded windows; they were cranked partially open, and a humid salty breeze filled the room. Giving her hostess a supportive smile Emma said, "Thus far my visit has been all I hoped. I wanted nothing more than to leave the confines of the metropolis, and I don't mind in the slightest that my uncle vanished upon our arrival. Rest assured, Uncle Torquil doesn't mind, either. He adores any chance for a hard ride across open country."

Of a sudden, the breeze picked up, attracting the ladies' attention to the scene outside. The line of poplar trees edging the lawns bent sharply toward the mansion, and twigs and leaves, borne on the wind, skittered across the close-cut grass. And inside the drawing room, brocade curtains ballooned out like old-fashioned hooped skirts while several letters atop an escritoire took flight and floated to the floor.

Lady Stanhope dashed to close the windows; she watched in horror as the fine gray rain that had blown in from the North Sea earlier in the day transformed into a torrential downpour. A jagged line of lightning blazed across the darkening sky, and a roll of thunder echoed in from the sea. "Dear heavens, 'tis pouring cats and dogs. How very rude!" She wrung her hands, her glance darting from the thunderstorm to Emma and Lady Wheatley and back to the weather. "These coastal storms play havoc with travelers. No more guests shall arrive this evening, and I fear Nigel and your uncle may be stranded and unable to join us for dinner."

"It isn't the end of the world," put in Lady Wheatley as she smoothed the skirt of her dinner gown. "They are grown men and know perfectly well how to take care of themselves."

"Oh, I'm not worried for them, ma'am," blurted out the new wife. "This is the first time I've entertained at Stanton Hall, you see, and I would so like it to be a success."

"Rain does tend to put a damper on things," observed Lady Wheatley.

Emma ignored this remark and addressed her hostess in a bracing tone. "And it shall be a rousing success."

From the depths of the Elizabethan manor house a dinner gong sounded, and several minutes later, those guests who had arrived before the weather turned sour began to descend from the second floor. The first to enter the drawing room was Major Arkwright, a retired military man and a widower of years sympathetic to Lady Wheatley.

Next Jules Heathcote, the Marquess of Cholmondeley, arrived with his wife. They were followed by the Honorable Freddy Pleydell, a young man of extraordinarily delicate good looks. Lady Stanhope made the necessary introductions, adding that the marquess's sister was also at Stanton Hall and would join the party shortly.

"Your sister-in-law isn't ill, is she?" Emma posed the solicitous question to the marchioness.

"Georgiana? Ill? Not likely. I'm certain she's merely lingering over her toilette," replied Lady Cholmondeley a trifle too scornfully. " 'Tis likely she heard the Earl of Cadogan shall be in attendance and is as determined as every chit in London to make a lasting impression on the gentleman."

"Cadogan is a much sought-after bachelor?" Emma speculated aloud.

"Surely you've heard?" the older woman whispered in disbelief.

"No, I don't know a thing about the man," came Emma's candid response.

The marchioness appeared taken aback. It was beyond her ken that any female of marriageable age had not set her sights on the earl, least of all that a lady might move within the realm of the beau monde and remain unfamiliar with the Cadogan heir. For a few moments, the marchioness wondered if Miss Fraser's ignorance was feigned and part and parcel of a shrewd plan to snare the earl; everyone knew the gentleman had been subjected to numerous and bizarre ploys this Season. But studying the younger woman's open countenance, the marchioness realized it was a harsh and ill-founded suspicion.

Lowering her voice, she told Emma, "He's dreadfully handsome. Only just inherited the title and has oodles of blunt. Positively the catch of the Season, and Georgiana's been dangling after him for weeks." Again scorn colored her words. "Girl's been behaving in a most shameless fashion, if I do say so, but my dear husband dotes on his sister and refuses to naysay the chit. Needless to say, Georgiana hopes this weekend is her chance to bring him round. Faith, here he is!" whispered the marchioness in a high state of excitement as the gentleman in question crossed the threshold.

Intrigued though Emma was to view this reputed nonpareil of masculine marriageability, she curbed her curiosity and did not peek about the corner of the chair. Lady Stanhope's voice rose in greeting, and Emma listened as their hostess escorted the earl through the room.

Nearing Emma, Lady Stanhope said, "I don't believe you're acquainted with Miss Fraser, my lord."

Emma smiled pleasantly and looked up to meet the sought-after earl. In the next instant, that simple smile transformed until her countenance was radiant with delight at the sight of her American. There he was, resplendent in a starched white shirt and burgundy superfine waistcoat, his ink-blue eyes gleaming in lively contrast to that bronzed and beautifully masculine face. *Miracles do happen,* was Emma's precipitous reaction. A wealth of girlish notions spun through her brain. *What a splendid weekend this is going to be! Imagine, my American is an earl. Surely, this is destiny! It wasn't going to be so difficult after all to marry before the end of the Season. Oh, won't Uncle Torquil be pleased?*

"Miss Fraser," Jeremy Wister drawled as he bowed and then accepted her extended hand, raising it to his lips.

"My lord," she answered with effort, her breath catching as his lips quickly brushed the top of her hand. His smile was warm, and there was a secretive glint in those compelling eyes. Demurely, Emma dipped her head, not wishing anyone to observe the flash of recognition from her eyes. She knew precisely what he was thinking; it was only natural that his thoughts were her own. *Hello, again. What a wonderful and unexpected surprise it is to see you. And what a pleasure it is to meet you at last.* At length, she turned to the nearby chair and forced out, "Lady Wheatley, may I present the Earl of Cadogan?"

"Charmed," said Jeremy, offering Lady Wheatley an elegant bow and causing her to blush furiously.

Introductions completed, the major continued his chat with Lady Wheatley, the marchioness turned to Lady Stanhope, and the Honorable Freddy engaged Lord Cholmondeley. Jeremy, pleased to have been left alone with Emma, inquired, "Shall I have the pleasure of seeing you in your plumed blue-and-silver bonnet this weekend, Miss Fraser?"

"Oh, no, sir," she gasped in genuine shock. "I did not purchase it."

"'Twas lovely," he drawled. He thought to add *as lovely as the lady I saw wearing it*, but he dared not, fearing to offend her. He had longed to learn her name and gain an introduction, longed for the chance to become acquainted with her and to find the answers to those questions she had roused within him. Knowing how rash he had been when he greeted her in the shop window, he vowed to do nothing to jeopardize this golden opportunity.

Emma smiled. "Yes, 'twas a lovely hat, and so said my guardian, who also said 'twas past the bounds of ladylike apparel, particularly for a quiet weekend in the country." There was an enchanting touch of levity in her voice.

Surreptitiously, Jeremy took a second look at the assembled guests to whom he had been introduced. They were all new to him, save for the Marquess of Cholmondeley, whose sister had been brazenly pursuing him from one end of London to the other. "Your guardian?" he inquired, experiencing the acute wish that Miss Fraser have no connection to the marquess. Her answer came as a great relief.

"Yes, my uncle. He's at Stanton Hall this weekend, but off with Sir Nigel on estate business at the moment. I fear they've been stranded in the storm and shan't return for dinner."

"You musn't worry, Miss Fraser. Likely, they're safe in a tenant cottage enjoying a hearty stew. I shall look forward to meeting your guardian upon his return," he replied with exquisite politeness, then added, "If not the plumed bonnet, tell me, what did you select?"

Astonishment played across Emma's face; she had never met a gentleman interested in bonnets. Wondering what sort of man this American was, she leaned forward in the Queen

Anne chair to gaze directly into Jeremy's eyes. In the next instant, the drone of chatter from the other guests seemed to come from very far away, and Emma watched as those unusual blue eyes dilated, their centers darkening to the same deep navy about the edges. She asked, "Are you truly interested in hats and fripperies, my lord?"

"No," he replied with a sincerity to match Emma's.

"Then why did you ask, sir?" she inquired softly.

Her question startled Jeremy, and he grinned. "I wished to converse with you, Miss Fraser, and thought to put you at ease. I chose a subject I hoped would be of interest."

What a little thing he offered in kindness, yet how easily it made her happy. On a rather breathless whisper, she replied, "That is perhaps the nicest thing I can recall any gentleman doing for me, sir."

Like invisible fingers, her ingenuous words touched Jeremy; they caused an unfamiliar constriction in the region of his chest. Although he favored honesty, he was not used to it, especially from ladies of the beau monde. Since his arrival in England, he had come to expect naught but guile and illusion, and such openness as Miss Fraser displayed was uncommon. She was, indeed, a lady of special value.

Emma continued, "You need not confine your conversation to such insignificant topics as bonnets and plumes, my lord. They're as boring to me as I'm certain they are to you."

"What then would you like to talk about?"

"My goodness, there's an entire world of fascinating things. For example," she suggested in a deceptively matter-of-fact tone, "who won the boxing match in Brickhill?"

Tossing back his head, Jeremy laughed. It was the sort of full-bodied, warm laugh that was shared between good friends. "Miss Fraser, are you truly a fan of pugilism?" he asked, enchanted by this lovely lady.

"In a manner of speaking," she began, experiencing an unfamiliar yet delightfully light-headed sensation. So this was what flirting was really like, she thought, realizing that all of the polite conversations she had heretofore enjoyed with attentive gentlemen had been only that... polite. She went on, "Having nearly lost my good health, if not my reputation, in that village, I own a certain curiosity in the outcome."

His laugh deepened. Not only was she pretty, she was clever. He wished to ask, "Do you ride? Do you enjoy walking through the countryside? Do you like to read? And who are your favorite authors?" Suddenly, he wanted to tell Miss Fraser about his home and family, and he wanted to discover everything there was to know about her. Instead, he simply responded, "Bill Neate was the victor in four rounds. And as for other outcomes, I believe the portly gentleman's friends bundled him off to the nearest coaching inn for a long nap."

Once more Emma's response was as charming as it was artless. " 'Tis exceptional news, though I'm not certain 'tis altogether proper to remind me of the ... gentleman," she quipped.

Another bell sounded from some distant room in the rambling manor house, interrupting their conversation. As did the other guests, they looked toward Lady Stanhope, who invited them to repair to the dining room. At the precise moment everyone rose to leave, the marquess's sister appeared. Lady Georgiana Heathcote was a vision in a lacy pink dress that pinched her tiny waist and suggestively molded her full breasts; immediately, she spotted her prey, and not pausing to greet her hostess, she cut a path toward Jeremy Wister, the Earl of Cadogan.

Halfway across the drawing room, the Honorable Freddy Pleydell moved into the lady's path. "I have been asked to escort you to dinner, Lady Georgiana," he was heard to say as he deftly slipped her arm through his and directed the lady, who looked as if she wished the Honorable Freddy might turn into a toad, toward the door.

Emma could have sworn she heard an audible sigh of relief escape the tall, blue-eyed man at her side. It must be odious, she decided sympathetically, for a gentleman to be hounded by females such as Georgiana Heathcote.

"May I ask a personal question, my lord?" she inquired as they exited the drawing room.

"Only if you stop calling call me 'my lord.' 'Tis a deuced awkward thing to get used to," he confessed. "Mr. Wister will suffice."

"In a roundabout fashion, that was my very question," she said, hesitantly adding, "Mr. Wister," to please him.

He raised his left brow in a quizzical fashion. "Yes?"

"Please don't think me forward, but I knew from the first you were an American. It is unusual in the least to meet an American earl."

"My mother, Lady Amelia Lytton, was the daughter of the Earl of Cadogan. Upon my grandfather's death, my uncle inherited, but he died last winter without an heir and after an extensive search of the family tree, the title passed to me." Feeling comfortable in Miss Fraser's presence, he added spontaneously, "Believe me, it was a distinct shock to receive the solicitor's letter. One moment, I was merely Jeremy Wister of Philadelphia, shipbuilder and banker; in the next, I was an earl on my way to London. Of course I don't intend to take a seat in the House of Lords. I will return to Pennsylvania shortly. That is my home and where I intend to spend my future. I shall always be an American, first and foremost."

"Oh," murmured Emma, wondering if he were here to find an English bride of suitable rank. If that was the case, she feared she would have little chance with ladies as pretty and sophisticated as Lady Georgiana about.

Upon reaching the dining room, Lady Stanhope directed her guests to their proper places, where tiny porcelain milkmaids held gilt-edged cards on which each guest's name had been penned in italics. Emma and Jeremy found themselves at opposite ends of the table, and it was not until the meal ended and the guests returned to the drawing room that they were able to converse again.

Having resumed her seat before the row of windows, Emma stared out at the wretched storm. It was worse than before. Rain battered against the glass panes, a low wind whistled about the manor house, and lightning accompanied by ferocious claps of thunder rent the skyline.

" 'Tis an awful night," remarked Jeremy. Standing beside her chair, he softly asked, "It doesn't frighten you, does it?"

"Oh, no," Emma answered. "Truth to tell, the night reminds me of my childhood at Heather House above the shores of Loch Fyne in the Highlands. I can't begin to recollect how many stormy evenings I passed in the library, listening to Mama's old nurse, Granny Campbell, telling ancient legends of ghosties and fairy folk."

"I seem to recall a few evenings like that myself. Had a crusty aunt who loved to frighten me and my sisters with a wretched tale about a headless horseman." Bestowing a warm smile on Emma, Jeremy stepped backward to lean casually against the wall, long legs stretched before him, arms crossed over his chest, and blue eyes twinkling at the fond memory of his great-great-aunt Augusta.

Major Arkwright had overheard the conversation between the two young people. "Ghost stories. Capital notion. Believe I know a few m'self. Wouldn't mind biding my time in such entertainment."

"That would be splendid," Emma agreed. "I'm certain each of us must own one from our childhood. 'Twould be curious fun to compare the tales, I warrant."

"Excuse me?" interjected Lady Stanhope, certain that she must have misunderstood.

"By my soul," muttered Lady Wheatley, praying that before too much more time elapsed, her charge would at last be a lady of irreproachable demeanor. A lady would have thought twice and stopped herself before voicing any enthusiasm for such an untoward pastime.

"Oh, no!" squealed Lady Georgiana, wondering what the dashing American earl could see in a girl as contrary as Miss Emma Fraser. Only a hoyden would admit to finding the slightest amusement in anything so juvenile as ghost stories.

"Capital notion," repeated the major. "Always did claim a fondness for spooky tales."

The other gentlemen agreed, Lady Stanhope relaxed as a majority of her guests appeared amenable to the suggestion, and the major launched into a rather lengthy narrative about the haunted guest suite at his ancestral manor on the Welsh border. Finally, after much descriptive prelude, the major revealed that the furniture in said chamber was known to dance on the eve of the summer solstice.

A collective sigh of relief was heard about the room, and Lady Georgiana scolded, "Shame, major, to frighten me so for naught but a waltzing clothes press!"

Ignoring Lady Georgiana's dramatically heaving chest, the major turned to Emma. "Have you knowledge of a haunting, Miss Fraser?"

"Indeed, I do. 'Tis a centuries-old tale about the death toll of the gousty bells, drowned and ringing from the depths of Loch Fyne," she said, her eyes brightening, and her voice taking on the musical lilt of her Highland home. Under Lady Wheatley's tutelage, Emma had worked hard to school her natural brogue, but at times like this she could not prevent the gentle rhythm from coloring her ardent words.

"Gousty bells?" repeated Lady Georgiana with a patronizing lift of her chin.

"Aye, gousty. Haunted," replied Emma, her language peppered with a healthy dose of Scottish phrases as she began the ancient legend. Verily, justice could not be done the ancient tale unless it was related in this fashion; instinctively, Emma slipped from her own sweet burr into the rolling cadence of the Highland crofter folk.

"Heather House is a mere century auld, but there has been a building on that bourock above the loch for more than nine hundred years. 'Twas first a monastery, built by the monks from Ireland, and though nothin' more than the crumblin' ruin o' a bell tower remains, 'tis said it was once as gawsie fine a holy site as Iona. Several hundred monks lived and studied and answered the call o' the bell to prayers. But 'twas no normal bell jowing from the tower o' that monastery. 'Twas a bell o' the purest gold." Emma paused for a moment to measure the effect of her words. She was pleased to see that her audience, save for Lady Wheatley, who appeared distressed by Emma's brogue, was listening in rapt attention.

"Word o' the monastery wi' the golden bell spread

through brugh and land and across the seas, and soon King Hakon's longboats were filled wi' Viking warriors and bound for Loch Fyne."

"Mercy," gasped Lady Georgiana, clutching at her frilly pink bosom.

"'Twas a cauld autumn mornin' when the longboats were sighted. A monk rang the bell in warnin', but there was no escape. The Norsemen were brutal. Every croft in the clachan was burned, the monastery plundered, and not a soul survived that dreadful day." Emma's voice dropped. She finished in the same deadly somber tones old Granny Campbell had used, "Aye, not a breathin' body survived. Not even the warriors who carried the golden bell down to the shore." Again she paused.

"Do go on, Miss Fraser," urged the major.

Jeremy added, "Yes, continue. You story is quite splendid, and we're eager to learn the fate of the Vikings."

Feeling an inner warmth at her American's praise, Emma resumed the tale. "The bell was so heavy a single boat couldna carry it. So the Norsemen tied the boats together and set a platform across them for the bell. Just as they weighed anchor, the lift o' the skies darkened, a cauldrife wind swirled out o' the hills until the waters o' the loch roiled wi' fury." A touch of feigned panic colored Emma's voice, her words coming quick as a Highland storm. "'Twas the work o' the deevil's buckie, a pollrumptious sight wi' waves near high as Ben Carron crashin' over the longboats, swampin' and sinkin' them, and drownin' the Viking warriors and the stolen golden bell. As suddenly as the weather turned hideous, the skies cleared and the waters settled." Slowly, quietly, she finished, "Silence descended on the loch. No man, nor beastie, nor rock gannet in the craigs aboon the shore could be heard. There was no sound save that o' a bell, muffled and distant, risin' from the bottom of the loch."

"Ooh," exclaimed Lady Stanhope in unison with Lady Georgiana.

"Excellently told, Miss Fraser. Haven't heard so authentic an accent since my own nurse retired to her cottage in

Grampian," remarked the Honorable Freddy. "But, Miss Fraser, why did you say the sound of the sunken bell was a death toll?"

In her normal voice, Emma explained, "Only after a storm upon the loch can the bell be heard, and the villagers believe 'tis a death toll for sinners. For when the drowned bell tolls, if a thief lives among them, that soul shall not survive the night."

"What happens?"

"Legend claims the spirits of the monks haunt the hills to fling thieves into the watery grave of the Viking marauders."

"And have villagers disappeared?"

"Granny Campbell told me Roddy Gowan stole the MacLeod's cattle and was punished for it. Fell more than one hundred feet into the loch and never came up for air. But that was three hundred years ago." She concluded with a mischievous grin, "I venture the tale has done much to preserve law and order on Loch Fyne."

"Indeed," muttered the major.

This was followed by a round of commendations for a tale well told after which the Honorable Freddy inquired, "Who shall go next?"

Without giving it a second thought, Emma directed her gaze at Jeremy. "Have you an American ghost story?"

"An American tale, you ask. Let me think," he said, pushing away from the wall, his gaze never wavering from Emma's expectant one. "Regretfully, I hold no claim to any ancestors who are specters, nor has any Wister home ever been haunted to my knowledge. However, I do know of a haunting—at one of the older country seats north of Philadelphia. And she has been sighted in the gardens near the river."

"She?" inquired Emma.

"Yes, the beautiful Susannah Stewart, famed for her fair complexion and midnight-black hair," Jeremy said to Emma as if there was no one else in the room. "She was but seventeen when she drowned in the Schuylkill and has not ceased searching the garden these past two score years for her lover."

"Aah," female sighs echoed about the drawing room as the door opened and in walked Sir Nigel with another gentleman, a stranger to Jeremy.

Jeremy nodded to his host and paused as Emma smiled at the taller man, who went to stand beside her chair; he would have liked to meet Miss Fraser's guardian, but the assembled guests demanded that he continue the tale.

"What happened to Miss Susannah?" asked the marchioness.

"And why does her spirit haunt the garden?" added Lady Wheatley.

So Jeremy, again focusing on Miss Fraser, began to describe the events that led to the tragic death of Susannah Stewart. "It was 1778, the year the British occupied the city, and as several British officers were living on a neighboring estate, Miss Susannah was confined to her father's property. It was May, and every morning Miss Susannah strolled down to the river to feed the swans, and it was there she met her officer." Jeremy went on to explain how the young people fell in love and how, when the British began to leave the city in June, Miss Susannah and her officer made plans to elope. "No one knows who betrayed Miss Susannah, but on that moonlit evening in June when she crept through the garden, her father was waiting. The young officer was nowhere in sight, and the panic-stricken Miss Susannah ran toward the river. Her father chased her, and in the excitement, she tripped. It is believed she must have knocked her head, for when she fell into the water, she never tried to save herself."

Lady Georgiana opened her reticule and withdrew a lace handkerchief. On a watery sniffle, she said, "La, my lord, 'tis a most romantic tale."

"Have you seen her, sir?" inquired Emma.

"Not I. But my youngest sister Augusta claims to have seen her several times. Says she always knows when she'll see Miss Susannah, for a single white swan swims to the water's edge where the gardens meet."

Emma smiled shyly. "That was a lovely story," she said and then led the company in a round of applause.

"Yes," agreed Torquil, offering a friendly smile to the gentleman at whom Emma had been staring in a most starry-eyed fashion.

"Thank you," answered Jeremy as he extended his hand in greeting. "Jeremy Wister, sir."

Taking the American's hand firmly in his, the Scottish earl responded. "Torquil Hamilton, sir, Miss Fraser's uncle and guardian, and I'm exceedingly pleased to make your acquaintance."

The American's smile froze and then vanished. Staring at the very rogue who had toyed with his Aunt Cressida, the rake who dared to flirt with married ladies, Jeremy nodded in a movement that bespoke nothing more than the merest civility.

Good God! Did no one here know about his aunt and the earl? Was it not unseemly to introduce him to the culprit's niece? Was it not ill-conceived to invite Hamilton and himself to the same gathering? Incredibly, he felt a rush of disappointment mingled with betrayal, and although he knew it was foolish to feel so, he did anyway. Of a sudden, he recalled Miss Sophie Hingham, and the painful truth that she had only been nice to him because her father, who was an inveterate gambler and in deep financial debt, had ordered her to marry a wealthy man. Now so many years later, Jeremy could not fathom why he had allowed himself to be swept away by the mere look and laugh of a lady. Like a raw lad, he had been beguiled into thinking that Miss Fraser was a different sort of female, but the niece of a man such as Hamilton could not be a lady of value. His experience with Miss Hingham had proved that a woman was but a product of her family. Given that fact, Miss Fraser, despite appearances to the contrary, most certainly could not be the sort of woman he desired.

Swiftly, he withdrew his hand from the earl's and turned to Emma. His voice was cold as ice. "Your pardon, Miss Fraser, I have taken your attention enough this evening. If you'll excuse me, I'll share a few moments with our hostess before retiring." He made a curt bow, turned on his heel, and walked toward Lady Stanhope, who was seated at the other end of the drawing room.

Emma dared not look at her uncle. She dared not move a muscle as she watched Jeremy Wister walk away. "Deuced odd chap," she heard Torquil mutter, but she did not say a word as she fought back the dreadful urge to cover her face with her hands. For the third time in her life, she experienced that empty feeling in the pit of her stomach. All at once she felt foolish for having allowed herself to entertain such silly thoughts about a man she did not know, and she felt wounded by a chain of events she did not understand. Perhaps it was her fault; Uncle Torquil was continually reminding her to think twice, yet she had begun thinking of him as *her* American without a second thought.

No! she decided as anger replaced hurt. It was not her fault. Inexperienced though she might be, Emma was not a dolt; she had not mistaken the sincere interest he had earlier displayed. She had not misread the offer of friendship in his smile, nor the warmth in his laugh. What, then, had happened? There was only one sensible way to discover the answer to that question. On the morrow, she would ask Mr. Jeremy Wister; she would not allow him to turn away from her so rudely. Honesty was always the best policy. Tomorrow, she would seek him out and demand to know why he had behaved in such a frigid fashion.

But he was gone in the morning. Departed before dawn, leaving a brief thank you for his host and hostess, explaining that his plans had unexpectedly changed.

Thus ended the very brief and unsatisfying encounter between Miss Emma Fraser and Mr. Jeremy Wister. Within a fortnight, Jeremy returned to Philadelphia, reaffirming his youthful pledge never to follow his instincts where the female sex was concerned; one could not form an intelligent opinion about a lady upon first sight, and one could never judge a lady without knowing her family. And Emma returned to London, where she stayed out the Season, no closer to wedlock than she had been at the outset, but immeasurably wiser about the flaws in her own character; she, too, vowed never to react so impulsively again.

That might have been the end of it, had not the Fatal Earl been forced by the repercussions of a dueling scandal to quit England and take Emma in his flight. Thus it was that in the unseasonable month of November, Emma and Torquil set sail for America, bound for Philadelphia where Lady Wheatley's cousin, Caroline Shippen, a matron of notable social rank, promised to introduce Miss Fraser to the society of that cosmopolitan city. Their ship would arrive at the Delaware River docks just as the Philadelphia Season plunged into full swing, and there was no better time, Mrs. Shippen had written to her cousin, to find a suitable husband for a single young lady than during the winter social whirl.

CHAPTER
FOUR

December 1817, Pennsylvania
Late afternoon sunshine slanted through the row of Palladian windows that lined the west wall of the Wister country house, Summer Cottage. An artist's easel was placed to allow an unobstructed view across the snow-covered lawn to the Schuylkill River. And before the easel stood Miss Melanie Wister. Her pretty gown was protected by a paint-splattered smock, and she was holding a palette of wintry grays and silvers, deep blue, and ruddy brown paints in her hand.

Sighing, Melanie stepped back the better to view her afternoon's work. Again, she glanced outdoors and squinted at the line of trees bordering the edge of the property. There was something wrong with the color on her canvas, and she sighed again in frustration.

This painting was to be the fourth in a set of seasonal

landscapes for her brother Jeremy, but this was the third time she had started the winter setting; and, having failed to capture the light and mood before, Melanie feared the quartet would never be finished. What a disappointment that would be, for she wished above all else to give the special gift to Jeremy, who loved Summer Cottage as much as she did.

With a nostalgic smile, Melanie recalled their childhood in this house by the river. Those had been splendid years, and her smile deepened at the thought that the name Summer Cottage was hardly an appropriate one for the house in which the Wister children had enjoyed such fellowship and love. The house was not a cottage; it was a stately stone-and-brick mansion situated on a hill that sloped to the banks of the Schuylkill. As newlyweds, Tony and Amelia Wister had lived in a town house on Walnut Street, a quaint structure that had been in the Wister family for several generations. But following the devastating yellow fever epidemic of 1793, in which more than four thousand citizens of Philadelphia perished, Tony Wister had been determined to protect his wife and children from future epidemics. They had been lucky that not a single loved one had succumbed to the dread disease, but they might not be so fortunate another time. A summer house away from the humid and densely populated city seemed the perfect solution. His wife, Amelia, designed Summer Cottage, and within a year, it was ready to serve as a summer residence. In no time, however, Tony and Amelia's brood had outgown the town house on Walnut Street, and by the time Melanie was seven or eight, they resided more at Summer Cottage than in town. And once the family had increased to six children, three of them lads, the children seldom left the countryside. Summer Cottage was their home.

The light began to shift as the sun slipped toward the horizon. Deciding that it was time to stop for the day, Melanie set the palette on a nearby table and began to take off her smock. Footsteps echoed through the large room, and Melanie glanced over her shoulder. Her aunt Cressida, resplendent in a magenta merino carriage costume, was walking across the parqueted floor. She had just come indoors. Her cheeks were red as apples and the tip of her nose was pink. She was followed by a young maid carrying a tea tray.

"Hello Aunt C-Cressy," greeted Melanie. She folded the smock and placed it on the table beside the palette.

"Hello, m'dear. Thought you might be stopping about now. Are you in the mood for a spot of tea?"

"Yes, thank you. 'T-twas considerate of you to th-think of it." She spoke slowly in an effort to prevent herself stuttering, but with each awkward repetition of a syllable that seemed determined not to leave her mouth, it became worse.

The ladies moved toward the far end of the long room, where a green brocade settee was set at an angle to a marble hearth and a crackling fire was blazing. Melanie's mother always called it the great room; devoid of the usual clutter of furnishings, it was where the large Wister clan could congregate and where banquet tables might be set out at holidays to accommodate friends and relations. This was the place where Tony and Amelia had often gathered with their children for an evening of storytelling; or where, on a rainy summer day, parents and offspring had staged puppet shows; and where, when the girls had been of age, their parents had held a series of elegant coming-out balls.

Melanie sat on the settee, demurely crossing her legs at the ankles. "Wh-where did you go this m-morning, Aunt C-Cressy? Jeremy and I could hardly b-believe you were up and out before b-breakfast." She poured a cup of imported Souchong for her aunt and teasingly added, "Jeremy r-remarked that you seemed out of character and w-wondered if you might b-be in need of a recuperative s-stay at the Pennsylvania Hospital."

Cressida tossed back her head and laughed with mirthful abandon. "He's right. I don't feel myself these days. But 'tis nothing to fret about. I was merely out riding with Mr. Rittenhouse. With the thaw opening the roads, Mr. Rittenhouse proposed an outing to the new leatherworks in the Northern Liberties. And though I must confess to nary an interest in factory machinery, I vow there's nothing I might not do if it permitted me the company of Mr. Rittenhouse. Nothing in the world," she concluded with affected breathlessness and a lovesick sigh.

A thin slice of fruit cake halted halfway to Melanie's mouth. "D-Don't tell me you're s-smitten with Mr. R-Rittenhouse!"

Cressida gave another dramatic sigh. "La, I fear I am, and further, though neither your brother nor my mama would credit it for an instant, I believe 'tis the real thing this time," she vowed.

"*I* b-believe you, Aunt Cressy," said Melanie sincerely.

The Mr. Rittenhouse of whom Cressida spoke and upon whom she was bound and determined to bestow a lifetime of affection was a serious-minded gentleman whose fine features were only surpassed by his family fortune. Melanie knew the elegant widower whose thick black hair was streaked with silver and could well understand her aunt's *tendre*. Truth to tell, Lady Cressida would not be the first female to have set her sights on Tench Rittenhouse. A dashing male specimen, a brilliant engineer, and a revered member of the Philosophical Society, he had long been one of Philadelphia's most eligible and evasive gentlemen. His wife had died childless two decades before, and it appeared Mr. Rittenhouse far preferred the bachelor state to matrimony. If Aunt Cressy could capture Mr. Rittenhouse's heart, she would be a much envied lady indeed.

"Thank you for your vote of confidence. It's gratifying to know someone takes me seriously." Cressida emitted another heartfelt sigh and glanced toward Melanie's easel. "The painting's progressing nicely."

"Not as n-nicely as I m-might wish. C-colors of the b-bare t-trees aren't r-right."

"Perhaps if you strolled down to the woods and got a small branch, that might help."

"What a wonderful idea!" Melanie exclaimed, the wretched stutter abandoning her in the onset of enthusiasm, her crisp, blue eyes dancing with delight.

This was not lost on Cressida, who endeavored to disguise a concerned frown for her niece. She spoke carefully, "Y'know, Melanie, my mama was right. She said you were an exquisite, and 'tis undeniably ture. I warrant you would be a Veritable Diamond of the First Stare at any rout, here or in London."

"Oh, m-ma'am." She blushed in disbelief. True, Melanie was a modest young lady, but it was not modesty speaking. Rather it was ignorance. Having not been out in society for more than four years, she was blissfully unaware of how she might shine in a group of young ladies. "I can s-scarce believe my l-looks are anything extraord-dinary. B-besides, surely m-my g-gruesome s-speech would be m-most unattractive to any man."

"Fiddlesticks. I'm not convinced it is an insurmountable condition. You managed to shed it once before, and there's no reason why you should not do so again," Cressida said, not making any mention of the role Charles Biddle had played in Melanie's overcoming her stutter, nor of Melanie's retreat and profound grief when Charles had died. In the kindest voice, she offered, "I'd like to help you, dearest Melanie. Why, we could practice elocution in the mornings, and it would give me the greatest pleasure to take you to several balls with me."

The sincerity in her aunt's voice moved Melanie. Usually when her mother or her sister, Louisa Catharine, made a similar offer, she dismissed it out of form. But there was something about the expectant sparkle in Aunt Cressida's eyes that prevented Melanie from refusing. Hesitantly, she answered, "I would like that, Aunt C-Cressy."

"Splendid." And to Melanie's surprise, the sophisticated older woman flung her arms about her in an enormous hug. "Oh, what fun we'll have, and won't Jeremy be pleased with the both of us? Why, the New Year's Ball is two days hence. Perhaps you might—"

"T-two days! Oh, no, Aunt Cressy. 'T-tis too s-soon."

Seeing the error of her enthusiasm, Cressida did not press the issue. "Mayhap you're right. But it doesn't hurt to try on a few ball gowns. I've an exquisite dancing frock of blue crêpe trimmed with artificial roses and tinsel leaves. The blue is, I venture, precisely the color of your eyes, and the gown would look divine on you. Never worn it myself, and soon as you say you're ready to go about, I would be most pleased if you'd accept it as a gift."

Again, Melanie was touched by her aunt's gesture. "Th-thank you. I would b-be pleased to accept the g-gown."

"Glad that's settled. By the by, drove past River Rest. Appears the new neighbors have moved in. Mr. Rittenhouse says he heard from Mr. Chew at the Fish House Club that they're British."

"Yes, 'tis t-true," confirmed Melanie. "And the g-gentleman is an earl. J-just imagine!"

"Oh, pooh!" Cressida exclaimed, giving her black curls a toss. "I've quite had my fill of earls to last a lifetime. Besides, m'dear, your very own brother is an earl, so you must see they're no different from you and I."

"B-but Jeremy's n-not a r-real earl. Not born one, at least."

"Faith, you'd never know that the way all those brainless chits flutter about him. Your poor brother. Never seen such a besieged gentleman. One would think there wasn't another eligible male within a thousand miles. Why, at the theatre the other evening, Elizabeth Baldwin thought to catch his attention by stumbling into his arms. Silly twit actually fell down the steps and landed at his feet."

Melanie giggled. "It c-can't be t-true!"

"Oh, but it is. Every word of it, I assure you, and Jeremy was quite perplexed by the ambitious young beauty."

Peals of laughter tinkled forth from Melanie. "Oh, I w-wish I'd seen."

"And so you shall. We'll have you out on the town in no time flat, and then you can see for yourself what a wretched existence the most popular man in Philadelphia has to suffer."

"No w-wonder he was so p-pleased to l-learn we'd an earl next d-door. He m-must be h-hoping this earl w-will take the attention away from him. He was off to c-call on them j-just before you came in."

"Suppose we'll hear all about it at dinner. In the meantime, why don't you come upstairs with me and try on that blue dancing frock?"

"Yes, I'd l-like that," Melanie responded. Although she was not certain she could ever stop stuttering or muster enough nerve to attend one of Philadelphia's subscription balls, there was no harm in trying on her aunt's dress. It had been ages since she had worn anything more elaborate than a dinner gown. It would be a treat to put on something fancier, even if it was only for a few minutes.

If one walked through the birch wood, River Rest was located several hundred yards from the sweeping front veranda of Summer Cottage. If one chose to ride, the distance was a full quarter of a mile along a winding dirt road. And although both mansions were situated at the same bend in the river, thick foliage and a small dip in the land deceived the residents of each into believing there was not a neighbor to be found for miles.

River Rest was the older of the two mansions and, though smaller than Summer Cottage, it was definitely more palatial in style. Built in 1763 by Captain James Stewart, a Scottish privateer, the brick-and-stucco mansion mingled classical Georgian details with the style of a Queen Anne manor house; above the white-columned front door was an elaborate pediment whose classic motif was echoed in cornices and chimney stacks. River Rest symbolizd Stewart's hard-earned wealth. It was one of the loveliest country seats north of Philadelphia, and it was the only home that Captain Stewart's beloved daughter, Susannah, had ever known; it was the place she had been born, and the place where she had perished. After her death, the captain left River Rest, and the house lay vacant until a Dutch sloop out of Antigua brought word that the captain was dead. The bank took possession of River Rest, leasing it to that variety of diplomatic missions and foreign visitors which came in an endless stream to Philadelphia.

The latest occupants had arrived two days before Christmas and were beginning to feel at ease in their new surroundings. Several wagonloads of trunks had been transported from the docks, the contents unpacked and aired. Various household supplies had been delivered from a general merchandiser on Front Street, and every room had new beeswax tapers and an aromatic dish of dried summer roses and lavender. One would never know that Torquil, Emma, and Lady Wheatley had not been in residence at River Rest for years. Their personal marks were already evident upon the mansion. In the hall, Torquil's and Emma's wellies were lined up by the elegant carved oak front door; Lady Wheatley, as was her practice, had ordered that liberal doses of lemon oil by applied daily to the furnishings and woodwork throughout the mansion; and Emma had insisted that an abundance of hothouse flowers be obtained to grace the common rooms on the first floor.

This afternoon, Lady Wheatley and Emma had resumed their London routine. They were cloistered in the sun-warmed parlor where Emma sat before a cherrywood pianoforte practicing her music lessons.

The parlor was at the rear of the mansion house, and from its recessed windows there was a commanding view of the river. Decorated in muted shades of green and blue, it was a comfortable room with an escritoire in the corner opposite the pianoforte. Twin fireplaces kept the parlor toasty warm year round.

"Lovely, m'dear. There's nothing to make the spirits soar with delight as music played with so delicate a touch," said Lady Wheatley when Emma had played the last chord of Mozart's piano sonata in A Major. "How fortunate that Cousin Caroline knew of such a handsome property and with a pianoforte so that you might continue your lessons."

This elicited a weak smile from Emma, who wondered if Lady Wheatley was partially deaf, for the piece had sounded decidedly stilted to her ear. She loved the "Rondo alla Turca" movement, but her skills as a musician were as weak as those as an artist or decorative seamstress. Lessons seemed quite futile to Emma, and she wished that she might have accompanied Uncle Torquil into Philadelphia this morning. But the earl was more adamant than ever about Emma following the proper dictates of society. It was no less important in America than in England for Emma to remember the importance of her reputation. Before departing for a meeting at the bank, he had lectured Emma that the world of business was for men, while her only business was to heed Lady Wheatley's tutelage.

Lady Wheatley prattled on about the merits of the rental property, and at length, Emma responded. "Yes, ma'am, your cousin did locate a splendid house. Though I do wish we might be in town, rather than in the middle of nowhere."

"Pshaw. I'm told the most fashionable Philadelphians have been living on the outskirts of the city for many years. And we do want to be fashionable, don't we? Further, the city's crowded and noisy. Whatever reason could there be for wanting to live there when it is a carriage ride away?"

Emma sighed. "I think it would be nice to look out the front door and see all that activity that makes so much noise. We've been in America nearly a week, and I know nothing more about my new home than when we arrived. Too, I should like to see other people."

"And so you shall. With the New Year's Ball two nights hence, we shall both be formally introduced to the society of this city."

At thought of the ball, a dark frown creased Emma's brow. Try as she might, she had been unable to prevent herself from worrying about Jeremy Wister. From the first moment Uncle Torquil announced his plans to sail for Philadelphia, Emma had *known* that sooner or later she would encounter Mr. Wister. And that thought left her thoroughly unsettled. Over the past months, she had learned to be less impulsive, and she had learned that the wiser course of action was to guard one's feelings from strangers. Although she knew this and had comported herself accordingly during the remainder of the London Season, Emma was not certain how she would react when she next saw Mr. Wister. What if she still found him attractive? It was an awful fear, and one of which she was, quite honestly, ashamed. He was a nobody, a little voice reminded her. A rude nobody, and it was ridiculous to countenance him in the least. But the sad truth was Emma could not stop thinking about the cad. Over and over she wondered why he had become so cold that evening at Stanton Hall. Over and over she reexperienced the mortifying moment when he had turned away from her as if she had the plague. Time and again, she recalled the moment when the unpleasant hollow ache had risen from the pit of her stomach, burning her like a relentless hunger. And over and over, she saw those beautiful blue eyes—eyes that had lied to her—turn as hard and frigid as ice.

Observing Emma's harassed countenance, Lady Wheatley continued, "We are not so isolated as it would seem, my dear. Cousin Caroline assures me there are neighbors all around. It is by careful use of the lay of the land that privacy is ensured and the pristine setting is preserved. Caroline says that river travelers can count more than five homes on the shores at this point in the river. Just look," she pointed toward a curl of smoke rising above the faint outline of a building on the opposite shore. "Let me recollect. I believe Caroline said the Plumsteads and the Brecks are across the river. And our own neighbors are very nearby. Summer Cottage is to our south. There's even a gate at the bottom of the lawn where the two gardens connect. And Cousin Caroline says our neighbors at Summer Cottage have an unmarried and highly eligible son. Good English family, she vowed."

"Lady Wheatley, you make it sound as if matrimony was our purpose behind taking this house. Honestly, I would like to enjoy Philadelphia and to make friends. Not to go about searching for a husband at every rout or musicale." She swiveled around on the pianoforte stool to gaze out the window. Tufts of dead grass, a sickly yellowish brown, poked up between patches of snow. The river was pitch black and frozen at the edges, where a thin line of silver-gray water rushed between the craked ice. While staring at the river, she added, "If there's one thing I learned this past summer, it was you can't expect to find love where and when it doesn't exist."

Lady Wheatley emitted a twitter of exasperation. "Never heard such a farrago of nonsense. My dear child, who said anything about love? Your Uncle Torquil and I wish to see you married to a suitable gentleman, not to tumble bug-eyed into a romance."

"You're right, ma'am," Emma said, looking over her shoulder at Lady Wheatley. "And rest assured, I harbor no intentions of falling willy-nilly in love with anyone. There was more than one lesson I learned this past season, and that was the utter foolishness of rushing into anything. Love at first sight is naught but a schoolgirl's myth." There was an odd, almost cynical edge to her words as she concluded, "Indeed, I believe that love, like trust, must grow on a foundation of years of sharing."

"Ah," was the full extent of the Lady Wheatley's response.

Emma pivoted on the stool, straightened her back, and positioned her fingers over the keys, but before she could begin another tune, there came a loud knock on the front door. There was the responding echo of the butler's footsteps across the entry rotunda.

"Who can it be?" asked Emma. Perhaps there was a house filled with young ladies her own age nearby, and they had come to strike up a friendship.

"Our first caller!" exclaimed Lady Wheatley. "Most likely a neighbor. Cousin Caroline has put about the word of our arrival, and it is high time we should be receiving callers." She fussed with the bodice of her gown and rose to her feet as the door opened and the butler announced:

"Mr. Jeremy Wister of Summer Cottage."

"My lord," exclaimed the older woman, recognizing at once the tall, powerful figure of the handsome American, who had inherited the title Earl of Cadogan. "What an unexpected surprise! La, don't tell me, we are to be neighbors. What a spectacular development!"

Stunned by the sight of the two women seated in the parlor, Jeremy halted midstride to stare keenly at the pair of them. Lady Wheatley's plump face was rosy with delight; Miss Fraser's countenance was as unreadable as he hoped his own was. Never in a thousand decades had he ever again expected to encounter Miss Fraser. That foolish episode in Brickhill and at Stanton Hall was a closed chapter, and he had very nearly succeeded in forgetting her since his arrival home. He blinked twice, wondering if he might be dreaming, but the two faces merely stared back at him.

Damn, but he wished that he had bothered to discover more about his neighbors before making this call. Well, he hadn't, and there was nothing for it save to deliver a gratuitous greeting and depart. Having recovered his powers of speech, Jeremy delivered a bland "Good day" to the ladies.

"What a delight to see you again, sir," bubbled Lady Wheatley. In an aside, she instructed the butler to bring tea and then, facing an unaccountably pallid Emma, she enthused, "Look who's come to call, m'dear."

Gone was Emma's daydream of a household of companionable young ladies. In its place remained the unpleasant fact that her closest neighbor was the very man who had treated her rudely and, whether by purposeful intent or not, had made her feel foolish and very young. Her tongue felt twice its size, and she could not utter a word. Answering with a nod, her mind flew back to the last time she had seen Mr. Wister. He was as tall as she recalled and as sinfully good-looking. His eyes were still that intriguing mixture of dark and light blue, and his expression was as frigid as when he had left the drawing room at Stanton Hall. Sadly, that warm smile she had once admired was naught but a daydream of a distant past. But the sorriest fact was that she could not help the sudden racing of her heart at the sight of this man with the ink-blue eyes. "Sir," was the best she could accomplish as she folded her hands in her lap.

"Come, Emma, join us by the fire for tea. 'Tis so exciting to have a caller, Mr. Wister," said Lady Wheatley. "I was just remarking to Miss Fraser that we are not as isolated at River Rest as it would seem. I am told we have neighbors all around, and I'm quite looking forward to making their acquaintance. By the by, will you be attending the New Year's Ball, sir?"

Trapped. Treed like an old coon up a tree. That was how

Jeremy felt as he mumbled all the proper niceties and took a seat beside the hearth. He heard the rustle of Miss Fraser's skirts as she rose from the pianoforte to join them.

"Lady Wheatley is correct, sir," she said in that musical voice he so well remembered. " 'Tis an unexpected surprise to discover we are neighbors."

Jeremy looked at Emma and experienced an overwhelming rush of self-disgust. Once before he had been blinded by her unusual beauty, and of a sudden, he found that it was happening all over again. He wished that he might look upon Miss Fraser with indifference, yet it was impossible. Those green cat's-eyes and rich plum-tinted lips were a lovely sight. Try as he might, he could not prevent his eyes from roaming over the pleasant picture she presented. What was wrong with him? He knew that she was the niece and ward of a notorious lecher, that she was not the sort of woman who deserved more than a fleeting notice. Still he was reacting in that same impulsive and boyishly immature fashion as he had the first time he encountered her. His jaw clenched in distaste. Studying her with cool regard, he noted that although she might be as pretty as he recalled, she did not have the same sparkle and vivacity he remembered. He must have imagined that. Evidently, Miss Fraser was not so unique after all.

He asked the obvious question. "What brings you to America? And," he further queried, already suspecting the dreadful answer, "is your uncle with you, Miss Fraser?"

"Yes, he is, though he's not at home at present. Uncle Torquil is in town, meeting with a Mr. Girard."

Stephen Girard, a merchant and banker, was reputed to be the wealthiest man in America. The elderly, crabbed, one-eyed gentleman was a genius at making money. It was not remarkable that an Englishman might seek him out, for one could not better invest one's funds than in one of Mr. Girard's ventures.

"So it was business which brought your uncle to Philadelphia?" came the cool query.

"Not precisely," was Emma's guarded reply. She loathed telling this man about the circumstances under which they had sailed for America. The entire incident had been a dreaful mistake; everyone knew Harry Brockton was a notorious bad loser at loo and when the cards were dealt against him, it was his practice to accuse his opponent of cheating. Emma knew how much it troubled Uncle Torquil to have been challenged by Lord Brockton. It had changed their lives, and she wished they might be able to forget it, for she suspected Jeremy Wister would not be in the least bit sympathetic.

Fortunately, Lady Wheatley intervened. "The truth is, sir, we departed under a most undeserved cloud." Seeing the suspicion in their guest's expression, she hastened to clarify, "Oh, 'twas nothing to do with Miss Fraser. Her guardian was called out by Lord Brockton, and though there wasn't a shred of truth in any of it, the earl had no choice but to accept the challenge."

In a deadly cool accent, Jeremy finished for her, "And am I safe in concluding that the earl mortally wounded said gentleman and was forced to leave England or otherwise face criminal charges?"

"Lamentably, you're correct." Lady Wheatley's hands fluttered through the air in a regretful little movement. She leaned toward Jeremy, her whalebone stays creaking audibly, "Let me add, dear sir, that I wouldn't share this intelligence with merely anyone, but as you're a previous acquaintance and as you and the earl share mutual friends in the Stanhopes, I'm sure my trust is not ill-placed and that we can depend upon your discretion. Upon my beloved husband's soul, I vouch 'tis a wholly unfounded allegation, and mayhap, if were not for Miss Fraser I would not be so bold to confide in you, sir."

Emma felt a blush heating up her neck. How could Lady Wheatley speak so forthrightly? Even Emma would not be so bold to speak this way. Whatever was she doing confiding in this man?

Jeremy, too, was uncomfortable with the turn of events. Far from distancing himself from Miss Fraser and her family, it appeared he was being drawn into her affairs as a principal player. With excruciating politeness, he said, "I'm not certain I understand your meaning, Lady Wheatley."

"The earl's decision to leave England was not so much to protect himself as it was to protect his niece and ward, our delightful Miss Fraser. My lord Hamilton has long suffered the sting of guilt that his own, let us say, frolicsome younger years might reflect poorly on his niece and her chances for a suitable match."

"Lady Wheatley, I don't believe Mr. Wister wishes to—" Emma endeavored to intervene, but was cut short with a stern look from the lady.

"I'm sure that you, my lord, see how coming to Philadelphia affords both his lordship and Miss Fraser a fresh start, and I'm hopeful that you'll agree to assist us in this matter." Lady Wheatley's words fell like dead weights upon the silent room.

This was definitely the most mortifying moment in Emma's entire young life. Never before had she felt such humiliation, nor such anger. This was beyond the line of toleration. In a fleeting moment of rationality, she supposed it was not Lady Wheatley's fault; the woman was only trying to do what she thought was best. Emma glanced from her plump and flushed expectant face to Jeremy's cool one, and what she saw reflected in his inky-blue eyes made her hastily lower her gaze to her lap. Again she experienced the uncanny feeling that she could read his mind. And this time what she read was not in the least bit pleasant. His thoughts were naught but negative and hostile.

Stunned though he might be, Jeremy could discern Lady Wheatley's blind enthusiasm for her charge. Obviously, the lady did not realize the impact her words had had on either himself or Miss Fraser, who appeared as genuinely dismayed as himself. Her suggestion was preposterous, yet there was no gentlemanly way he could refuse. Any excuse would be pure sham.

As the silence lengthened, Lady Wheatley added, "I would merely hope that you might introduce Miss Fraser to suitable young gentlemen. We would not wish her to make any inappropriate connections."

"No, of course, not," he mumbled, then feebly, offered, "If you've any questions about anyone in particular, I should be happy to tell you what I know." Egad! Where had that come from? What was in his mind to actually volunteer to become embroiled in Miss Fraser's quest for a husband? Of a sudden, he heard a voice of conscience saying that there was no danger in helping Miss Fraser. Although *he* did not wish to align himself with a lady whose guardian had a stigma attached to his name, she might be highly attractive to any number of other young men in Philadelphia. Young men, he amended cynically, who did not have an innocent younger sister or any female relative who might fall prey to the Fatal Earl.

"Oh, sir, you are too generous," declared Lady Wheatley. "We shall forever be indebted to you for your kindness. Isn't it kind of Mr. Wister, m'dear?"

Emma did not appear in the least bit grateful. She bit her lower lip and glared at Lady Wheatley. A deep frown distorted her lips and patches of scarlet—that clashed horrendously with her coppery curls—splotched her forehead and cheeks. She had the look of a truculent and temperamental child.

"Yes, ma'am, we are most indebted to Mr. Wister," she said tonelessly, not daring to glance in that gentleman's direction.

Truth to tell, Jeremy could not help wondering if he had imagined the enchanting creature he had seen in Brickhill.

Night was falling over the countryside when Torquil returned to River Rest. The winter air was crisp and clean after the closed-in odors of the city, and he paused on the path between the stable and the house to enjoy the last moments of lingering light that reflected off the icy waters of the Schuylkill.

It was beautiful here, and although Torquil detested having to leave England amid scandal, he did not regret his decision to travel to America. This was a vital country, and after meeting with Mr. Girard, he was certain that he was going to stay here for quite some time. He loved this house, elegant and serene on a sloping hilltop above the Schuylkill, and he liked the gentlemen to whom he had been introduced by Mr. Girard. This was not an exile; it was a chance for a new beginning. And Torquil relished the opportunity he had been offered to enter into a partnership with several local gentleman, who were forming a company to mine the anthracite fields on the upper Schuylkill. Stephen Girard was a genius at spotting profitable investments, and Torquil was inspired by the older gentleman's enthusiasm for the project; there was more than personal gain to be found in this enterprise, a man might even affect the shaping of the world about him. Never before had that possibility occurred to Torquil, and he was intrigued by the prospect. He was confident that his stay in Philadelphia would be positive and productive. His single wish was that Emma might soon feel as comfortable as he had upon first stepping ashore.

Black riding boots crunching on the frozen ground, Torquil continued toward the house. Welcoming candlelight flickered from the windows, and he recognized Emma's silhouette standing before a pair of French doors. She was staring toward the river, and he waved to his niece, but she did not notice him. Curious as to what held her attention, Torquil followed the direction of her gaze and stopped dead in his tracks, transfixed by the ethereal sight of a slender figure moving through the bare trees.

Was it really a person? He could not tell for it seemed lighter than air, floating in and out of the mists like a mirage. Or was it nothing more than mists, swirling upward and moving delicately through the woods? On December days such as this when the air warmed, but the river remained frigid, 'twas not uncommon for eerie cloudlike figures to rise along the shoreline. Or was it, he wondered with an onset of whimsy, the spirit of Miss Susannah?

No, 'twas no chimera he saw reach up to pull a branch from a tree. 'Twas the figure of a woman, he concluded, though who she was, and why anyone might be out plucking bare branches, he did not know. Impulsively, he strolled in the direction of the copse of trees and waved at the woman, who was swathed in a pale gray cloak, her face hidden beneath a full hood.

Torquil was near the bottom of the lawn when, as if she had sensed his presence, the woman turned. He caught his breath. For a very brief instant through the half-light of dusk, Torquil tasted a glimpse of a rare, near ethereal beauty. She was intensely fragile, such a faint image wavering through the fog, and he thought she could not be of this world. Then she was gone from his sight; it was as if she had vanished into thin air. Common sense dictated that she must have slipped into the darker recesses of the woods, but the swiftness of her disappearance mystified Torquil as much as the sight of her had done. And as he turned up the hill toward the house, he could not help wondering if, indeed, he had seen a ghost.

CHAPTER
FIVE

In Philadelphia, as in Paris, the best society seldom attended balls before Christmas. A smattering of modest assemblies were held as early as November, when the theatres raised their curtains, and Mr. Philipps, the music impresario, began his concert series; however, the first gala of the season was the New Year's subscription ball. Caroline Shippen, whose husband was one of the managers of the ball, had been assured by her spouse that her friends from England would be issued invitations. True to Mr. Shippen's word, and to Lady Wheatley's delight, a footman arrived at River Rest the morning after Jeremy Wister's visit bearing the following invitation in gold lettering:

> *New Year's Ball*
> *Masonick Hall*
> *The Honour of*
> *Miss E. Fraser's*
> *Company is requested at a Ball on Wednesday*
> *Evening the 30 of December 1817*
> *Introduced by Mr. G. Shippen*
> *Subscriber*

Each manager was allowed to introduce two ladies, and a similar invitation was also delivered for Lady Wheatley. Mr. Shippen, with Mr. Girard acting as seconding sponsor, had placed the earl's name before the managers' committee so that he might purchase a subscription, that being the procedure required for a gentleman to gain entry to the event.

Thus it was amidst high expectations that the formally garbed trio embarked on the carriage ride from River Rest to town, the evening of December 30. Lady Wheatley was in high alt that she and her young charge would be soon introduced to some of America's finest families; Torquil was confident that Emma, in this country where men chose to test the scientific and geographic frontiers of their world rather than idle away their time in the pursuit of pleasure, would soon find a gentleman to her liking; and Emma was eager to make the acquaintance of the young ladies and gentlemen of Philadelphia.

Tonight, she had chosen her ensemble with care, selecting a flattering cream-colored gown of corded silk. The bodice and hemline were stitched with seed pearls, and brocaded flowers in muted yellow and green decorated the skirt. The creamy silk accentuated her delicate complexion, and the bright green leaves that trailed between the flowers highlighted the vibrant hue in her sparkling cat's-eyes. Over it all, she wore a stylish Witzchoura cloak. A Christmas gift from Uncle Torquil, the wrap was lined with an abundance of deep auburn fur, and a standing pelerine collar with fox fur was high enough to keep her ears warm no matter how low the temperature plummeted.

The carriage turned down Chestnut Street, the pair of matched Maryland bays snorting with exertion, clouds of frozen breath rising about their heads, and the clip-clop of hooves echoing through the still night. Emma pressed her nose to the frosty glass window as they passed the domed neoclassical structure that housed the Academy of Fine Arts; in the next block the carriage came to a halt before the Masonick Hall. The building that combined both medieval and gothic styles resembled a cathedral with two levels of enormous arched windows and a crenellated roof over which rose a great spire. Statues carved by William Rush and representing the figures of Faith, Hope, and Charity adorned the structure. Candlelight beckoned from those tall arched windows, and a liveried footman hurried forward to open the carriage door and assist the ladies to the sidewalk.

Inside, several of the managers, distinguished by the white-ribbon sashes across their chests, and their wives were receiving the guests. Torquil, Emma, and Lady Wheatley were welcomed by the Shippens, who led them through an arched doorway draped with evergreen boughs. Sprigs of holly and red-velvet ribbons festively decorated the grand saloon in which some one hundred ladies and gentlemen mingled. At the far end of the room the members of an orchestra on a platform carpeted in deep green velvet were tuning their instruments.

Emma and Lady Wheatley marveled at the prodigiously elegant scene, and the older woman added to her cousin, "Faith, Caroline, Philadelphia is quite as stylish as you've always claimed it was."

"Glad you approve," replied Mr. Shippen, his wife smiling at his side.

"Oh, look, Uncle Torquil!" Emma exclaimed. "Do you see what I see? I believe 'tis Lady Cressida, over there on the arm of that distinguished gentleman with silver streaks in his hair."

Torquil frowned. "Believe you're right, puss. Though I hadn't realized the lady was in America."

Several paces ahead was Lady Cressida, magnificent in a décolleté gown of flaming red satin with matching scarlet plumes swaying from a topknot of Grecian curls. She carried a red lace fan with which she was bestowing numerous gentle pats upon her partner's forearm.

"Should have known you'd be acquainted with Lady Cressida," commented Mr. Shippen. "Small world, isn't it?"

His wife added, "If you know Lady Cressida, then you must know her nephew, Jeremy Wister, our own Philadelphia earl. You're neighbors with the Wister family. Did I tell you that?"

In avid tones, Lady Wheatley informed her cousin about their previous acquaintance with Mr. Wister and of his courteous call at River Rest. While the two older women waxed eloquent about the gentleman's favorable personage and suitable fortune, Emma glanced about anxiously, hoping that the particular gentleman was not in attendance this evening. She was determined to make friends and to enjoy herself; another encounter with Mr. Wister was not her notion of the way to ensure a successful evening.

A familiar English accent brought Emma back to her immediate surroundings. Lady Cressida swept toward their group. "Darling, see who's here," she cooed to her companion. "It is a dear old friend, the Earl of Gairloch, and his niece, Miss Emma Fraser. La, Hamilton, I can scarce believe my eyes, but it really is you. What a glorious surprise."

The earl bowed. "Lady Cressida, 'tis, indeed, a surprise," he said with the appearance of pleasure. "Did your nephew not inform you? We are neighbors. I've taken River Rest for the Season."

"Neighbors, you say? And Jeremy knew about it! Shame on him for not sharing the good news. Sometimes I wonder about his manners. He should have known how much it would please me. Oh, this is, indeed, good news," she chattered on excitedly, waving her fan this way and that, scarlet plumes bobbing up and down. And with each movement the flowery aroma of some exotic Eastern perfume became more and more evident. "Miss Fraser, Hamilton, allow me to introduce my special friend, Mr. Tench Rittenhouse." This was said with such a surfeit of adoration that only an idiot would not have realized how besotted the lady was with Mr. Rittenhouse, and only that same idiot would not have noticed the immense relief that crossed the earl's expression at this revelation.

Mr. Rittenhouse bowed to Emma, then faced Torquil. He had heard of the Scottish earl's involvement in Mr. Girard's anthracite venture, and being an engineer, Mr. Rittenhouse had a great curiosity about the plans. While the gentlemen conversed about the development of the coal fields along the upper Schuylkill, Cressida gossiped with Emma.

Unbeknownest to the amiable group of partygoers, they were being observed by a tall gentleman at the opposite end of the ballroom. Jeremy, who had gone to fetch a glass of punch for Miss Ann Morris, had nearly spilled the pink liquid down his white shirtfront at the sight of the Earl of Gairloch conversing with his aunt. Egad, what a bad turn of luck this was! Blindly, he thrust the punch cup toward a petite blonde.

"Thank you, Mr. Wister. I mean, my lordship," she lisped fawningly.

"Please, Miss Morris," came the barely civil retort. "I am as American as you and prefer you to address me as you always have."

Holding the crystal cup to perfectly pursed lips, Miss Morris batted her eyelashes. "But, sir, your lordship, 'tis a most thrilling event to have an earl in our midst. Why, I don't believe we've had such renowned company at our New Year's Ball since the young Bonaparte visited Philly."

Impatiently, Jeremy sighed. He had thought that of all the blushing misses in attendance this evening, Ann Morris possessed a modicum of common sense and would not be dazzled by his newly acquired title. Obviously, he was mistaken; she was as beguiled as every other young lady who insisted on "milording" him at every opportunity. And the flirtatious ploys to which he was subjected were just as endless. One might actually wonder if the academies of this city had stooped to teaching their female pupils the art of casting out lures to ensnare a husband. It was worse than London! One slip and he was bound to find himself the victim of some scheming mama and betrothed to her giggling, spotty daughter! What was he to do?

It was senseless to argue the truth with Miss Morris. She was bound and determined to make him an earl, no matter what he said. Of a sudden, a brilliant notion took seed in his mind. "But Miss Morris, you are mistaken. I'm not the only earl here." He saw a glimmer of inquisitiveness spring to her eyes. "Verily, there's a real earl, born and bred to the title, gracing our ball this eve."

"Who? Where?" she gasped.

"Over there, Miss Morris." He nodded toward Torquil. "The tall gentleman conversing with Mr. Rittenhouse."

"Pray, sir, tell me all," she lisped, eyes pinned on the impressive sight of all six feet three inches of Torquil in evening black, his golden brown hair falling about his shoulders like a lion's mane. "Who is he? And who's the pretty young lady by his side?"

"'Tis the Earl of Gairloch. Just arrived from England. And his niece, Miss Emma Fraser."

"And you know them, sir?" inquired Miss Morris with no little awe.

"Yes, they're leasing River Rest. Would you like an introduction?"

"You would do that, sir?" He had already taken her arm to guide her across the floor. Nonetheless, she lisped on in a high state of excitement, "Oh, yes. I'd love an introduction, my lord, Mr. Wister. 'Twould be grand."

When Lady Cressida spotted Jeremy and the petite blonde walking across the floor, she suspected right away her nephew's purpose in joining their group. Likely Miss Morris was proving tiresome, and he was seeking safety in numbers. That was not uncommon. What was different and most intriguing was the remarkably stern grimace that shadowed Jeremy's countenance as he regarded Miss Fraser; the young Scottish girl's distinctly uncomfortable reaction was equally fascinating to Lady Cressida. Though Miss Fraser tried to maintain her smile, Cressida watched it wobble and then vanish altogether as her nephew approached. This was most interesting. Until now, Cressida had no reason to think Jeremy and Miss Fraser had met before his visit to River Rest, yet it was clear from their behavior that some emotion of consequence existed between them—an emotion that could not be born of so brief a meeting—and Cressida was determined to flush it out.

Focusing an assessing eye on her nephew, Cressida rushed into conversation. "Shame, Jeremy, for not telling me that Lord Hamilton and his niece are our new neighbors. What a bad boy you are! You weren't keeping it a secret from me, were you?" she asked with mock innocence, giving his elbow a healthy thwack with her closed fan.

If looks might smite one senseless, the narrowed gaze that Jeremy fixed upon his aunt could have done so with razor sharpness. Emma did not miss this. It was a dreadful stare, leading her in the next instance to realize that Mr. Wister had, indeed, kept the news of their arrival secret from his aunt. Plainly, Jeremy was furious with Lady Cressida for broaching the question. And as Emma watched, his looks darkened further; that narrowed, dangerous gaze shifted from the demure smile upon his aunt's face to Uncle Torquil and back to Lady Cressida. Of a sudden, Emma understood the reason why Jeremy had kept the news of their arrival from Lady Cressida. The odious man actually wanted to keep his aunt away from her Uncle Torquil! Her ire at the discovery was instantaneous and red-hot. Just who did Jeremy Wister think that he was to act in such a superior fashion? Her dainty bosom swelled resentfully.

Lady Wheatley broke the silence. "Mr. Wister did not tell you then, Lady Cressida, of his kind offer?"

"No, he breathed not a word to me. And what offer might that be?" Lady Cressida flashed her nephew a speculative grin.

"He has agreed to guide me in selecting suitable gentlemen with whom Miss Fraser might strike an acquaintance," replied Lady Wheatley.

"La, Jeremy, I had not known you were such a neighborly sort. 'Tis a kind offer, indeed." Curiosity devoured Cressida, and she glanced between her livid nephew and Emma; the indignant outrage that was reflected in Miss Fraser's eyes and the firm set of her nephew's jaw confirmed her initial suspicion. Jeremy and Miss Fraser were not strangers to one another. In a most calculating tone, she proceeded, "But before my nephew can begin any introductions, he must have the first dance with Miss Fraser himself. That alone should guarantee her success. Don't you agree, Jeremy?"

Five pairs of eyes focused on Emma and Jeremy. Mr. Rittenhouse exclaimed that Lady Cressida was brilliant; Lady Wheatley beamed with satisfaction; and the earl, who had heretofore heard nothing of Lady Wheatley's request, thanked Mr. Wister for his kind offer.

Emma flushed unbecomingly. Her cheeks aglow with embarrassment, she looked up at Mr. Wister and watched his blue eyes darken with the same angry resignation that she was feeling. There was no way she could cry off. She was as trapped as Mr. Wister, and they had no choice save to comply gracefully.

Stepping forward two paces, Jeremy gave a stiff bow. A nerve ticked along his jawline. "Miss Fraser, would you do me the honor of standing up with me for the next dance?"

"Thank you, sir," she accepted, holding up her head with dignity and smiling as though she could want for no more charming a partner. He took her elbow, and they proceeded onto the floor as the musicians began the chords of a waltz.

"You are out, Miss Fraser, and have already waltzed in London?" he inquired in a voice so composed that Emma wished to step on his toes, if only to wipe that bland expression from his face.

"Yes," she answered evenly.

"Then you don't object to waltzing with me, do you?"

Wishing that she could think of an appropriately withering retort, she quietly answered, "No, sir, I do not object." Quickly, she averted her eyes from his. For, truth to tell, Emma had just made a most unsettling discovery. Far from wishing to escape this man's presence, she possessed an acute desire to be held in his arms and to waltz with him. There was no accounting for such a shameless and senseless fancy. Emma knew better than to behave like a schoolgirl in her first Season, yet she could not prevent the rapid pattering of her heart. Ashamed and discomfited, she could not look at him as he took her right hand in his and set his other about her waist.

Eager couples were milling about them as the orchestra began the lilting melody. Music filled Emma's ears, and all rational thought fled her as Jeremy guided her into the sea of dancers. They circled the ballroom in silence. Emma's smile was brittle, and it seemed time had altered to an intolerably slow pace. She struggled to concentrate on matching her steps to the music. She fought to prevent herself from thinking of anything else except for the glittering ballroom, but she could not hinder the stunning, almost overwhelming awareness of Mr. Wister that grew with each sway and turn of the waltz. She was acutely aware of a sensual masculine aura emanating from him. This was not supposed to happen; she was not supposed to care. But she could not deny his strength, and its assault on her senses. There was a smoky woodsy scent about him that was most pleasing, and with each step, Emma sensed the rippling of shoulder muscles beneath her fingertips. She had never felt so confused, and a kind of panic came over her. Instinct warned her not to let her glance stray from the other dancers to those inky blue eyes. He was so cool and superior. He held her and dear Uncle Torquil in the lowest contempt, yet she could not prevent wildly foolish thoughts, similar to those she had conjured up in England, from rushing through her brain.

She had to say something. She had to put a stop to those unwanted and ridiculous thoughts. Without thinking, she hurried into speech, "You might do well, sir, to learn to school your features. 'Twas written all over your face that you detest my uncle and wish to keep an ocean's distance between him and your aunt."

Jeremy was speechless. Her words were astounding, but the affect she had on him was even more so. This woman had done nothing to entice him, in fact, she had just insulted him, yet, looking down into her upturned face, all he could think of doing was kissing her upon those rich, plum-colored lips. Had he become a complete fool?

"Don't try to deny it," she snapped as Jeremy continued

to stare at her in that uncanny way. "There's no sense in it, for 'tis far and above the most ludicrous assumption and one which only a jackanapes would make," she declared valiantly. Her face was glowing, and her green eyes were dazzling with emotion. "Uncle Torquil has not a fig of interest in Lady Cressida. Truth to tell, he warned me away from her company in London."

This statement had the effect of any icy bucket of water being dumped over his head. Immediately, Jeremy regained control of his wits, his passion was doused, and two sharp blue eyes bore into Emma. In a lethal voice, he inquired, "He did what?"

"My uncle did not think your aunt was a suitable companion for a young lady such as myself," was Emma's straightforward response.

"How dare he? And how dare you repeat such insults!"

"Please, sir, I hasten to amend that I don't share his opinion of Lady Cressida. I think she's a singular lady whose sense of independence is most admirable," she concluded with a definitive nod, her coppery curls bobbing about her flushed face.

To her astonishment, Jeremy threw back his head and laughed. Hostility faded from his eyes, and genuine pleasure lit his countenance at the sight of the vital beauty before him. His words were as surprising as his laughter:

"Ah, at last, I see the young lady I recall. 'Tis a relief, you know, for I had wondered what happened to the young lady who told the tale of the gousty bells."

"I beg your pardon, sir," Emma said, all animation gone from her voice. How could she have been so careless? How could she have let her guard down? How could she have spoken in such a forthright fashion? And she was not the only one behaving erratically. Why would the cool and disdaining Mr. Wister care in the least about the girl who had told the old Highland tale? While Emma could not answer for Mr. Wister, she should be able to control her own conduct. She had to be more careful; impetuosity was ill-conceived, especially in the presence of Mr. Wister. In her demurest voice, she said, " 'Twas an unladylike slip of the tongue. I have often been warned not to speak so impulsively, and it's a habit I hoped to have outgrown. I had no right to speak of your aunt and shall not be so frank again."

A frown creased Jeremy's brow. With a scowl, he looked down at Miss Fraser, but she had turned away. Gazing onto her crown of shiny auburn curls, Jeremy wondered what had caused such a change in the bright young lady he had met in England? That she was sadly subdued was a fact. It was likely the result of some callous and uncaring dandy. Young ladies were fragile creatures; reflecting upon the ups and downs his sisters had suffered, he knew that the most insignificant event could wound deeply. Evidently, young Miss Fraser had suffered such a blow. It was a good thing her uncle had brought her to Philadelphia; time and distance were the best medicine, and soon she could be as spirited as he recalled. In fact, there were a number of young men present this evening who might speed her recovery.

In a softer voice, he said, "I'm forgetting my duties. My promise to Lady Wheatley is one that I intend to keep. Miss Fraser, your attention please. Do you see that pair of gentlemen in the doorway? 'Tis Mr. Ethan Breck and his cousin, Mr. Jonathan Logan. They are both unattached, of the finest patriot stock, and engaged in profitable trade with the Celestial Kingdom. Would you care to meet them?"

"If you think it suitable," was the best Emma could respond. The truth was, she did not wish to meet the eligible bachelors of Philadelphia. She wished to return to River Rest. The evening was hardly begun, yet she was decidedly out of spirits. And it was all Mr. Wister's fault.

"You don't sound terribly enthusiastic," cajoled Jeremy as he might tease one of his sisters.

Promptly, Emma forgot her promise to avoid forthright speech. "My notions of matrimony are rather contrary ones, sir, and they do not include being introduced about like prize cattle. I have never thought marriage should be a means to an end as so many other young ladies believe. It seems they perceive marriage as the way to achieve wealth or status or a title. In my case, it is not so. When I marry, it must be for the life I'll share with my husband."

Those simple and sincere words had the most unsettling influence upon Jeremy, and as they spun about the dance floor, he pulled Emma as close as propriety permitted. The sweet scent of rose water assailed him, and he closed his eyes. He wanted to wrap his arms about her and enfold her in an all-encompassing embrace; he wanted to kiss those sweet plum-colored lips and run his fingers through those fine, coppery curls. He shook his head to clear his mind, and with an all too noticeable catch in his voice, he responded, "You're correct, Miss Fraser. Yours is a unique opinion of marriage, although I would not call it contrary."

Emma sighed. Conversing with Mr. Wister made dancing with him so much easier. Relaxed, she replied, "If not contrary, sir, then what would you call it?"

"Wise," he said, lowering his voice until it seemed almost intimate.

"If that is a compliment, sir, I thank you," she replied, a trifle out of breath. Of a sudden, Emma could not help remembering another time when Mr. Wister had made her feel special. It had been that evening at Stanton Hall when he confessed to discussing bonnets in order to put her at ease. Emma did not want to remember that, nor did she wish to put any stock in this moment, for Mr. Wister's actions had proved him a far different man than his kindly words.

The music stopped, and Emma spoke. "I may not be searching for a husband, but I would nonetheless like to make the acquaintance of Mr. Breck and Mr. Logan, if you please, sir, for I am new in Philadelphia and wish to make as many friends as possible."

"Naturally, Miss Fraser. I should be delighted to make the necessary introductions," he said, leading her toward the two gentlemen and all the while feeling an odd desire that she might change her mind.

In no time, a crowd of gentlemen appeared. Mr. Wister made the introductions, and Emma's dance card was filled for the evening. The orchestra began a rousing country dance, and Mr. Breck, a broad-shouldered gentleman with a thatch of wheat blond hair, claimed Emma.

As they moved onto the floor, Jeremy observed that Miss Fraser appeared most animated in Mr. Breck's company. She was no shy miss, thought Jeremy as he watched the expressive way her cat's-eyes widened and narrowed. Oddly, Jeremy could not help wondering what it was they were discussing. Oddly, too, he thought, it was a shame her family was so unsuitable. Truth to tell, under different circumstances Miss Fraser would have appealed strongly to him.

It was past one in the morning. A long line of carriages had left Masonick Hall and dispersed throughout the city, returning the revelers to their homes on Society Hill and in the countryside. At River Rest, Lady Wheatley had already retired to her bedchamber, and soon Emma would climb the staircase to her pretty room on the second floor. But for now, as had been their custom in London, Emma and Torquil shared a few moments at the end of the evening. They were seated in the library; Torquil cradled a brandy between his palms, and Emma sipped from a cup of warm chocolate. It was a habit they had gotten into when Emma was younger and used to wait up for Torquil's return, eager to hear every detail of his evening on the town. Of late, their talk had a tendency to stray toward Emma's opinion on the various young men with whom she had danced or conversed.

"Well, puss, was it a good evening?"

"Splendid," she said, ending with a tired little yawn.

"Precisely the response I would have expected from the belle of the ball," came the earl's proud and affectionate response.

"Faith, you mustn't utter such a farrago of nonsense. I'm no belle," insisted Emma.

Torquil grinned. "Think what you like, dear puss, but I don't believe another young lady received as much attention as yourself. Particularly not from Ethan Breck."

"Yes, he was attentive and most charming, but..." she

began to add, knowing her uncle wondered if every gentleman she encountered was at last the gentleman whom had attracted her romantic fancy, "he was no more so than Mr. Logan or Mr. Rittenhouse or any of the other gentlemen with whom I danced."

"Hmm," was the earl's response as he thoughtfully nodded. "And what do you think of Jeremy Wister?"

"He's a prig," she answered without prelude.

The earl laughed. "By jove, I believe you're right. He never did think I was good enough for that flibbertigibbet of an aunt."

"You know that?"

"Of course."

"And it doesn't bother you?"

"Not a jot. Glad for it, in fact. Helped to sever Cressy's interest in me. Cressy complained bitterly about her nephew, for he managed to keep her away from me on several occasions. Said he had some starched-up notions that were almost as bad as her mama's."

"Or it may be that he's merely as concerned about his aunt's reputation as you are about mine," she said pensively.

Torquil shook his head. "P'raps. Anyway, he ain't all that bad, and I'm glad to know we've neighbors we can count on. Though I wish Lady Wheatley hadn't imposed on him, I'm sure he'll be a help to you, puss."

"If it makes you happy, I'll accept his help. But I'll not seek out his company. He has an odiously unpredictable temperament, and I intend to avoid him whenever possible," she said with a surfeit of bitterness mingled with determination.

"Ah, so that's the drift of it, is it?" Torquil remarked. Befuddled by this remark, Emma frowned, but the earl did not elaborate. For he was deep in thought, wondering if Emma, in her naïveté, understood the reason for her reactions to Mr. Wister. In Torquil's experience, such emotions usually portended some other and distinctly contradictory emotion. Could it be that his niece had developed a *tendre* for Mr. Wister? He would have to keep an eye on Mr.

Wister; he did not want Emma hurt by the man. Concernedly, he inquired, "You are happy here, aren't you?"

"Of course. How could you ask? I'm always happy wherever we are," she replied, rising from her chair. She crossed the room and kissed her uncle on the forehead. "And you, dearest uncle, are you happy?"

"Mightily. Particularly since Cressida is so besotted with the Rittenhouse chap. Though—thanks to Mr. Wister—it don't seem I'll ever be free from those cloying petticoat types. Remind me I must someday repay him for that introduction to Miss Morris. Egad, the chit makes Cressy seem a paragon of sensibility." Together, they laughed at the memory of Miss Morris, who had remained glued to the earl's side the entire evening, pouting and posing and batting her eyelashes as if her very life depended on it.

Emma controlled her giggles long enough to ask, "Did you hear Miss Morris call you her earl?"

"Afraid I did." Torquil gave a sign of Drury Lane proportions.

On an affectionate grin, she concluded, "Well, I shall look forward to seeing how you deter the avid Miss Morris. Mayhap you can find a way to return her to the Philadelphia earl." Again Emma dropped a kiss to his forehead. "Good night, Uncle Torquil." Then she left the library.

Alone in the silent room, Torquil poured a second snifter of brandy. Leaning back in a great leather chair, he propped his feet on the desk and glanced out the window. Emma seemed so guarded these days and even though she said she was happy, he did not really know how she felt about her new home. It caused him great pain to think that she might be unhappy or never come to feel as welcome as he did. For too many years he had not thought of Emma; now she was the sole motivation behind most of his decisions.

Outside, a sudden movement caught his attention. There it was again! At the edge of the lawn. A sliver of white moved between the trees. Quickly, he set the brandy snifter upon the desk and rose to slip through the French doors. Quietly, he moved across the light layer of snow that had fallen earlier that night. At the edge of the trees, he stopped at a spot where, hidden by a bare oak, he might view this midnight apparition.

The moon slid from behind the clouds, and a burst of light illuminated the woods at the precise moment the figure turned to stare up the hill at River Rest. The hood of the great cloak fell back, and Torquil caught his breath. He remained motionless, fearing to effect the disappearance of the ethereal sight before him.

It was, indeed, a female, and faith, the most beautiful lady he had ever beheld. Moonlight bathed skin as white as a lily. Ink-black hair was wound at the nape of her neck in an ageless style that recalled the madonnas devotedly painted by Italian masters. Her features were delicate, as finely drawn as the most aristocratic in London, and her enormous eyes, wide and innocent, shimmered with a mist that could be naught but tears.

Never before had Torquil been so moved. There was not a sight nor an experience in all his years that had touched him as deeply as the sight of this lady. And it was more than her unspoiled beauty. He was not merely drawn to her because of her loveliness. Without saying a word, her gentle spirit spoke to Torquil. He knew that she was lonely, and he felt her pain as if it were his own.

She blinked, and a single tear slid down one flawless cheek.

Devil a bit! She was no ghost. The lady was flesh and blood, as real as he, and as he watched her raise a shaking hand to her eyes, Torquil resolved to meet her the next time she appeared.

On New Year's Day, unfettered girlish laughter tinkled through the library. Pale green brocade curtains were pulled back to admit sunshine, a fire crackled in the paneled hearth, and the room was as pleasant as the company that had come to call. Lady Cressida and Miss Melanie Wister had arrived at River Rest after noon; it was nearing three o'clock, and they had not stopped talking in all that time.

"I can't tell you how apprehensive I was about coming to America," confided Emma as she stared at the last of the ham and jelly sandwiches on a pewter tray. "When I was a little girl, our travels seemed such an adventure, but somehow this time, it seemed a step into the unknown."

" 'Twas only n-natural, and I th-think you're very b-brave," assured Melanie, smiling kindly. From the moment she entered River Rest, Melanie had known that she had met a true and lasting friend in Miss Fraser. "Why, th-think. You c-came all the way across an ocean while I c-could barely make it d-down the lane to m-meet you this morning. Aunt C-Cressy had to p-push me much of the way."

"But you did come, and that's all that matters. And I do hope that you'll call frequently."

Cressida, who had not been following this conversation, gazed at Emma and blurted out, "I can't help wondering about you and Jeremy."

"What?" Emma replied in a voice that sounded more like a squeak.

"I can't help wondering if you and Jeremy have met before. In England, mayhap?"

Unable to prevaricate, Emma responded with the truth. "Yes," she said pithily. "We were introduced at a weekend in the country last Season."

"Tell us everything!" declared Melanie.

"There's little to tell," was Emma's cautious reply. "We met one evening, and in the morning he was gone."

Cressida remarked, "Nevertheless, you must have formed an opinion of him."

"Our acquaintance was too brief. Of course, I found him a handsome gentleman, but I suspect there's very little we have in common."

"Y-you shall s-soon get to know him b-better," put forth Melanie enthusiastically.

Emma fidgeted with the lace on the end of her right dress sleeve. "I don't imagine we shall see each other that often," she mumbled.

"Oh, b-but you sh-shall," continued Melanie with that same enthusiastic fervor. She was as fond of her brother as he was of her, and she was, of a sudden, anxious for her new friend and her brother to like one another. "Why, the s-sooner the b-better. Why d-don't you and your guardian c-come to dinner t-tomorrow?"

"Oh, no!" burst out Emma much too impetuously. Avoiding Mr. Wister was the one certain way to squelch those wretched feelings he aroused in her, and that would not be possible if she were forever traipsing over to Summer Cottage. She had to keep her distance from him, if she wished to be happy. "I believe my uncle has already made plans for us. Another time, perhaps."

"Yes, another t-time," agreed Melanie, disappointment lacing her words.

An all-knowing "Aah" was heard to escape from Lady Cressida, who had been studying Emma.

Feeling most uncomfortable, Emma abruptly changed the direction of their chat. She faced the younger of her two visitors. "And you, Melanie, speaking of the ball, I didn't see you there. You weren't ill, were you?"

"N-no. I d-don't go about much. 'Tis the st-tutter, you see."

"Oh, Melanie, I can't credit that!" exclaimed Emma. "You can't mean you stayed home because of that?"

Coloring, the black-haired young lady nodded in the affirmative.

"I did not mean to meddle," went on Emma. "But it was a superlative ball, and you can't mean to miss the entire Season. Can you?"

Again Melanie nodded a weak response. She could not bear to tell a soul how she had cried in the garden last evening, lonely and heartbroken and wishing from the bottom of her heart that she might spin about a ballroom floor as carelessly as other young ladies surely did. But the more time passed, the more impossible it seemed to return to society. " 'Tis almost four years since I've b-been out in s-society."

"But that's dreadful."

"I quite agree," put in Cressida. "And Melanie has consented to practice elocution with me in the hopes of soon attending one of this Season's balls."

"Oh, I should love to help, too," said Emma with much enthusiasm.

"Perhaps we might begin with a shopping excursion. I'm sure Emma would like to tour Philadelphia's shops, and you, dear Melanie, would be able to get out without having to meet anyone." Seeing the interest upon both of the younger women's faces, she continued, "Afterwards we might stop at Franklin Garden. 'Tis a lovely little tea room. Mr. Rittenhouse took me there, and one can watch the ice skaters on the pond while enjoying a hot chocolate and freshly baked pastries."

They agreed it was a perfect plan, and a date was set for a week from Friday.

"There's no use in putting it off," pointed out Cressida, who was suddenly seeing a myriad of possibilities in the arrival of Emma and the Earl of Gairloch vis-à-vis the romantic futures of her niece and nephew. She was so much in love with Mr. Rittenhouse, and wanted to do something to bring similar joy into the lives of her family and friends.

CHAPTER SIX

Torquil's chance to encounter the mysterious lady of the woods came two mornings after the ball. It was barely nine, and he was bound for a business meeting at the bank when he spotted the familiar slender figure at the bottom of the winter-brown lawn.

It was she. Even from the top of the hill with the early morning sun glinting off the icy river, he could tell it was the same lady. So dark was the sweep of hair in contrast to the milky whiteness of her face, so delicate was her figure among the massive gnarled oaks, that it could be none other than the ethereal beauty he had glimpsed the night of the ball. She was standing on the frozen bank, the hood of her cloak folded about her slender neck; there was the hint of a smile upon her lips as she tossed bread crumbs to a single white swan.

On instinct, Torquil went down the path. He had to reach her before she slipped away. The desire to exchange a simple greeting with this lady was a compulsion he could not deny, and a queer little pain rippled through his chest at the thought that she might flee from him. He was very near, less than fifty paces when a branch snapped beneath his boot. The sharp sound was magnified and carried on the wind; it startled the woman, who turned away from the swan. In a single motion, she pulled up her hood and began to move toward the shelter of the trees.

He took a deep breath and moved closer to her. In an unexpectedly ragged voice, he called out, "Don't run away. Please, don't go."

She halted in her flight and tilted her cloaked head to one side. But she did not face him.

"I've seen you several times before," he began, softly, speaking instincitively and from some secret and unbound corner of his soul. His words were snatched up by the crisp breeze, and he wondered if she had even heard them. Raising his voice, he added, "The other night, I watched you. Y'know, you shouldn't be alone as you were then. 'Tis far too fine a morning to be by oneself." He paused, hoping for a response, but the only sound he heard was the gurgling of the river. At length, he asked, "Might I feed the swan with you?"

At that, she turned partially, and her hood slid back, allowing Torquil a glimpse of flawless porcelain skin, a dainty nose and long black lashes. Her luxuriant black hair was braided into a demure coronet; there was a touch of red upon those lily white cheeks, and her lips were full and a startling contrast to the serene beauty which she radiated. In expectation, he held his breath, for he thought that she was about to speak. He saw her lips part, and a puff of frozen breath escape, but she picked up her skirts and without a word hurried through the woods.

Watching her go, Torquil experienced a disappointment the likes of which he had never known. It seemed as if something immeasurably precious had slipped between his fingers. Strangely, he recalled that summer so many years ago when he had first ventured forth to London; that summer when he had been young and optimistic and certain of the goodness that life had to offer. Such hopefulness was a priceless, enviable state of mind, and briefly, it had returned to touch his heart when his phantom lady had listened to his words. It was glorious, and for a moment, his spirit soared with a rare purity of faith. Yet it had only been temporary, and silently Torquil pledged that he would do everything within his power to change that. He would never allow goodness and hope to escape him again.

It was a good thing there was not adequate light to work on her landscape, for Melanie was not getting anything done. She had donned her smock and picked up her palette as if to paint, but her brush had not made a single stroke across the canvas. Every time she glanced from the canvas to the stand of trees that separated Summer Cottage from River Rest her mind wandered. It was there that the handsome man with the lilting, deep accent had talked to her, and instead of concentrating on blending her grays with the light blues and browns, the memory of their morning encounter rushed back to her.

With a sort of wonder, she set down the palette and walked to the Palladian window to gaze at the woods. There was no one there now, but the sound of the man's voice and the image of his imposing figure were crystal clear in her mind's eye. His soft-rolling words were as smooth and ripplingly sensual as the richest velvet. And the brief peek she had dared to take had revealed a masculine and dangerously attractive man. He was magnificent. His thick golden brown hair and those intense, deep-set eyes reminded her of the ruthless pirate kings or Highland lairds in storybooks. With a romantic sigh, Melanie decided that he must be the sort of man who would not let anything stand between himself and the woman he loved. It was, she admitted, an extremely fanciful notion. However, it was pleasing to think that such men existed, and there could be no harm in weaving fantasies about her handsome stranger.

Oh, how Melanie had longed to return his greeting and to linger by the river! She knew it was not the first time he had seen her, and she was as curious about him as she suspected he was about her. But she had dared not say a word. For her keen artist's eye had discerned a hopeful light in his gaze, a glimmer of desire that had mingled with open admiration. No man, not even Charles Biddle, had looked at Melanie with such mysterious and tender longing, and she did not want anything to destroy that extraordinary moment. Encountering the gentleman was like a dream, and for an instant it wiped out the years of loneliness and grief. It was an exquisite dream from which she never wished to awaken. But she knew that one word from her, one dreadful, awful stutter, and that dream was bound to disappear, making her solitude more unbearable than before. And Melanie was not prepared to take that risk.

She closed her eyes, and the image of the gentleman became clearer. She heard his low voice, little more than a whisper, and trembled at the recollection of the way it had reverberated through her senses. It did not take a great amount of intelligence to discern who he must be. The tall gentleman must be Emma's uncle, Torquil Hamilton, the horrid earl whom Jeremy had lectured Aunt Cressy to avoid. She had heard Jeremy tell Lady Cressida that the Earl of Gairloch was a hard, false man. Once again, Melanie sighed; this time it was a sad, wistful sound, for she knew her brother was wrong. Although she did not know the earl, Melanie sensed that he was neither a callous nor a dishonorable man. He was sensitive and gentle, and as she opened her eyes and turned away from the window, the unbidden realization that he was as lonely as she was struck Melanie with the impact of a physical blow.

Dazed, she sat upon a settee as tears trickled down her cheeks. Last night, she had believed it was the serene beauty of the still night that had caused her tears. That was not the truth; she had been deceiving herself and hiding from reality. Verily, she had lived in isolation for so long that Melanie had forgotten what true pain was like. She had remained sheltered from the world until she thought that she did not care to be a part of it. But now she knew that was not so. Above all else, Melanie wished for something more. It was time to depend on someone other than Jeremy, and she would start by relying upon herself. Of a sudden, she was determined to succeed at those elocution lessons and to leave the confines of Summer Cottage.

"D-do you like this h-hat?" Melanie inquired in mock seriousness. A hideously overdone velvet bonnet in the latest and most fashionable shade of peach-down sat upon her head; on the underside of the brim velvet peaches framed her face and gold tassels bobbled about her ears as she spun to face her companions.

"You look like a bowl of fruit," said Emma, whereupon she and Lady Cressida burst into a bout of companionable laughter.

The three ladies were in the establishment of the Messrs. Vanuxem and Lombaert at No. 79 North Water Street. This was their third stop of the day, having already made purchases from Monsieur Baptiste, the umbrella maker at the sign of the sun, and from the stationers, Caldeleugh and Thomas, where Melanie selected four sable pencils, a bottle of poppy oil, and several of the latest French colors for oil painting.

Here, at Messrs. Vanuxem and Lombaert, the latest spring fashions were on display, and Emma, Melanie, and Lady Cressida were trying on the newest fancy chip bonnets and willow hats. Lady Cressida glanced from her niece to Miss Fraser, and an affectionate smile settled upon her features. The change in Melanie was remarkable; she was gaining back the self-confidence that had been hers as a child. Thank goodness that the retiring young lady, who had greeted Cressida upon her arrival from England, was now jesting with an uncommon ease. Lady Cressida had never felt a single maternal instinct in all her years, but she experienced an altogether unfamiliar yet undeniably pleasant glow of pride as she watched the two young ladies. It was a miracle to see Melanie in such a carefree mood. Cressida also suspected that this afternoon was equally pleasurable for Miss Fraser, for the older lady could not help thinking that the pretty Scottish girl had not often enjoyed young female companionship.

Recovering from her fit of the giggles, Melanie, still wearing the velvet fruit bowl, picked up a bonnet and placed it upon Emma's head. "Look, Aunt Cressy, w-will this one d-do for Emma?"

"Assuredly, you would be in the vanguard of fashion, Miss Fraser," asserted Lady Cressida, who herself was sporting a thoroughly ridiculous Como turban of pale blue crêpe from which four long ringlets of false curls were suspended.

Studying her reflection in a mirror, Emma grinned at herself. The hat resting upon her head bore an uncanny resemblance to the blue-feathered creation she had admired in Mme de Rigny's shop. It was of deep blue satin, and there was panache of blue-and-silver zebra feather sprouting from the top. "Oh, my uncle would never approve. 'Tis quite similar to one I liked in a London shop, and although he admitted 'twas fetching, he would not allow it."

Lady Cressida offered an understanding nod while Melanie's eyes lit up at mention of the earl. "Y-your uncle is a strict g-guardian?" she inquired circumspectly.

"Oh, he's not in the least bit tyrannical, if that's what you're wondering. He's merely obsessed with protecting my reputation. Claims a fancy hat would ruin my chances of marrying a proper gentleman," explained Emma. Observing, though not questioning the curiosity burning within Melanie's eyes, she elaborated, "Y'see, his reputation was sadly blackened when he was younger, and he wishes to prevent that happening to me."

Unwilling to let this opportunity to learn about the earl escape her, Melanie rushed to ask another question. "Whatever d-did your uncle d-do that was so d-dreadful?"

"Nothing, I assure you. Yet still the tabbies gossip, and he frets continually about the way he raised me. Y'see, when my mama and papa died, he did not send me to boarding school or leave me alone with a nanny. He took me to live with him."

"W-what nonsense! 'Tis n-not so t-terrible a thing," burst forth Melanie, knowing that she had been correct in her assessment of the earl's character. He was, indeed, a compassionate man. "He m-must own a very l-loving heart."

" 'Tis precisely what I tell him, but he doesn't listen, for there's also the matter of the scandal in his youth." Addressing the older woman, Melanie asked, "Do you know of it, Lady Cressida?"

"Indeed, I do. And it was both an unjust and tragic affair for your dear uncle," said Cressida in her melodramatic style.

"Please tell me," urged Emma, "for he would never do so himself, and I'm certain I'm quite old enough to hear the truth."

Cressida hesitated a moment before launching into the story. "Your uncle was seventeen or eighteen and had just inherited the title when he came to London for the first time. La, fresh from Rugby, and he was far too inexperienced to realize the power of his good looks or to know that his fortune made him the object of many a calculating mama." She offered a lamentable pout and then went on, "Indeed, it makes me feel quite ancient to recall the first time I saw Torquil Hamilton. It is no Banbury tale to say conversation halted when he walked into Almack's. He was as tall and elegant as he is today, but a youth, the promise of his strength was unfulfilled, and the trusting light of inexperience still shined in his gaze. I fear his head was turned by all the female attention, and soon his name was associated with naught but the loveliest ladies of the *ton*."

"B-but that's n-not so t-terrible."

"Melanie's right," Emma agreed. "Surely that can't be the whole of it. What did he do that was so wrong?"

"And w-why is he called the F-Fatal Earl?"

" 'Twas not your uncle precisely, but the wife of the

Duke of Warwick—Amanda Croyden, the Duchess of Warwick—who was responsible for hanging that name about his neck." Cressida gave a little mirthless laugh. "Amanda was nothing more than a contemptible parvenue who had seduced the elderly duke into marriage. And she was a schemer who spotted your uncle's trusting nature from the first. He was her victim."

"What happened?" Emma prompted.

"Amanda, it seems, had a lover, and the two of them were anxious to hasten the duke's demise. So she chased after your uncle. They were seen dancing frequently, and I believe that was the extent of it. But the rumors started flying and the old duke discovered certain evidence—planted, to be sure—that led him to believe he'd been cuckolded by your uncle. Naturally, the duke reacted as the treacherous Amanda had hoped. He challenged your uncle and was fatally wounded in the ensuing duel, leaving Amanda to inherit a fortune and to marry her lover."

"Oh, poor Uncle Torquil," exclaimed Emma, beginning to comprehend the intensity of her uncle's convictions. " 'Tis grimmer than I ever thought. How horrid to be so ill-used. He must have been devastated."

"D-did no one r-realize how evil the d-duchess had been?"

"Of course they did," replied Cressida, derision ringing in her words. "But people are not always fair. Though the *ton* knew very well Amanda had used your uncle, they would not forgive him for killing the aged duke."

"And th-that's why he's c-called the F-Fatal Earl?"

"Initially, yes," said Cressida. An enigmatic grin curved up at the corners of her glossy, tinted lips. "As the years passed, I think many called him that because of his effect on the ladies."

Emma giggled. "Faith, he has often complained about their relentless ploys."

"And I must confess to having behaved as shockingly forward as the lot of them," said Cressida. An uncharacteristic flush rose upon her cheeks, and she looked away from the two younger women.

"You d-didn't, Aunt C-Cressy!" cried Melanie, drawing back in shock. With inexplicable hesitancy, she shyly inquired, "W-were you and the earl v-very close?"

Nonchalantly, Cressida replied, "Oh, it was nothing. A mere dalliance of unfortunately short standing." She waved an elegant hand as if pushing away a bothersome insect. A mantle of cloying perfume hung heavily upon the air. "Truth to tell, he took me in distinct dislike. I was too forward by far. But that's my style, and I'm not changing for any gentleman, not even for the most dangerously attractive earl in the realm."

Melanie sighed. " 'T-tis a t-tragic story. The p-poor dear man has suffered m-most unjustly." This was said with such warm sentiment that Emma and Lady Cressida stared astutely at Melanie, who immediately realized she had nearly revealed her interest in the earl. Quickly, she exchanged bonnets with Emma. "C-come, you must try on the bowl of p-peaches for us. Mayhap p-peach-down is your color."

Good-naturedly, Emma complied. She offered a curtsy to Melanie, then lifted her skirts and began a dramatic turn so that her friends might view the velvet fruit bowl from all angles. Halfway round the shop, she halted. A dreadful chill spread through her limbs, and her hands flew to her face, her skirts dropping to the floor with a whoosh.

Gadzooks! It was none other than a forbidding Mr. Wister standing on North Water Street! Grim-faced, he was staring through the window at herself and the other occupants of the shop.

If Emma did not know better, she might think the gentleman spent the better portion of his time spying on ladies. That he should once again catch her in the midst of such a sad and unladylike romp was enough to astonish St. Anthony, and she could do no more than stand there, her mouth agape, as he proceeded up the steps and into the shop.

The door opened, and a gust of air, as frigid as Jeremy's voice, followed him inside. "Good afternoon, Melanie, Aunt Cressy."

To Emma's disgrace, he ignored her. Nonetheless, she

forced a pleasant smile to her lips and gave a little curtsy in his direction.

"I did not know you were going to town." He spoke only to Melanie.

"You did not ask us," Cressida replied with a touch of asperity as she met her nephew's stormy blue eyes. She did not know what had come over him, but she did not like it in the least.

Jeremy did not countenance his aunt's curt words. Instead his lips hardened into determined lines, and he said to his sister, "Come, Melanie. I'll take you home now."

"B-but, J-Jeremy, there's n-no need," began Melanie. Her voice faltered, and her stutter was worse than it had been in days. "We c-came with Miss F-Fraser, and *h-her* coachm-man is w-waiting to take us home."

As if he had not heard a single word, he picked up a pelisse from the counter. "Is this yours, Melanie?" And when she nodded yes, he slipped it across her shoulders and began to escort her to the door.

"B-but w-what of M-Miss Fraser?" stammered Melanie.

"Yes, what of Miss Fraser? And what of me?" demanded Cressida.

At mention of her name, Emma looked toward Mr. Wister at the same moment he turned toward her. This was the first he had glanced at Emma since entering the shop, and he visited a lingering stare of such intense dislike upon her that Emma gave an involuntary start as if she were about to flee. But there was no place to go. She merely stepped back and wrenched her gaze away from Mr. Wister's. Stricken, she stared down at her feet, a lump in her throat, and tears sparkling on the tips of her long eyelashes.

"Aunt Cressy can ride home with her," was his brisk and altogether impersonal reply. Then, glowering over his shoulder, he snapped at his aunt, "And take off that garish turban before you leave."

In the next instant, they were gone. The door slammed behind them, and Emma expelled a caught breath.

"Oh, my dear Miss Fraser, my dear Emma," began Lady Cressida. Her eyes softened with concern as she observed the younger woman's ashen face. She hurried to her side. "Please accept my deepest apologies. I can't understand what came over Jeremy to have behaved no better than an ill-bred cit."

Clasping her shaking hands together to steady them, Emma took a deep breath before she might respond. Her anguish was as profound and as inexplicable as it had been at Stanton Hall. Feeling wretched and quite alone, Emma longed to confide in someone. In a tiny shaken voice that was little more than a whisper, she said, "I should be used to Mr. Wister's moods by now."

"What?" asked Cressida in astonishment, scarcely believing that Miss Fraser had, in truth, just confirmed her earlier suspicions. Not only had they met before, but, indeed, something of a personal nature had transpired between them.

"'Tis not the first time he has snubbed me," came the bitter confirmation. Emma paused to take another breath and to swallow back the tears that threatened to overflow her glistening eyes.

Once again that oddly maternal feeling came over Lady Cressida, and she could do no less than wrap a comforting arm about Emma's fallen shoulder. Kindly, she said, "I did not think it was. And though I've no explanation for his behavior, I pledge to help you to forget it. Now don't cry, for he ain't worth it."

"But, ma'am, 'tis so difficult. I had thought I didn't care one jot for his good regard, but it appears I do," she confessed gloomily, managing to hold back a sniffle. She had never been as crestfallen than she was at this moment.

"Then what is the quandary? If you know what you want, you must go after it."

Emma's cheerless countenance darkened further. "It isn't so easy a thing to accomplish. Tell me, Lady Cressida, what does one do when one's heart says one thing and one's common sense says something else?" she asked, disclosing the whole of her predicament.

Cressida frowned, then emitted an overly gay trill of laughter as she reached out to smooth back a coppery curl that had tumbled across Emma's pale brow. "In my case, I've always followed my heart. But then, mayhap, you'll not wish to heed my example." Her tone sobered. Most pensively, she added, "For look at me, my dear. My heart's given me two husbands who were perfect rats and nothing but a great deal of trouble."

To that dismal intelligence, Emma had no response. In twenty years' time, she did not wish to be like Lady Cressida. In twenty years' time, Emma wished to be a happily settled wife and mother and grandmother. It appeared that minding one's common sense had to be a better path than listening to the erratic pangs of one's heart. It did not matter that she wanted Mr. Wister's good regard, that she wanted him to be kind and to favor her with a warm smile as he had once done. That was a thoroughly impossible notion, and her earlier vow had been correct; at all cost, she must avoid Mr. Wister until she had managed to recover from this impossible *tendre*. It could not last forever. Could it? Emma dropped her head to stare at her feet while Lady Cressida gathered up their cloaks and reticules.

Having said quite enough for one afternoon, the older woman remained silent. She wrapped a comforting arm about Emma's shoulder and led her outside to the waiting carriage.

"How c-could you d-do that?" Melanie demanded of her brother. She was seated in the corner of the carriage farthest away from him, a scowl upon her pretty face, and her arms belligerently folded across her chest. " 'Twas t-totally senseless, n-not to mention rude. At last, I've m-made a friend and have g-gotten into town. W-wasn't that what you w-wished?"

"Yes, but not with Miss Fraser," was Jeremy's crisp reply.

"B-but whyever n-not?"

"She's not suitable." He gave her a quelling glare.

Melanie blanched, but did not retreat. "I d-don't agree w-with you."

"And I don't wish to argue with you, Melanie," he said

dismissively, assuming a pose similar to Melanie's, arms folded across his chest, as he stared out the window.

That was more than Melanie could take. Mild-mannered and soft-spoken she might be, but she was neither witless nor a child. She could not remain silent in the face of such arrogance from her brother. Her eyes flashed. "Well, you aren't m-my parent, J-Jeremy, and I'm of an age t-to make my own decisions. You're b-blind as a bat and cruel into the b-bargain. Never thought my own favorite b-brother could be such a thoughtless and callow n-ninnyhammer. Miss F-Fraser is my friend, and I w-won't stand for it. Did you see how you hurt her?"

"No," he grumbled, listening to the rattle of the carriage wheels over the cobblestones and wishing that he did not feel that Melanie was correct and that he was wrong. What Melanie though was of no account, he reminded himself; it was his promise to Charles Biddle that mattered and nothing else. He was bound by honor to watch over his sister and to guarantee that she have nothing but the best that life could offer. The Hamilton family were not suitable company, and if Melanie intended to disregard him, he had no choice save to share his feelings directly with the earl.

The following day, Jeremy wasted no time in searching out the earl. He found him in an office adjacent to Mr. Girard's on the second floor of the bank. Without preface, he strode into the small room and pronounced, "I don't wish my sister mixing company with your niece, sir."

Torquil glanced up from the document he was perusing and stared at his unannounced visitor. "And why is that?" he demanded to know, his eyes narrowing ominously and a muscle twitching in his tightened jaw.

"Because I don't think your niece is a proper companion for my sister. And I don't wish Melanie falling into her orbit."

"Well, we're even, for I don't think your aunt a proper companion for either of them," came Torquil's scathing retort.

"So Miss Fraser told me." Jeremy's words were precise and cold.

Torquil's right brow quirked upward in unpleasant surprise. "She did? Am I to believe you had a similar conversation with her?"

"Not exactly."

"What then did you say to her? For 'tis abundantly clear my niece does not like you, sir. She has told me so herself." Torquil pushed away from the desk. His chair grated on the bare floor, and frowning, he stood to confront Jeremy eye to eye. In the confines of the cramped office, the two tall men dominated the room. On a derisive snort that was barely a laugh, Torquil remarked, "And to think I believed you sincere and honorable in your offer, that you honestly intended to introduce her to suitable young gentlemen."

"I am sincere, and I will keep my promise to Lady Wheatley. I simply don't wish Miss Fraser to keep company with my sister."

"Christ's nails!" Torquil ran a hand through his hair and strode around the desk, a menacing scowl upon his hardened features. "And what has Emma done? She has had but one Season, never had a beau, and is quite innocent. What evil, pray tell, might she inflict upon your sister?"

Evenly, Jeremy said, "I hasten to explain that it is her family of which I disapprove."

"I take it you mean myself," offered Torquil dryly.

"Bluntly stated, yes."

Torquil gave vent to full blown and wholly contemptuous laughter. A mocking smile played upon his lips. "I'm astonished to hear such rubbish spew forth from the mouth of an American. You are a fool, Mr. Wister." Again his right brow rose in sardonic displeasure. He frowned. "Sir, I admit to owning a less than sterling reputation; my niece's, however, is without flaw. And to hold my errors against her is unjust and unfair. I had thought that in coming to America we might leave that behind us. I ask you, sir, as a gentleman, to reconsider your request."

"Why should I?" Jeremy bristled beneath the other man's denunciation.

"What harm can Emma do your sister? She's but a young girl, who for the first time has found a friend near her own age. Sir, you may believe it makes perfect sense to introduce my niece to society while you refuse her the company of your sister. In truth, it makes about as much sense as my pledging to be a good neighbor and then putting the word out about the Lady Cressida."

A muscle jumped in Jeremy's right cheek, and he clenched his teeth. "Are you threatening me?" he ground out.

"No, I don't make threats," replied Torquil with deadly calm. "I'm endeavoring to illustrate how misguided you are, and how serious is my intent to prevent Emma from ever suffering for my folly. I have dueled with men over matters far less consequential than Emma and her happiness. My niece is as important to me as any daugther to a devoted father, and let me warn you, sir, I would not hesitate to cut down the man who hurt her in any way." He paused to measure the effect of his words. Jeremy Wister disguised his feelings well, and for final measure, Torquil added on a low and ominous note, "And there are methods other than resorting to duels or fisticuffs. Should you hurt Emma, I vow, you'll live to regret it."

Jeremy did not respond. Crisply, he bowed and turned on his heel.

Upon his return to River Rest, Torquil spotted a female figure walking through the bare trees at the edge of the lawn. Magically, his foul humor abated like vapor into thin air, and that glorious sense of hope and goodness encompassed him. For an instant, he wondered if it were a trick of his imagination. To see her now would be a blessing, he thought as he lengthened his stride toward the trees.

When he reached the woods, she was seated on an octagonal wooden bench built around the trunk of a massive oak. Her high leather boots barely touched the frozen ground, and her back rested against the tree. A pad of sketching paper—like those Torquil had seen used by the artists in Green Park and along the Thames—was in her lap, and in her hand was a charcoal stick that moved over the paper bringing alive the shapes of trees and an outline of the opposite riverbank.

Several paces away, Torquil paused. He waited a few minutes, enjoying the unrestricted sight of her. Then he coughed into his hand and spoke. "Good afternoon."

The pencil stopped feathering the branches of a tree. She inclined her head in silent greeting, and to his delight, Torquil saw the unmistakable hint of a smile upon her lips.

He moved a single step nearer. Quietly, he said, "I've always admired those talented and sensitive enough to translate the world into a thing of everlasting beauty to be prized by others." Cautiously, he sat down on the bench halfway round the other side of the tree. He wished to sit beside her and to gaze into her eyes, but he sensed that the anonymity provided by the massive trunk afforded her a sense of safety. She made no attempt to flee or hide beneath the cloak, and he watched as she drew, clouds forming in the space above the trees.

She spoke, and he thought that it had been a trick of the wind, nothing more than the creaking of a dead branch overhead, so hushed was her voice. The two tiny, quietly uttered words had been, "Thank you," but she might as well have confessed her entire heart to him, so great was Torquil's joy at this first sign of communication from her.

"Oh, you're very welcome," he returned. "And I assure you, 'tis most sincerely meant."

Two more little words as quiet and as carefully spoken as the first two floated around the tree, "I know."

Again her hand moved across the piece of paper. Torquil watched as the woods came alive beneath her touch, and after several moments of silence, he spoke again: "I'm exceedingly pleased you didn't turn away from me this time."

Her hand continued to sketch. In that unhurried voice, she answered, "And I'm pleased," she paused for what seemed an eternity, "you're here."

Each word was like a precious gem. Her whispered responses pierced Torquil with such warmth that he struggled to prevent himself from jumping to his feet and pulling her into a tender embrace. She seemed so fragile that he longed to take her in his arms and comfort her, to let her know that she was safe with him. But he could not touch her, could not even move another inch nearer. This opportunity to converse with her was a godsend, and he would not let it get away; he could not frighten her.

A bit awkwardly, he coughed. "You'd never know it, but I was in a tremendously foul humor until I saw you. Had an unpleasant encounter with a gentleman this afternoon. Seems he thinks my niece ain't good enough to keep company with the ladies of his household." Torquil spoke to this woman as if she were his closest confidant; he told her about Emma, and his fears that even here in America his past might destroy her chances for happiness.

Several moments of silence passed between them. A cool breeze blew off the river, and Torquil pushed his hands into his pockets. The lady pulled her cloak tighter. In the distance a dog barked.

After some time, she spoke. "But what of yourself?" She set aside the sketchbook, and in that hesitant, ever-sweet voice, added, "'Tis tragic to ignore one's own happiness. Is it not?"

"I never thought of it like that," remarked Torquil, leaning forward to catch the expression upon her face.

She was deep in speculation, her dainty features clouded by distress as she stared up the hill toward Summer Cottage. Ever so slowly, she spoke, each word coming quietly and deliberately after the other, "One can only do so much for others without hurting oneself." She paused, and Torquil watched as she laced her fingers together in a steadying motion. "My own brother is a victim of such overconcern, I believe."

"And you're worried for him?" he put forth with uncanny perceptiveness, realizing that his mysterious lady must be Wister's sister.

She nodded. "He seems much changed. And I can but pray he realizes this before it's too late." She turned and lifted her gaze to Torquil's. Her eyes, blue as a summer's sky, reflected a deep and abiding affection. "We can each of us do no more than wish the best for those we love."

Those quiet words lanced Torquil's chest with the force of a bullet. His lady of the woods was kindhearted, selfless, and thoughtful. And with each sweet-spoken word, he knew she was a woman to be treasured. They faced one another, and as he returned her gaze a slender thread of friendship—unspoken, undemanding, and untainted—wove back and forth between them, and that long lost hope within Torquil's soul grew stronger with each heartbeat.

Having missed her lessons with Lady Wheatley the day before, Emma was busily attending to two afternoons' worth of chrysanthemums. The order of business was flower arranging—the only domestic task that Emma enjoyed. Lady Wheatley had set Emma the task of making new displays for the trio of marble-topped consoles in the hall, and Emma was humming a pleasant little tune as she went about her work.

Snip. She cut off the wilted leaves near the bottom of a stem. Snip. She sliced the stem at an angle and then placed the yellow-blossomed flower in a porcelain vase. There were several dozen other bursting yellow beauties already in the vase, and Emma stood back to assess her handiwork. She had an excellent sense of height and depth in the matter of floral arrangements, and she moved two of the blooms from the back center to the side. Lastly, she filled the background with a generous supply of greenery, and, satisfied with her creation, she carried it to the table beside the rear door.

She glanced out the window, did a double take, and squinted in total disbelief at what she spotted in the woods. She blinked twice, even rubbed her eyes as if to improve her vision, and still, it was the same. There, on a bench in the woods between River Rest and Summer Cottage was Melanie, and there, taking a seat on that same bench was her uncle.

Then, from the corner of her eye, Emma saw Jeremy Wister. He was on the stable path and had not yet rounded the bend that would afford him a view of the woods and river. Emma's breath caught in her throat, and her eyes flew back to the scene in the woods. It appeared Uncle Torquil was conversing with Melanie, and although Emma was not certain what to make of this encounter between her uncle and her new friend, she was certain that she could not allow Mr. Wister to intrude. If the shopping excursion had put him out of sorts, this would assuredly thrust him into an apoplectic rage.

Emma threw a paisley shawl about her shoulders. Without considering what it was she intended to do, and forgetting all about her pledge to keep her distance from the man, Emma burst out the door and dashed off in the direction of Mr. Jeremy Wister.

CHAPTER
SEVEN

The blue-and-maroon paisley shawl slipped off Emma's left shoulder as she picked up her skirts and dashed toward the stable path, her kid slippers skimming over the rutted walkway, the hem of her petticoat trailing along the ground. Only when she sighted Jeremy did she slow her pace. He had progressed several yards down the path; in another second, he would gain an unobstructed view of the lady and gentleman on the bench beneath the oak tree.

Oddsbodikins! She had to divert him before it was too late.

"La, Mr. Wister! Good afternoon to you, sir," she called, thinking that she sounded uncommonly like Lady Cressida and feeling utterly foolish as she catapulted herself to stand before him. Her chest was heaving, two errant copper curls tumbled across her forehead, and try though she might, she could not check the great puffs of frozen air that burst forth from her parted lips. She saw astonishment upon Jeremy's face and cringed as those ink-blue eyes narrowed in sardonic perusal of her untidy gloveless and hatless condition. On she babbled in a high and unnatural voice, "I, too, was out for a stroll. Such a perfect afternoon. Don't you agree?" she inquired in a simpering tone as she dared to slip an arm through his. It seemed her pledge to maintain a reasonable distance from this man was ill-fated at best.

"Miss Fraser," muttered Jeremy, wondering what had come over her. She did not seem herself, not in the least, he thought as he felt her patting his forearm while she chattered on at a mad pace.

"Why, I said to myself, 'Look 'tis Mr. Wister. How fortunate. Mayhap he, too, is fond of birds, and we can compare sightings.' Are you a naturalist, sir?"

He mumbled a response, regarding her flushed cheeks from beneath raised eyebrows. Perhaps she had a fever, for she did not heed his negative reply and continued in the same vein.

"Sir, you seem a gentleman of much knowledge. You must tell me what bird that is," she said, pointing into the bare boughs of a lime tree. "Is that a wren or a warbler?"

Jeremy squinted at the bird, one dark eyebrow arched upward——even he knew it was a woodpecker——and then he studied Miss Fraser, a slight frown forming upon his countenance. Even at her brightest, he had thought she was a sensible young lady, but this sudden coquettishness was most peculiar. The unique young lady who did not wish to marry for status or wealth was gone; in her place, there was a chit as fatuous and as incorrigible a flirt as the rest. She might be fatally prone to frolicking in shop windows, but she was not a tease. Was she?

" 'Tis a woodpecker, Miss Fraser."

"Ah, yes. Of course. How silly of me not to see that myself." A perfectly inane giggle escaped from between her lips. "Well, I believe I've had enough. Would you escort me to my front door, Mr. Wister?"

Perplexed by this bizarre conduct, Jeremy allowed her to guide him along the less direct route to the mansion house.

"And what brings you to River Rest, sir?" she asked with an excessively chipper smile. "Do you walk this way often?"

In a most formal tone, he replied, "The fact is, Miss Fraser, I was coming to see you."

"Me?" was Emma's astounded response. This was the last thing she expected to hear, and she lowered her lashes, hoping to disguise her emotions. After his rude intrusion upon the shopping excursion, she scarcely expected Mr. Wister ever to seek out her company. And though she wished to confront him with that precise sentiment, she held her tongue. Forcing another ebullient smile to her lips, she glanced sideways at him. The serious set to his face was formidable. "Why, Mr. Wister, whyever would you wish to see me?" she asked, her blasé tone revealing none of her suspicions and bitterness.

"I believe I owe you an apology, Miss Fraser."

Her smile softened until it became genuine. Her green eyes widened and brightened with a mixture of exhilaration and triumph. *Ah, ha, so the man is not so imperious after all; he is able to admit his mistakes.* This discovery pleased Emma immensely, and her smile deepened. The preposterous accent fled her voice. Seriously, she responded, "Yes, I believe you do owe me an apology, sir."

This was the Miss Fraser whom Jeremy knew. Clever, forthright, and perceptive. It was an unexpected delight to watch those green cat's-eyes twinkle in lively counterpoint to her solemnly spoken words. And strange though it might be, this glimpse of her outspoken character put him at ease.

After his confrontation with the earl, Jeremy had perceived no choice for himself save to apologize to Miss Fraser. He admitted that his behavior in the shop had been unconscionable. Melanie was right, and there was no excuse for such ill-mannered conduct; he did not usually act like a boor, and it did not sit easily with him. Furthermore, having earlier surmised that Miss Fraser had been ill-treated by some insensitive London dandy, Jeremy did not wish to contribute to her heartache. Again, Melanie was correct. He had hurt Miss Fraser, and there was no justification for such thoughtless behavior. Too, there existed a selfish reason for wishing to apologize. He wanted to blunt Torquil Hamilton's wrath. Jeremy did not doubt the earl's every intention to protect his niece, and he did not wish there to be any reason for retaliation on the part of the Fatal Earl.

It was an unpleasant situation all around, and the sooner it was settled and over, the better things would be.

They reached the front entrance to River Rest. Emma paused on the first step, her hand on the wrought-iron railing. Below her, Jeremy shifted his weight from one foot to the other.

"Might I come inside, Miss Fraser?" he inquired politely.

"Of course, 'twas rude of me not to have suggested it," replied Emma. She was at once intrigued by this display of contrition and grateful for an excuse to get him inside, where she might prevent him from seeing Uncle Torquil and Melanie.

They entered a spacious vestibule, and after Emma had ordered a tea tray, she led Jeremy into the front parlor. It was a sumptuous room, appointed in a style befitting the fortune Captain Stewart had accumulated. The walls, painted a pale rose, were trimmed by marble white woodwork; pediments above the windows and doors were cast in sea eagles; and the mantel pilasters were carved with honeysuckle vines. A Turkey carpet in shades of gold, deep rose, and blue covered the mahogany floor; at the windows were hung curtains of the same pale crimson brocade with which the eight-leg sofa and matching side chairs were upholstered; the gold in the Turkey carpet was repeated throughout the room in gilt mirrors and wall sconces; and on the panel above the hearth, there was a pastoral fantasy in rose and muted blues depicting a shepherdess with her flock on a hill above the Schuylkill. Emma loved the opulent style of this room, but for the moment, she loved it best because it had no view of the river.

Settling into one of two crimson chairs before the hearth, she took a moment to tuck a curl behind her ear and then faced Jeremy, who remained standing. He approached the hearth to warm his hands. From the side, his profile was unreadable; at least, he was not angry, Emma thought as she mentally prodded herself to speech. If she did not speak her mind now, she might never have the chance again. After three steadying breaths, she managed to say: "You surprise me, sir. Although your apology and visit are not unwelcome, I had thought from your attitude in the shop there was nothing to be said between us."

Now that was the sort of candid statement Jeremy expected to hear from Miss Fraser. He faced her and leaned one shoulder against the mantel. Arms folded casually across his chest, there was the trace of a smile upon his lips. His blue eyes focused on her flushed heart-shaped face in warm appraisal. Yes, it was a shame that circumstances were not different between them. Indeed, he readily admitted that he admired her buoyant spirit and unpretentious nature, but that did not change facts. It was far too dangerous to allow a friendship to develop between her and his sister. And there could be no question of a liaison between himself and Miss Fraser.

"You're correct. I know I gave that impression," he replied in a voice devoid of that arctic quality Emma so loathed.

Cocking her head to one side, Emma stared at Mr. Wister in puzzlement. Why, he almost sounded friendly. But that was wholly unlikely. Wasn't it?

He pushed away from the mantel and stood at attention, hands grasped behind his back. "Verily, Miss Fraser, I treated you in a most ungentlemanly fashion, for which I apologize. You must understand, it was such a shock to see my sister out of the house, and as she had not told me of her plans, I'm afraid I reacted without thinking."

"And I, sir, can well understand your predicament. It is far and away the easier course to speak one's mind rather than to weigh one's words. You can't begin to comprehend how many times I've been guilty of that same offense," she said with unforeseen affinity.

To Jeremy's embarrassment, a hot flush rose upon his cheeks. How was it that this young and inexperienced woman could make him feel like a perfectly inept dolt? He replied, "You're very understanding, Miss Fraser."

"Mayhap far too accepting for my own good. You see, sir, I don't deceive myself as to the real reason behind your disagreeable humor. I'm well aware of your sentiments for my guardian; however, I didn't imagine they extended to myself nor any friendship I might have with your sister."

The flush on Jeremy's cheeks darkened, and in a nervous gesture, he ran both hands through his black hair. This was not the way he had anticipated the interview to progress. He had expected to have the upper hand, but he should have known that Miss Fraser was not a lady to meekly accept his feeble explanation. It was not going to be as easy to finish this conversation as he had planned.

There was a noise behind them, and they both swerved around as a plump young maid entered the parlor with a tea tray; Jeremy breathed a sigh of thanks at the temporary interruption.

"Come, Mr. Wister, please sit and enjoy some refreshment," offered Emma as if they had not been discussing so thorny a subject. "Or would you prefer something stronger? My uncle keeps a fine stock of rums and brandies in that cabinet to your left. You're welcome to help yourself."

"No," he said, taking the opposite seat. He leaned back in the chair, managing to relax as he extended his long legs and crossed them at the ankles. "Tea would be fine."

Silence descended over the parlor while Emma poured boiling water through a delicately crafted silver strainer into Rose Medallion cups. The young maid moved about the room. She drew the heavy curtains across the recessed windows and then stoked the fire, tossing on several pine cones. A cedar log hissed, the blue-and-gold flames jumped higher, the soothing incense of burning pine drifted through the room, and the metal poker rattled as it was replaced on its brass stand.

Curiosity got the best of Emma. She peered over the rim of her cup, took a fortifying breath, and then rushed into speech. "I've the distinct impression there's something left unsaid between us."

Wishing that Miss Fraser did not have the uncanny ability to discompose him so thoroughly, Jeremy set his tea cup on the pie-crust table at his side. It was almost as if she could read his mind. Stalling, he again threaded his fingers through his hair and sat straighter. "Yes, there is," he stated with awful dignity.

"Well, whatever it is, it can't be any more mortifying than what transpired yesterday," she blurted out, immediately regretting the haste with which she had spoken. "What I meant to say—"

He cut her off, "Don't bother to explain. Please allow me to continue. 'Tis about my sister, Melanie. As you know, she has led a sheltered life for several years. After the death of her fiancé, she was much changed. 'Tis when that unfortunate speech affliction returned, and I'm concerned she may be taking on too many activities, too soon and too quickly."

As if they were discussing nothing more consequential than the most preferable time of the year to plant tulip bulbs, Emma listened to Jeremy, an agreeable smile on her face. She nodded and held a plate of gingerbread squares toward him. After he accepted one of the cakes, she replaced the platter on the tea tray. With deceptive casualness, she said, "What you're really trying to tell me, Mr. Wister, is that you don't wish there to be any association between Melanie and myself." As she watched, his features hardened, and the implaccably harsh look upon his face confirmed her statement. Stalwart in her convictions, she went on, "I am afraid, sir, that I cannot agree. Your sister's companionship is as important to me as I believe mine is to her. If you're truly sorry for your conduct yesterday, and if you truly wish for your sister's improved spirits, then I'll take your consent to our friendship as a sign of goodwill," she dared to conclude, quite startled by her own audacity, but not regretting a single syllable if it meant ensuring her friendship with Melanie.

At a loss for words, Jeremy stared keenly at Miss Fraser. It mattered little that she had not meant to be impudent, nor manipulative. Her proposition was outrageous, and he did not intend to comply with such blackmail.

Just then Torquil stood on the threshold.

"Heard we had a visitor," the earl said jovially, entering the parlor and stopping short at the sight of Jeremy. In a less welcoming voice, he added, "But I didn't know it was you, Wister. This is an unanticipated surprise." He visited a shrewd glance upon his niece and then upon the man who had dared to confront him at the bank; he took a longer, second look, studying them as if seeing them together for the first time. Worry etched his brow, and concernedly, he asked Emma, "How are you, puss? Your afternoon has been without incident, I trust."

Jeremy seethed at the innuendo in the other man's suspicious question. He would be damned, if he would sit by while the earl insinuated that he had been harassing his niece. Motivated by an angry desire to thwart Hamilton, Jeremy blurted out, "We were discussing Miss Fraser's friendship with my sister." He paused to watch as unspoken threat sprang to his adversary's eye. Not flinching beneath the earl's penetrating gaze, he experienced a rather trivial elation as he elaborated, "Miss Fraser has assured me she's sensitive to Melanie's situation and I believe she wishes nothing more than to be her friend. My sister has long needed a companion her own age, hence I approve."

If this pronouncement surprised the earl, he disguised it. He merely nodded a silent approval.

Emma, however, was flabbergasted. Befuddlement clouded her countenance, and she glanced in disbelief, first at Mr. Wister, next at her uncle. Inexplicably, she could not help feeling there was more to Mr. Wister's words. It was almost as if he had said them for Uncle Torquil's benefit, and that puzzled Emma. "I may call at Summer Cottage on the morrow, then?" she asked, half fearing that he might rescind his approval.

And Jeremy, furious at himself for having been goaded into making such a declaration, replied, "Melanie would be pleased to see you, I'm certain." With a vengeance, he took a bite of gingerbread, wondering why his behavior listed toward the unpredictable and uncharacteristic whenever he was in Miss Fraser's company. He was not normally explosive or rude, nor was he as spineless as he had just demonstrated. Yet every time he was about Miss Fraser, he did something for which he could find no logical explanation.

Hastily, he stood, almost upsetting the teacup on the table beside him. "Well now that we've got that settled, I must be going."

"I'll walk with you to the door," said Torquil in a tone that brooked no argument. When they reached the hall, he addressed Jeremy, "I'm pleased you changed your mind. I thank you, sir, in behalf of my niece, whom you've pleased enormously."

Jeremy accepted his greatcoat and beaver hat from a hovering manservant. His reply came in the most frigid tone of voice. "I did it for my sister and no other reason," he stated, although deep inside he could not quash the sentiment that he had in some incomprehensible way done it for Miss Fraser as well. Instinctively, he had known how to bring that animated sparkle to her lovely green eyes. There was no denying he admired the girl who had told the Highland tale. And there was no denying the tiny warm spot that glowed within him at the sight of the girl he had aided at Brickhill, the girl who had a penchant for outlandish bonnets.

Torquil extended his hand in farewell. "If you say 'tis devotion to your sister, I accept that, sir, for such devotion is something I can well understand and respect."

Feeling like a perfect nincompoop, Jeremy accepted the earl's hand. "Thank you, sir. At least in one thing, we are of the same mind."

Torquil nodded, but he did not smile as Jeremy bade him goodbye and departed River Rest.

Shortly after dusk, snow began falling over the Pennsylvania countryside. It continued through the night, and in the morning, a soft white drift was piled high upon Emma's windowsill. Dashing from the warmth of her canopied bed, she pulled open the sash and poked her head outside. She shivered and took a deep breath, filling her lungs with the frosty air. It was magnificent. As far as she could see, the trees and fields on both sides of the river were blanketed in white. A steady wind had blown the storm clouds eastward, and the sun shone resplendent in a clear azure sky.

On sudden impulse, Emma scooped up a handful of snow. She held it to her lips, tasted it, and then tossed it in the air, watching it separate into a thousand sparkling slivers of light that flew upward to disappear into nowhere. Grinning, she closed the window and turned away from the beautiful scene as a maid entered to lay out her clothes. The day reminded Emma of winters in Argyll; eager to enjoy every moment of it, she completed her toilette in less than fifteen minutes and hurried downstairs.

Torquil was already in the dining room, and together they indulged in a hearty breakfast of Philadelphia scrapple, eggs, and freshly baked corn muffins. Ebulliently, she talked about the snowfall; they reminisced about winters past in Scotland and joked about the time Emma taught several of Torquil's more staid friends how to make snow angels. Emma was about to butter her third muffin when a servant entered the dining room to deliver a note from Summer Cottage.

Addressed to Emma, it was an invitation from Lady Cressida, who was organizing an afternoon sleigh ride; Emma was invited to join their party. The stable boy who had trudged through the snow from Summer Cottage, waited for Emma's response, that was, of course, an acceptance. And after the messenger had departed, Emma, who had nearly four full hours until the sleigh would arrive, hurried upstairs to select the perfect ensemble for a winter outing.

What fun it would be to sail across the fields of snow! What a treat it was to be included in Lady Cressida's party and to see Melanie without the threat of Jeremy Wister's censure. It was going to be a wonderful day. 'Twas as Granny Campbell had often said; she could feel it in her bones. And Emma hummed a Highland tune as she delved through the satinwood armoire.

No, the brown cloak would not do, she thought; it was far

too somber for so bright a day. Reaching farther back, she pulled out a pale blue velvet pelisse, only to push it aside; it had never looked quite right with her coppery hair. Next she studied a wool ensemble in the Fraser tartan. No, no, no. The plaid was not flattering. 'Twas too overwhelming a pattern. With a female vanity she had never before exhibited, Emma rejected that outfit as well and rang for a maid to bring the trunk down from the attic.

If it took all morning, she was going to find the perfect outfit for what was bound to be a perfect day. Though she did not pause to consider why, she was determined to be at her best.

CHAPTER
EIGHT

Promptly at half past noon, a great red-painted sleigh with gleaming runners and deep black leather seats glided up the circular drive to River Rest. Emma had chosen a hooded cloak of Forester's green wool lined with fox fur; she carried a matching muff, and upon her feet she wore a pair of high, fleece-lined boots. As she exited the mansion house, she pulled the hood over her head. She had chosen well. A halo of auburn fur mingled with russet curls about her face, and the green fabric was a soft and enchanting contrast to the excitement in her eyes.

"Hello, d-dear friend," called Melanie. She was seated across from Lady Cressida and Mr. Rittenhouse, who were snuggled side by side beneath an enormous fur rug. Atop the driver's seat was Jeremy Wister, wrapped in a dark cloak, a plaid muffler about his neck and a beaver hat upon his head. He was gripping the heavy leather reins and concentrating on keeping the anxious pair of dapple-grays steady; he did not turn to greet Emma.

Mr. Rittenhouse stepped from the sleigh. He tipped his hat. "Good day, Miss Fraser. Glad you could join Lady Cressida's outing. You're in for a treat. There's nothing better than a swift ride through the countryside after a new snow. Why, I've been out since dawn."

"Mr. Rittenhouse trekked all the way to Summer Cottage on his snowshoes," informed Cressida, a rather girlish look of blind adoration creeping into her gaze.

"Snowshoes?" repeated Emma as she climbed into the seat beside Melanie.

"Marvelous invention, they are," began Mr. Rittenhouse as he reached into a space between the seat and the driver's box to pull out two oddly shaped objects made of leather strips and wood. In a professorial tone, he explained, "They disperse a body's weight so one can walk on top of new-fallen snow."

"How clever. Did you invent them?" asked Emma.

"Oh, no, that credit goes to the Indians. Deuced clever devils when it comes to being downright practical. I merely took a lesson from them. Crafted mine after the pair on display at Mr. Peale's Museum. Ojibwa design. Brought back from the Lewis and Clarke expedition."

Lady Cressida, bored by this second dissertation on snowshoes of the afternoon, jumped into the conversation. "La, Mr. Rittenhouse, 'tis enough of snowshoes for one day. Let me look at Miss Fraser's pretty cloak," she said in a little voice that sounded like a child asking her parent for one more piece of rock candy. She pursed her lips, slipped an arm through Mr. Rittenhouse's, and pulled him into the seat beside her. "Though your snowshoes are most practical, sir, and most excellently made, I confess the cut and color of Miss Fraser's cloak is much more to my interest." She cast an assessing eye in Emma's direction. "Green is your color, dear Miss Fraser. You look lovely."

Mr. Rittenhouse and Melanie concurred, and as Emma wrapped a bearskin rug about her legs she thanked them for their kind words.

Raising her voice, Cressida addressed her nephew's back. "Do look round, Jeremy. You must see Miss Fraser. Doesn't she look divine?"

"Is everyone settled?" Jeremy inquired without budging. "The horses are eager to run."

Miffed by what appeared to be nothing short of wholly intentional disregard, Emma spoke up in her most dulcet voice, "Good afternoon, Mr. Wister."

He responded with the minimum acknowledgement dictated by good breeding.

Well, Emma thought, trying to ignore her indignation, Wasn't that what she wanted? If she had to go on this outing with Mr. Wister, wasn't it fortunate that he was going to leave her alone? Just because he had said she might cultivate an acquaintance with his sister, it did not mean he intended to become her bosom bow. Again, her heart battled with logic. Of a sudden, she confronted the reason why she had devoted an inordinate amount of time to dressing; she could not deny that she still yearned for his approval. Such a desire was as ridiculous as it had always been, and there was only one sensible course. Emma should have been prodigiously pleased that she was not going to have to sit next to the man and converse with him; but that did not blunt that tiny, niggling hurt which his icy demeanor stirred within her.

"Ready?" Mr. Wister repeated, staring straight ahead. He had noticed Miss Fraser and she was breathtaking swathed in fur nearly as soft and glossy as those coppery curls that framed her heart-shaped face. But he had no intention of being beguiled by that alluring sight. This afternoon, he intended to be himself. Ever since he was a small lad, there was nothing he liked so much as a sleigh ride, and nothing was going to ruin his pleasure. Too, he had heard the genuine pleasure in Melanie's greeting, and he did not wish to upset his sister again. This afternoon, he was not going to do anything out of character because of some word or look from Miss Fraser. He was a man full grown, and it was ridiculous that anyone, least of all a girl barely out of the schoolroom, should affect him in such unmanageable ways.

The quartet of passengers chorused "Yes," they were ready to depart, and Jeremy flicked the reins. The dapple-grays sprang forward, and the jingling of harness bells rose about the sled as it moved away from River Rest. Trees fled by, and Emma and Melanie giggled, burying their faces in their muffs as soft winter air whipped past them. The horses trotted through the woods until they reached the open country, where they picked up their pace.

Emma had never experienced anything as exhilarating as this unleashed sense of speed. They were flying like leaves on an autumn gale, and she decided Mr. Rittenhouse was correct. There was nothing better than a sleigh ride over newly fallen snow. She forgot all about Mr. Wister. Smiling, she pulled the rug higher up about her neck and closed her eyes, content to listen to the music of the bells and enjoy the wind upon her cheeks.

It seemed they went for miles and miles until they came to a stop at the Germantown pike. At the crossroads, there was a coaching inn. The Rebel and Patriot was a simple two-storied fieldstone house with bright red shutters and a sloping roof. Snow had drifted to the eaves along the south wall, but at the front, a path had been cleared to the door. Although there were no other vehicles in the yard, a thin gray line of smoke curled in welcome from the chimney. Jeremy leapt down from his seat and secured the reins to a half-buried hitching post while Mr. Rittenhouse assisted the ladies.

They stayed at the inn for less than an hour, barely enough time to warm their hands before a crackling fire and to enjoy steaming mugs of spiced cider. Then they bundled up once more and headed outside for the return ride.

"I've a stupendous idea!" declared Lady Cressida. She skipped ahead of the others, scrambling up to the driver's box. "La, Jeremy, I think you ought to let one of us ladies take the reins."

"Absolutely not, Aunt Cressy," he responded, hurrying forward to fetch her down.

"Oh, pooh!" With a willful toss of her head, she waved him away.

"Come, ma'am, you've no experience." He managed to haul her from the sleigh. "Handling a sleigh isn't the same as a phaeton, and I can't allow you to put he rest of us in jeopardy."

"Double pooh!" she exclaimed with a stamp of her booted foot and spun away from her nephew. A mysterious smile played upon her lips as she slipped an arm through Mr. Rittenhouse's. "But then I really did not want to leave your side, sir."

Beneath the lady's fervent regard, the gentleman blushed a vivid scarlet. Two paces to the rear Emma and Melanie suppressed a serious bout of giggles.

Jeremy, wishing that he had not sounded so inflexible, made an astounding offer, "On second thought, perhaps one of you ladies could sit beside me and hold the reins for a few moments."

Cressida removed her bewitching gaze from Mr. Rittenhouse. "Not I, dear boy. You've made me see the error of my ways. But as I recall, my lord Hamilton oft touted Miss Fraser's ability with the ribbons. Mayhap she would like to have a go at it."

Thunderstruck, Emma stopped in her tracks. Her mittened hand flew to her throat, and she gaped at Lady Cressida. Indeed, it might be splendid fun to sit upon the driver's seat, but not with the disapproving Mr. Wister. The outing had been quite pleasant thus far, and she did not wish to spoil it.

"Oh, no!" cried Emma, her soft-spoken words of aversion drowned out by Melanie's enthusiastic agreement.

"W-what a splendid idea, Aunt Cressy. Oh, Emma, s-say you w-will!"

"Yes, Miss Fraser, you must say 'Yes,' and demonstrate those skills of which your uncle talked," added Cressida, giving a catlike smile of satisfaction that her spontaneous scheme was working. Success was within reach, and soon Jeremy and Emma would be sitting side by side. They had managed to avoid one another in the Rebel and Patriot, but such stubborn behavior could not be ignored any longer. Despite her own sad history, Lady Cressida was no fool in matters of romance. She knew when two people were suited to one another, and she was resolved that her nephew and Miss Fraser get past whatever obstacle was between them. Progress could not be made, if they ignored one another. It was of vital import that they sit together. Batting her eyelashes, Lady Cressida stared up at her beau. "Miss Fraser must accept Jeremy's offer, mustn't she, Mr. Rittenhouse? It will be a perfect way to end such a spectacular ride, don't you agree?"

Unable to naysay Lady Cressida, Mr. Rittenhouse mumbled his assent. Melanie and Lady Cressida glanced from Emma to Jeremy with high hopes written upon their pretty faces.

"But——" began Jeremy, who bit back his opposition at the sight of his sister's gay expression. Melanie wished him to be kind to her friend, and to refuse to allow Miss Fraser on the driver's seat would appear spitefull. In his most charming voice, he said, "Well, Miss Fraser, we must not disappoint your friends." He offered his arm to assist her. "Come, it would be a pleasure to have you ride beside me and handle the reins for a spell."

Emma stood stock-still, wondering how it was that she had been somehow tricked into this. Wondering, too, why she allowed herself to feel the stirring of elation at his genial words.

"G-go on," urged Melanie, giving her friend a prod in the back.

She stepped forward and accepted Mr. Wister's hand to climb up to the driver's seat. Once settled, Emma looked down at him, a tentative smile upon her face. "Truth to tell, it would be rousing good fun to handle the reins," she confessed.

"That's the spirit," chimed in Lady Cressida.

Jeremy visited a dubious look upon his aunt, who shrugged at his dour countenance and emitted a flighty laugh. Ignoring her audacity, he bounded up beside Emma. "Ready?" he inquired.

"Yes," she replied, and they were off once again.

"Watch how I hold the reins," Jeremy said above the

jingling of the bells. And for the next mile, he explained the technique of driving a sleigh.

"Might I try now?" asked Emma when they reached the open countryside.

"Yes, but let me steady you," he said, slipping an arm about her waist as he did when he permitted his younger brothers to guide the sleigh. He passed the heavy leather reins to Miss Fraser, keeping his hands poised above hers as a precaution. But she needed no help. It was no wonder the earl had boasted of her ability. She was an able coachman, holding the reins with confidence as she urged the horses to a canter.

The snow began as they topped the hill that led toward the final stretch for home. At first, only a few very large flakes drifted out of the sky. Then, in a matter of seconds, it seemed the world had turned white, and they were enveloped in a flurry of dense white.

"Oh, Mr. Wister, should you take charge?" asked Emma, a notable reluctance lacing her question. She was already slowing the horses.

"'Course not. You're doing a superb job," he said, pleased by the grin upon her shapely plum-colored lips and the dazzle in her eyes.

From the passenger seat, Lady Cressida let out an unladylike whoop of exhilaration as the sleigh raced down the tree-lined drive. Emma laughed; her hood fell about her shoulders as she gazed into his approving face, and her heart soared at the perfection of the moment. Sitting atop the sleigh was like no other experience she had known, and observing approval in those inky-blue eyes was exhilarating beyond her wildest dreams. Emma laughed again.

Snowflakes whirled into her face. "Oooh," she exclaimed as a large flake landed on the tip of her nose. Several more clung to her eyelashes, and she blinked.

And in that lightning-quick moment, Jeremy felt his resistance to Miss Fraser vanish into the swirl of snowflakes. Beholding her, he was reminded of a bright star in a summer sky. He was mesmerized by the sound of her light laughter, and those twinkling green cat's-eyes. The snow-draped woods faded away, and the jingle of the sleigh bells dimmed; his every sense focused on Miss Fraser as they glided to a stop at the entrance to River Rest. It was as if they were the only two souls in the world. Time stood still, and in that magical moment, he lifted a hand to caress her wind-pinkened cheek.

The reins fell from Emma's grasp, but she did not move away. There was a curious light in the back of his eyes, and for a long, loaded moment, he looked at her. Then her dearest wish was answered; he was smiling at her. It was that same warm grin that had so beguiled her last summer, and her heart somersaulted with ecstasy as he raised both hands to frame her face.

In a low, husky voice he asked, "And did you enjoy your sleigh ride, Miss Fraser?"

With ingenuous delight, Emma returned his smile. "Oh, Mr. Wister, it was marvelous. Verily, it was my first sleigh ride, and it far surpassed my expectations."

"Your first sleigh ride?" There was astonishment in this question, and a touch of admiration, for Miss Fraser had handled the reins with assurance.

"Yes, indeed, and I shall always remember it, sir. What good fortune to have been able to venture forth on this glorious day, and to sit here beside you and take the reins. Thank you for your kindness to me."

Impulsively, he raised her gloved hand to his lips. His voice was hoarse. "Well, then, here's to many more sleigh rides and splendid winter days!"

So surprised was Emma that she could not answer him immediately. Her throat was dry as parchment, and as he let go of her hand, she wondered where that cool and distant gentleman had gone. On a whisper, she managed another, "Thank you, sir."

Jeremy's smile deepened until little lines flared out at the corners of his eyes. It was mightily pleasing to take some credit for her happiness. Indeed, he experienced the unforeseen impulse to invite her again. It was not often that one encountered a lady who enjoyed a sleigh ride without complaining about the wind or how the snow might damage her boots. Yes, it might be pleasant to take Miss Fraser on another outing.

But Melanie's voice intruded upon his consciousness; he came to his senses and stopped before he did anything so foolish. The less contact he had with Miss Fraser, the better. His shoulders stiffened. More than ever before, it was hard to do the right thing and keep his distance from the earl's niece. But he had to for Melanie's sake. His smile faded, his eyes clouded with sad reluctance, and he drew away from Emma. It did not matter that they had shared something special this afternoon, nor that he had sat beside the girl from Brickhill and Stanton Hall and knew her to be the true Miss Fraser. It mattered only that contact between their families be kept at the barest minimum. Leaping from the sleigh, he did not see the brightness dim in Emma's eyes.

Pain exploded in Emma's heart. Wretchedly, she tweaked at her gloves. It had happened again; she had listened to her heart instead of remaining aloof. Mutely, she allowed him to help her down. Quickly, she said her thank-yous to Melanie and Lady Cressida and Mr. Rittenhouse, and then she dashed up the steps and into the mansion house.

Leaning against the closed door, she shut her eyes and listened to the jingle of sleigh bells fading in the distance. Tears burned her nose and throat, and she bit her lower lip to prevent herself from sobbing aloud. What a fool she was to have thought Mr. Wister might change. What a blind and naive fool! Plainly, she was no closer to a mature and sensible change of heart than she had been last summer, and vowing to avoid his company was not going to solve her woes. She needed to broaden her circle of male acquaintances; she needed to find someone who might take her mind off Jeremy Wister. With the back of her hand, she gave an angry swipe across her cheek, dashing away her tears, and deciding, in that same moment of bitter frustration, that Mr. Ethan Breck would do quite nicely. He was handsome and eligible and had been most attentive the night of the New Year's Ball. Certainly, a friendship with Mr. Breck was just the ticket to help her forget Mr. Wister. Thus before the sun set that evening, she dispatched a note to Mr. Breck, inviting him to dine with her and her uncle at his earliest convenience.

The storm continued for several days. At River Rest the windows were white, frozen blurs of madly swirling snow. Wild winds drove snow against the mansion house with such force that Lady Wheatley feared they might all be blown down the river and out to sea. By local standards it was a blizzard, and for more than a fortnight Emma, Lady Wheatley, and Torquil were isolated at River Rest. January turned to February, and Emma, accustomed to the solitude of the Highlands, was content to sit by the fire and read. Lady Wheatley, on the other hand, spent her time berating the stupidity of Americans, who would schedule their social season in the dead of winter. In less than two weeks' time, they had missed two cotillion parties, the Philadelphia Theatre production of *The Sultan: A Peep into the Seraglio,* and, at Mr. Peale's Museum, the viewing of the celebrated sea serpent taken from Loblolly Cove in Massachusetts. As for Torquil, who had developed a fondness for the American practice of going to work every day, he was anxious to get back to town. As the days passed he grew more and more restless. He missed the intellectual challenge of solving how to transport anthracite from the frontier; he also missed the lady in the woods, for he had not seen her since the snow began.

There were two lulls in the storm, and during those times messengers managed to make it through the drifts to River Rest. To her delight, Lady Wheatley received three notes from her cousin, who described the boredom on Society Hill, where hostesses were homebound, and the mayhem along the Delaware waterfront, where several oceangoing vessels had become frozen to the piers. One day, there was a pamphlet on canals for Torquil from Mr. Rittenhouse, who had joined the anthracite partnership and was advocating the construction of a canal system throughout the whole of Pennsylvania. And for Emma, there was a letter from Melanie, who was faithfully practicing her elocution, and one from Mr. Ethan Breck, who was pleased to accept her gracious dinner invitation and hoped that in return he might escort Miss Fraser to an equestrian performance at the Olympic Theatre, where Mrs. Williams and a company of rope dancers were scheduled to perform on a slack wire.

On the fifth of February the clouds drifted away. The winds died down, and the sun sparkled against the crusty snow like a hundred thousand diamonds. Overnight the citizenry resumed the social whirl with the vengeance of porridge-starved orphans presented with an Easter feast.

Within twelve short days, Lady Wheatley managed to attend three of Shakespeare's tragedies, all of the plays of Mr. Sheridan, and two concerts at Washington Hall. The schedule she arranged for Emma was equally hectic. It included three cotillion parties, a concert of sacred music for the benefit of the Female Hospitable Society, and a performance by Mr. Cartwright on musical glasses at Mansion House.

To her relief, Emma did not encounter Mr. Wister in that time. 'Twas the attentive Ethan Breck who occupied her attentions. During the day, he took Emma riding through the snowy woods and on tours of the various museums and points of interest in Philadelphia. And at night, he often dined at River Rest before escorting Emma and Lady Wheatley to the evening's activity.

As February drew to a close, Lady Cressida was a permanent fixture upon Mr. Rittenhouse's right arm. At the Fish House Club, gentlemen wagered on the date of the nuptials for the besotted pair, and across Society Hill, matrons wondered at the speed with which the lady had tamed the city's most elusive bachelor.

And the quiet visits in the woods by the edge of the river became a daily event for Melanie and Torquil. 'Twas by unspoken agreement that they met each morning to feed the swan, who had been joined by a mate, and stroll along the snow-covered riverbank. They exchanged childhood tales and confided the wishes they used to make upon the first evening star in a blackened sky. And it was a marvelous discovery to ascertain they both enjoyed the outdoors and animals and poetry.

Each morning, it was as if two halves of a whole were reunited, and their brief moments together nourished their souls for the rest of the day and the long hours of the night until they might meet again.

"Say you'll be at the Birth Night Ball, Mellie," said Torquil in a subdued and anxious voice. He tossed down the last of the bread crumbs to the elegant birds and took one of her hands between his.

Melanie smiled. She loved it when he called her Mellie, and she loved it when he made her feel so needed. "It would please you?"

"Ah, Mellie, how could you even ask? 'Twould be an occasion for much celebration. Don't you know, my dearest, how I long to show you off to the world?"

"Yes, I do. And I should l-love to stand atop the belfry at Christ Church and announce our friendship to all of Philadelphia. But," assailed by a nagging self-doubt, she broke off and stared across the frozen river, "I may not be ready for so p-public an event."

The hope in Torquil's eyes flickered like a dying candle. In the next instant, it flared with renewed strength as his grip about her hand tightened. "Not ready? You mustn't fret about such things. You have nothing to fear, dearest Mellie."

"But w-what about my st—?"

"Your voice?" he asked in a shockingly intimate tone. With one hand he reached out to cup her chin, gently turning her face so that she might see his tender smile. "Your voice is the sweetest I know. You shall be among the fairest of the fair. As the London dandies in the bow window at White's would assert, A Diamond of the First Degree."

A delicate pink tinted Melanie's porcelain cheeks. Her black eyelashes fluttered against ivory skin, and then her eyes fixed upon his. "I want you to be proud of me, my lord."

"Ah, dear Mellie." Torquil's words were thick with

emotion. "To have a lady as kind and sensitive, as forgiving and understanding and talented as yourself upon my arm is what shall make me the proudest man alive. I need nothing else save you by my side."

Tears shimmered in Melanie's blue eyes as she raised a hand to run shaking fingers along the length of his rugged jaw. "You d-do not care what others might s-say?"

"Not any longer. What the tabbies might say is of no importance. I care only what your brother says, for 'tis his blessing which I seek."

A tear of joy slipped down her cheek, and she laughed with gay abandon. "Oh, my dearest friend, yes, yes! I say yes to everything you ask. Yes, I shall be at the ball, and yes, I shall always be by your side."

And beneath the lacy canopy of gray branches, Torquil pulled Melanie into his embrace. He buried his face in her hair and held her to him with the passion of a man who has found home after a raging storm.

That afternoon when Melanie returned to her easel, she eagerly picked up the palette and a broad brush. With quick feathery strokes, she went to work on the landscape. The world had never been so beautiful; she was not lonely anymore, and she would never be lonely again, for she had found the man upon whom she could depend for a lifetime. At last, she knew what to do, and within ten minutes the entire texture of the painting had transformed. It was airy and bright, silver and delft blue. There was no mistaking it as a winter scene, for the branches were heavy beneath ice and snow. At long last, she had captured the proper light and mood in the reflection of the sun off the frozen river and the delicate white drifts that covered the hedges in whimsical shapes.

CHAPTER
NINE

Two thousand wax candles illuminated the grand saloon at Washington Hall on the eve of the Birth Night Ball, February 23. The room had never looked as splendid as it did that evening. Purple damask curtains, festooned with chains of evergreen, had been hung for the occasion at each of the recessed windows. Gilt chairs were placed about the circumference of the dance floor, and in the four corners, enormous bouquets of hothouse flowers were perched atop marble pedestals. At the far end of the grand saloon an orchestra of twenty-seven gentlemen in black was tuning its instruments, and on a dais was conspicuously placed Rush's statue of the late President Washington.

The ball was a gala military affair managed by the Colonels Biddle, Prevost, and Raquet, and the Captains Swift, Scott, Roberts, and Stevenson. The rooms were crowded with a brilliant assemblage of the fair of the metropolis; a greater display of beauty and elegance no republic could boast. Even persons not normally admitted to the elite ranks of the Philadelphia Assembly were welcomed into polite society this glorious evening, for no one who had the price of a subscription and was a true American would miss the annual Birth Night Ball. The custom of celebrating George Washington's birthday had begun in 1792, when Philadelphia was the capital of the new nation, and on that evening, the President had given the following toast: "To the Dancing Assembly of Philadelphia. May the members thereof, and the Fair who honor it with their presence, long continue in the enjoyment of an amusement so innocent and agreeable."

Thus the practice continued after the great man's death and into the new century, each gala being more splendid than the last, boasting finer musicians, a finer presentation of collations, finer decorations, and a greater crush of celebrants. This year was no different, and by seven-thirty, when Emma, Torquil, and Lady Wheatley entered the grand saloon, some four hundred guests had already arrived.

"Lady Wheatley, would you care to dance?" inquired Torquil with a flourishing bow.

"Nay, sir. Though 'tis most kind to inquire, you know better than to ask. I see my cousin and shall be perfectly content to join her," replied the older woman, giving a nod in the direction of several of the city's more distinguished matrons. They were seated on spindly gilt chairs, heads wrapped in elaborate brocade and satin turbans, and lorgnettes raised to peruse the crowd.

Ethan Breck appeared and after exchanging civilities, he asked Torquil's permission to stand up with Emma, who accepted his offer. Taking the fair-haired gentleman's arm, she bade farewell to Lady Wheatley, who went to join Mrs. Shippen, and to Torquil, who wandered off in the direction of several of his acquaintances from the bank.

"I'm honored, Miss Fraser, to dance with the loveliest lady at the ball," said Mr. Breck. Like the other gentlemen this evening, he was in full military dress; his blue naval officer's jacket smelled of cedar shavings, and the gold epaulets were slightly frayed, but he cut a nonetheless dashing figure. He bowed in a courtly manner as the orchestra began the opening chords of a popular country tune.

Emma curtsied in reply. "Thank you, sir. And thank you, too, for the lovely flowers. They arrived yesterday. 'Twas a most thoughtful gesture. Lady Wheatley and I both enjoy their beauty. I was prodigiously impressed, sir, that you remembered my telling you how fond I am of flowers."

Charmingly, Mr. Breck smiled at Emma, his golden eyes warm with admiration. "Any gentleman would do no less for a lady such as yourself," he said smoothly. The dance steps separated them for a few quick beats as Emma circled to the left, turning on the arm of an elderly gentleman whose ancient uniform proclaimed him a veteran of that infamous winter at Valley Forge. When they returned to face one another and link arms to promenade about the room, Mr. Breck spoke again, "I hope when the weather turns, you'll accept my invitation to ride through the countryside. Our American springs are most colorful, and a jaunt over the hills is a delightful way to pass an afternoon and collect wild flowers."

"I would like that very much," said Emma, thinking that Ethan Breck was in many ways all that she had ever wanted in a gentleman. It had not been such a bad decision to cultivate her acquaintance with him. Like her papa, he had been a military man, and like Uncle Torquil, he was an outdoorsman and he expressed naught but approval at Emma's interest in riding and hunting and marksmanship. And lastly, he was a man of the highest character, who did not countenance rumor nor stoop to petty snobbery. Emma felt exceedingly comfortable in his presence. Ethan Breck did not discompose her as did Mr. Wister; her limbs and heart never reacted in an overly peculiar fashion when he said her name, and she was never goaded into uttering things that were best left unsaid when she was upon his arm.

Having completed a full promenade of the dance floor, the pattern began to repeat itself. Mr. Breck bowed, Emma curtsied, and once more they moved through the steps. At the conclusion of four promenades, the musicians ended the rousing number, and polite applause rippled through the grand saloon as couples socialized with one another.

From out of the crowd walked Mr. Rittenhouse, a starry-eyed Lady Cressida on his right arm. Jeremy Wister and his sister were directly behind them.

"Evening, Miss Fraser, Breck," said Mr. Rittenhouse jovially.

"Evening," responded Mr. Breck, executing a gallant bow to Lady Cressida and Miss Wister, who was as delicately beautiful as he recalled. She did not appear a day older than she had been the season of her betrothal to

Charles Biddle, and she was the only female who held a candle to Miss Fraser's heretofore unsurpassed beauty.

Jeremy bowed in greeting, but he did not speak, his cool blue eyes pinned upon the exquisite sight of Miss Fraser. She was stunning this evening, in a ball gown of white satin with thin gold diagonal stripes and a brocade ribbon tied beneath her bodice. A golden ribbon was threaded through the soft auburn curls about the crown of her head, and the pearls about her neck were as flawless as her skin. She reminded Jeremy of a Greek goddess, tall and composed and perfectly lovely. It was difficult enough to remain collected each time he was in Miss Fraser's company, but it seemed harder when she was smiling so brightly on the arm of Ethan Breck. Yes, he had introduced them and encouraged the liaison, but that did not vanquish his disgruntled reaction. He had not seen Miss Fraser since the sleigh ride, and he had not expected to react so strongly to the sight of her with another man. Breck was a decent enough fellow, but Miss Fraser, he decided, needed a more stolid gentleman, someone older and wiser to balance her irrepressible ways, and he scowled at the pair of them.

In truth, Emma was not smiling at Mr. Breck in any meaningful fashion. Hers was a wobbly smile made fragile by the disconcerting mixture of emotions she experienced at the sight of Jeremy Wister. She had managed to avoid him in all those weeks since the sleigh ride, and she had hoped in that time to have grown out of her senseless attraction. Yet, seeing him now, she realized that was not the case. He was still the handsomest man she had ever seen. But that was not the worst of it. Looking at Mr. Wister, Emma again experienced the unsettling feeling that she could read his thoughts. And it was little consolation knowing that he was as uncomfortable as she was at that moment. Why should it matter? And how could the Fates so cruelly allow such a hopeless attraction to persist?

The orchestra began to play again, and in a series of deft moves Lady Cressida managed to send Melanie and Mr. Rittenhouse off for punch, to wrangle an invitation to dance from Mr. Breck, and to place Emma on Jeremy's arm.

As Lady Cressida disappeared with Mr. Breck, Jeremy drawled, "We are hoodwinked again, Miss Fraser." On a wry expression, he pulled Emma into a light embrace for a waltz. "I could not help noticing that it appears you've developed a *tendre* for Mr. Breck."

Emma's frail smile quivered. "And why would you think that?"

"Perhaps I'm mistaken. I had heard from Melanie that you were spending a noticeable amount of time in his company. I've even heard the tattles attach your name to his. In fact, you put me in mind of a young lady considering matrimony. And, I might add, for someone who recently professed not to be possessed with marriage-mart fever, your conduct is most confusing."

"I've changed my mind," she informed him in aloof tones.

The hint of a smile touched Jeremy's countenance. "Pray, Miss Fraser, don't disappoint me and say that you've succumbed to the lure of wealth and status like all the others here tonight."

"Nay, 'tis merely the acceptance of my duty," she replied honestly.

"Your duty?"

"To my Uncle Torquil. He has had full responsibility for me these last eight years, but I cannot continue to be a burden to him forever. Recently, I've come to realize he'll never have his own life—a wife and family and children— unless I marry. 'Tis my duty to wed and have a life of my own. I owe that to him."

"So you'll settle for Mr. Breck? Just like that?" he queried curtly, omitting to say that he thought her sense of duty was commendable.

In a bracing voice, as much to convince herself as Mr. Wister, she said, "I see no reason why not. We share much in common, and my uncle likes him and," she could not help adding, "he likes my uncle."

Of a sudden, her attention snapped to their surroundings. From the corner of her eyes, she spotted Torquil. He was bowing before Melanie, who was pretty as a porcelain doll in blue satin. Again Emma was seized by the same impulse that had prompted her to fly out of the house and prevent Mr. Wister from seeing them in the woods by the river. Instantly, her own trepidations vanished.

"La, Mr. Wister," she simpered, staring directly into those ink-blue eyes and holding their gaze. No matter what, she could not let his glance stray from hers. On a dazzling smile, she continued, "Tell me, sir, of your American springtimes. I understand they're prodigously unique."

She was doing it again. Behaving in that silly and distinctly un-Miss Fraser manner. Perplexity creased Jeremy's brow. "Our springs? Why, yes, they are quite lovely, particularly on the river."

"Tell me more," she prompted, continuing to look up at him as if her very life depended upon it. Flirtatiously, she smiled and nodded her head in time to the music. Then, sensing that Mr. Wister was about to twirl them toward Uncle Torquil and Melanie, she intentionally lost her footing, preventing the turn.

"Miss Fraser, are you all right?" he inquired, annoyance apparent in his concerned yet curt tone. That she had deliberately stumbled, he did not doubt, though why she had, he was not certain. If it had been Miss Morris or one of the other young ladies who had been vying for his favors, he would think it a ploy to effect physical closeness. But this was not the case with Miss Fraser, who immediately righted herself and maintained a proper distance from his person. Scowl lines returned to his brow as he studied her closely, observing that for the first time since the dance had started she allowed her eyes to waver from his.

Jeremy followed the direction of her gaze. His breath caught at the unholy sight of his lovely, innocent sister waltzing with Torquil Hamilton, the Earl of Gairloch.

Swiftly, Emma turned back to him. He had sighted them!

"You knew," he whispered urgently, holding back the urge to shake Miss Fraser senseless. Condemningly, he added, "And you were purposefully preventing me from seeing. Weren't you?"

Her smile was gone in an instant. Her complexion became chalk white. "Yes," she barely managed to reply.

Abruptly, Jeremy's grip about Emma tightened, he pulled her closer, as close as any man dared to hold a conniving strumpet, and with a vengeance he whirled her furiously about the dance floor.

"Mr. Wister," gasped Emma in alarm. She tried to push away, but he only held her tighter. This was wrong. When a man held her, Emma knew it was supposed to be out of tenderness and affection, not anger. It was not supposed to happen like this, logic protested miserably. She felt robbed; it was as if Mr. Wister had cheated her out of something special. In supplication, she looked up at him and repeated his name, managing to break his attention from Melanie and her uncle.

Oblivious to the misery etched upon her features, his words were as bitter as acid. "This is what you were about that afternoon you were dashing along the path at River Rest with naught but a shawl about your shoulders, isn't it?"

Reluctantly, she nodded, wincing as his fingers dug into her right arm

"And have you aided and abetted untold trysts since then? Since that afternoon when I so gullibly allowed you free access to my sister's friendship?" he demanded tauntingly.

"No. I swear not." Hot tears burned her nose and throat, and she closed her eyes. "You make it sound far worse than it is. I did not mean to deceive anyone, merely to—"

Following an ascerbic laugh, Jeremy retorted, "Your notion of deception is, indeed, intriguing, Miss Fraser."

The music stopped. Emma halted where they stood, wondering how she might escape Mr. Wister, but Jeremy gripped her elbow and pulled her toward the other couple.

Melanie caught sight of her brother. Gaily, she called out, "Jeremy, Emma! Hello again. Isn't it a wonderful ball?" Her voice was beautifully and evenly modulated. Her eyes were sparkling, and delicate accents of high color touched her cheeks and forehead. "I'm so glad I came this evening. I'm having a glorious time."

In the next instant, Jeremy did not know what amazed him the most. Was it the sudden realization that Melanie, radiant on the arm of Torquil Hamilton, had spoken without a single stutter? Or was it Miss Fraser's quick little voice whispering in his ear: "Please, sir, don't destroy her happiness."

He saw no choice save to reply with infinite politeness. "Good evening, Melanie. Hamilton." He gave a terse nod. His eyes narrowed, and he added suspiciously, "Didn't know the two of you were acquainted."

"Acquainted? Yes, you might say that. It seems we share a fondness for feeding wildf-fowl," said Melanie, her lips twitching with merriment. "The earl has been most kind to me, Jeremy. Why, 'twas he, who finally persuaded me to attend this evening. And, of course, I could do naught but promise him a waltz," she finished on a distinctly coquettish note.

"For which I shall be eternally indebted to you," replied Torquil, who had eyes only for the fragile onyx-haired exquisite on his arm.

Egad, Jeremy thought, pursing his lips in disapproval, his sister was about to be swept off her feet by one of England's most infamous rogues. If the Fatal Earl had been poison for his worldly Aunt Cressy, he was surely as deadly as the plague for sweet, vulnerable Melanie. It was tantamount to sending a lamb among a pack of wolves. Damn, what was he to do? Jeremy glanced from the earl to his sister, who glowed with a loveliness that had been buried for more than four years.

Melanie observed her brother's penetrating stare and flashed him an enchanting smile. "The earl and I are going for refreshments, Jeremy. Won't you and Miss Fraser join us?" she invited with the skill of a seasoned hostess.

"Yes," he agreed, deciding this was the best way to keep an eye on his sister and the earl. No matter what, he would not leave their side. He did not bother to ask Miss Fraser what she wished to do; he merely pulled her along with him.

Emma stole a sideways glimpse at Mr. Wister's granite-like expression. His features were puckered in displeasure. She whispered, "My mama's old nurse, Granny Campbell, always said if you scowled too much, one day your face would stay like that."

"Are you again telling me to school my features, Miss

Fraser?" he replied without removing his gaze from his sister and the earl.

"Yes."

"It's so obvious, then?" he inquired, looking down at her and thinking that Miss Fraser was the only one who dared to speak to him so directly. It was remarkable how truly undesigning and candid conversation could be between them... at times.

"Yes, it is. And 'tis patently obvious to anyone else in the room. Furthermore, the object of your displeasure is evident as well. For someone who wishes to protect his sister, you'll have tongues clackiting about her in no time."

Jeremy frowned. He did not like being transparent, particularly with Miss Fraser. "Didn't you once tell me your uncle was forever cautioning you not to speak your mind?" he inquired, unable to stop himself from needling her.

"Yes." She blushed at his setdown and opened her mouth as if to say more.

"Is that all you have to say?" came his sardonic query.

"Not by a long chalk."

"Well?"

"Only that I hope you'll do nothing to ruin Melanie's evening."

"You've already asked that of me, and I believe my actions indicate my consent," he replied tersely. "I can see how important this ball is to her, but let me make it abundantly clear that I'll tolerate it for this evening only."

From behind them came Lady Cressida's voice. "What a marvelous sight that was, Jeremy. Don't you agree, 'tis a wonder to see Melanie out and so brilliant? Do you think the earl has worked some miracle on the darling girl?"

This last was asked teasingly, but Jeremy did not appear to find it amusing. He scowled at his aunt.

"Oh, come, don't be such a gorgon!" pounced Cressida, who was prodigiously pleased that Melanie and Torquil had found one another. At least in that quarter, there was no need for intervention. She returned her nephew's scowl. "One would think you a creaky ancient. 'Tis often hard to fathom what those ladies who flutter about you are so attracted to."

Casting a sideways glance at Mr. Wister, Emma observed a dark red flush upon his high cheeks, and she felt the sting of his mortification at Lady Cressida's tactless statement. Poor Mr. Wister. He was merely trying to do what he thought right, and though he was somewhat overzealous, he was no creaking ancient. Not really. Truth to tell, he put her in mind of Uncle Torquil; Emma could well imagine Torquil behaving similarly under comparable circumstances.

Mr. Rittenhouse was saying something about aqueducts. Cressida was gazing at him wide-eyed as if she understood every word he spoke. And Jeremy was endeavoring to cut a path through the crowd, for he had lost sight of his sister and was anxious to return to her side.

"Would you care to join us with my uncle and Miss Wister in the refreshment room?" offered Emma in the hopes of lightening the mood.

Lady Cressida and Mr. Rittenhouse accepted the invitation, and the four of them pushed forward, but when they reached the refreshment table Torquil and Melanie were not there. Instead they saw Mrs. Shippen. She scurried toward them a worried expression on her face.

"Oh, dear. Oh, dear. 'Tis my cousin, Lady Wheatley," exclaimed the matron. "The most dreadful attack of the megrims came over her without warning, and I quite feared she was going to faint into her plate of pistachio cream, but your considerate uncle and that darling Miss Wister kindly offered to take her home to River Rest at once."

"They've gone?" shot out Jeremy.

"Yes, thank goodness. 'Twas such a relief when they volunteered to attend to her," said Mrs. Shippen.

"But that means Melanie and Hamilton are—" Jeremy was on the verge of launching a full-blown protest that the two of them should be out of his sight.

"Are chaperoned," put forth Mrs. Shippen. "My cousin is not *that* indisposed. And I, sir, would never have accepted their offer, if I thought it might hurt Miss Wister in any way."

"Well, yes, ma'am, I'm certain you're correct," mumbled Jeremy, fully rebuffed and feeling quite the gorgon that Cressida had accused him of being. But he could not help himself.

Mrs. Shippen moved off into the crowd, and the four of them—Emma and Mr. Wister, and Lady Cressida and Mr. Rittenhouse—stood there in silence for a few moments.

"You, Miss Fraser, shall, of course, ride home with Jeremy and myself," said Lady Cressida, seizing the unexpected opportunity to put Emma and her nephew into one another's company.

Reluctantly, Jeremy agreed.

And Emma, who was thoroughly mortified to have been thrust upon the good graces of Mr. Wister, but aware that she had no alternative, politely acceded to the arrangement.

Two hours later, when the clock struck one and it was time to depart, Emma sought out Lady Cressida. The older woman was, however, not to be found anywhere on the premises of Washington Hall. Hesitantly, Emma approached Mr. Wister, who had spent the latter half of the evening standing at the edge of the dance floor. He had not danced with any of the young ladies who had fluttered about him, nor had he conversed with any of the doting mamas who had endeavored to draw his attention to their daughters, each reputed to be the singularly most talented, if not the loveliest, in the city of Philadelphia.

"Mr. Wister, I'm ready to leave whenever you are, sir," said Emma, wishing that he would not scowl. It ruined the perfection of his fine features and made him appear far more ferocious than she knew him to be.

"Have you seen my aunt?"

"No, sir."

He swore aloud. "If I didn't know better, I'd swear she planned this entire *fiasco* of an evening entirely to try me."

"I don't understand," said Emma.

"Never mind," replied Jeremy in a more civil tone. "I've been charged with your care, Miss Fraser, and shall see that you arrive home safe and sound." He offered his arm, and they proceeded to exit the hall.

As they emerged into the crisp February night, Emma's spirits lightened. Snow was falling from the coal black sky and dusting the brick sidewalk like sugar on a gingersnap.

Wordlessly, Jeremy assisted Emma into the carriage.

They sat across from one another, bundled in blankets and their feet propped upon hot bricks, as the vehicle wheeled through the city. Emma turned away from her silent traveling companion to gaze out the window. The snow was coming harder now, and the carriage swayed uneasily on the slick ground. Soon the sound of the horses' hooves was entirely muffled as they left the paved roads of the metropolis and headed into the countryside.

It was a still night. The woods were shrouded in white, and the only sound carried on the air was the intermittent cracking of branches. Wet snow lay heavily upon the boughs of spruce and oak, maple and hemlock. Emma watched as the great bushy limb of a fir tree dipped to the ground, then cracked and snapped off. Suddenly the woods echoed with the sound of breaking wood. Outside, the coachman hollered, and the carriage lurched and swayed to one side. The horses neighed in panic, and Emma, gripping the leather strap, looked at Jeremy as another round of splintering limbs coincided with the impact of something large and heavy upon the carriage.

Everything happened at once. A section of the roof caved in, causing snow and twigs to fall upon Emma and Jeremy. Emma gasped and gripped the strap more tightly. Instinctively, Jeremy threw himself forward to shelter her as the entire vehicle toppled over amid the shattering of glass and the shrieking of horses.

The carriage rocked twice, then settled on its side. The horses were quiet; snow sprinkled down into the carriage, and Emma dared not move. She lay very still and listened. First, she could hear nothing more than the pounding of her heart. Then she became aware of Mr. Wister; she heard the shallow rhythm of his quickened breath. Outside, there was no noise. Where were the horses? And what had happened to the coachman?

"Miss Fraser! Emma? Are you all right?" Jeremy asked through the darkness, panic sharpening his words of concern.

She gulped and took a steadying breath. "I believe I'm fine."

"Nothing broken?" His voice came from somewhere behind her.

"Nothing broken," she whispered. "And you, Mr. Wister, are you all right?"

"Yes," he replied.

"Hello, in there!" It was the coachman's voice. He was standing above them and speaking through the broken window.

"Jamieson, good to hear your voice. You're uninjured and the horses are fine?"

"Yes, sir. I jumped clear of the accident and the horses, praise the Lord, are only frightened. But I'm sorry to be sayin' I won't be able to get you and the lady out without assistance."

"What do you mean? Just open the door and reach in for Miss Fraser. I'll come after her."

"Sorry, 'tain't possible, sir. A large branch fell onto the carriage, and 'tis blocking' the door. Can't budge it, sir, and so I'll be having to leave and get help posthaste."

"Of course."

They heard Jamieson jumping off the carriage. Then it was quiet again save for their mingled breathing.

"Can you sit up, Miss Fraser?"

"I believe so." She shifted to one side, and pressing her back to the bottom of a seat, drew her legs up before her. In another moment, Mr. Wister sat beside her in a similar fashion.

"There. That's much more comfortable," he said with false levity, tucking the tumbled blankets about their feet and shoulders. "Lord, Miss Fraser, you're shaking like a leaf. Are you certain you're not injured?"

"Yes, quite certain. 'Tis nothing more than shock, I suppose," she managed, all the more discomposed by the feel of his hand moving about her arms and legs, checking for broken limbs.

"Here," he said, turning slightly and rearranging the blankets. "I believe it would be better if we shared a blanket."

"Share a blanket?" she barely got out, her trembling worsening with each passing second.

"Yes. Under the circumstances, I'd be less than a gentleman, if I didn't do everything within my power to make you as comfortable as possible."

In the next second, he had slipped his arm beneath her blanket and wrapped it about her shoulders, so that her head was cradled against his upper torso. Mr. Wister seemed to envelope her, and the warmth from his body radiated about her like a noonday sun. A comforting, woodsy male scent curled round her, and at length, Emma's quaking subsided. Outside, the winds mounted and swirled about the carriage, an occasional gust rocking the vehicle dangerously, making more twigs and snow fall upon their heads.

The silence between them was excruciating, and Emma cast about for anything to say. As usual, she said the first thing that came into her mind. "I do not think my uncle intends to hurt Melanie in any way, sir."

Into the darkness, Jeremy asked, "Are you pleading their case?"

"No. Merely stating the truth in the hopes you'll accept it."

"And I take it that in addition to accepting your uncle's honorable intentions, you expect that I must also accept the relationship between them?"

"Sir, you make it sound dreadfully tawdry. Has it never occurred to you that each of us is never whole, that we all lack some part, and that only another person, someone perhaps very different from ourselves, can fill that vacant space for us?"

"You sound as if you are vastly experienced in love, Miss Fraser."

"Nay, sir, I'm not. But I've sensed that vacant space within myself, and I've seen the same in Melanie and my uncle. Yet when I saw them together this evening, I realized that void was vanquished. There's perhaps no accounting for it, but you can't deny Melanie was alive with self-confidence tonight, and as for Uncle Torquil, he seemed, well, he seemed not so lonely anymore."

"Lonely? Your uncle lonely?"

"Yes. When I was little I didn't see it, for his life was

gay, and he had many friends. And here, in Philadelphia, he's busy with his anthracite plans, but that will never be enough. Yes, he's lonely." She paused and tilted her head upward to stare at Mr. Wister's profile. He was staring straight ahead into the blackness, and although she could not see his expression, she sensed he was seriously listening to her words. Emboldened, she went on, "Haven't you ever been lonely, Mr. Wister? The handsome and eligible Philadelphia earl, surrounded by beauties and the center of every young lady's attention, hasn't he ever been lonely?" She waited for his answer, but it did not come. "I've been lonely, sir," she confessed. "Sometimes when I watch Lady Cressida and Mr. Rittenhouse. And this evening, when I saw Uncle Torquil laughing with Melanie. It seems they have something that's denied to me, and although you may think it peculiar, I allow there was a great empty spot within me, so hollow and cold it actually hurt."

A spasm of pain tightened like a metal band about Jeremy's chest. He knew precisely what she was saying. And then as frequently happened in Miss Fraser's presence, he was moved to speak the truth. "Yes," he replied, his voice laden with raw emotion. "Yes, I've felt it, and 'tis exactly as you describe."

This was the man Emma had sensed existed beneath the cool facade. Tears pricked her eyelids. A great shudder of sentiment seized her, and when his bare fingers caressed her cheek and trailed down to her mouth, she did not move away. Her heart was racing, the tips of her toes were tingling, and she was lightheaded as she sat breathlessly, allowing Jeremy to trace her lips. His gentle touch, his warmth, his nearness, and his smoky woodsy male fragrance were the only reality there was, and Emma could not deny him.

"Ah, Emma."

She heard him say her name as if it had been wrenched from his soul.

"Yes?" she whispered, and in the next instant his lips were upon hers.

It was a sweet kiss, featherlight and teasing across her barely parted mouth. A small sigh of wonderment escaped Emma. She closed her eyes and reveled in the unknown sensations pulsing through her. This was everything her heart had ever dreamed, and nothing else mattered save this moment.

Foolish girl! The ugly thought surfaced. Logic invaded her heart and mind, ruining the beauty she had sensed in the joining of her lips to his.

Abruptly, she pulled away. "You forget yourself, Mr. Wister. I don't believe this is proper, sir," she said faintly.

He did not argue with her, and for a while the only sound between them was his breath, deep and harsh and ragged. His encounters with Miss Fraser exhilarated him, touched him, but nothing before compared to the moment when he had felt her mouth, soft and pliant, beneath his. That she was so sweet a creature, he had not imagined. Indeed, he did not think that he would ever know everything about this lady, and he experienced a pang of regret that he might never really know Miss Fraser. Several minutes passed before he spoke into the darkness. His voice was tinged with melancholy. "Proper or not, it seemed, though, that for a moment it helped to fill that void. Did it not?"

Voices outside the carriage prevented her from answering. It was Torquil and the coachman.

"Are you all right, Emma?" called Torquil.

"Yes," she managed to reply

"Hold on while we get this branch off."

The coach shifted as the two men removed the limb. In the next instant, the door opened and the light of a lantern blazed upon Mr. Wister and Emma.

Torquil squinted down at Emma, who was white as a ghost, her hair disheveled and her lips slightly swollen to a deeper shade of plum. "My niece is all right, sir? You have protected her in every way?" he asked the gray-faced gentleman at her side.

The nature of the earl's question was clear. Jeremy answered, "Yes," although as his gaze rested upon Emma, he was not so sure of his reply. There was confusion in her wide sad eyes, and as he helped her to stand, he sensed an awful trembling in her limbs. In a hushed voice, he spoke to her alone. "I did not mean to upset you, Miss Fraser. You have my word as a gentleman. Nothing like this shall ever happen again."

Emma could not utter a word. Suddenly the whole of this evening assumed gigantic proportions, and she was very close to tears as she realized the answer to his question. Yes, his kiss, his touch, and his tenderness had, for that one brief space in time, filled the void. What Emma felt for Mr. Wister was no passing *tendre* from which she would soon recover. Verily, she was in love with him, and her heart constricted with anguish, for it was a love that was destined to forever go unspoken, a love that would remain unrequited.

"My apologies, Miss Fraser." His voice seemed to come out of a distant fog.

And trembling beneath the impact of her discovery, Emma allowed her uncle to hoist her out of the carriage.

CHAPTER TEN

"Faith, Emma, one would think you were off to the gallows, instead of a skating party," clucked Lady Wheatley as she bustled about Emma's bedchamber. "Come now, you should smile more often, particularly when Mr. Wister is to escort you. You did have a pleasant evening at the theatre last night, didn't you?"

"Yes," Emma replied listlessly.

"Why the blue-deviled looks then, my dear?"

Dismally, the girl glanced toward the fire crackling in the hearth. She gave a shrug. " 'Tis nothing."

Although Lady Wheatley was one of the kindest persons she knew, Emma was not about to confide in her. Truth to say, she was not going to reveal her dilemma to a living soul. It was bad enough that she was in love with a man who barely tolerated her presence, but to reveal such a weakness would only compound her plight. She was going to have to suffer this alone. No kind words from Melanie, nor judicious advice from Uncle Torquil would cure the ache. Besides what would Lady Wheatley say? Likely something horrid and thoroughly leveling and to the effect that love was naught but romantic twaddle for silly twits, and she was a complete nodcock to give it a second thought.

Mayhap that was true, thought Emma with a chilling bitterness that was filled with self-condemnation. She was certainly behaving like a mindless twit. Jeremy Wister had not given her any reason to love him, yet inexplicably, he had touched that hollow spot within her soul, and she willingly ignored the fact that he was a thoughtless prig. Her heart had triumphed over logic, and she saw only that he was a devoted brother, respected citizen, and charming companion—when it suited his purpose.

The pucker across Emma's brow deepened, and she moved toward her dressing table. Staring into the gilded mirror, she gave vent to a fully fledged frown. It was unimaginable that love would be like this. Somehow she had thought that it would be a rational and reasonable emotion.

"'Tis nothing of import," she repeated as she fluffed the short coppery curls that framed her heart-shaped face.

From across the bedchamber, Lady Wheatley emitted a distinct harrumph of doubt. She did not believe Emma for one minute. Ever since the Birth Night Ball her young charge had been out of sorts. Despite a full social calendar and a notable increase in attention from Jeremy Wister, Emma did not seem happy. Why, any other young miss would be thrilled to have been escorted to the theatre on three consecutive evenings by Mr. Wister. But not Miss Emma Fraser. Although she continued to accept the gentleman's invitations, she did so with little joy. Something was troubling the girl, but Lady Wheatley knew better than to press her.

"Turn around, my dear." Lady Wheatley's voice broke through Emma's reverie. "Let me see how you look."

This afternoon Emma was wearing a new costume from Mme Fournier, the mantua maker on Market Street. The heavy wool gown of mazarine blue with a matching pelisse was fastened with snow white silk frogs. The collar and cuffs were trimmed with white fur.

"'Tis lovely, my dear. That shade of blue is perfect against your skin."

"Yes," Emma agreed without much enthusiasm. She reached for the hat that had been designed especially for the outfit. It was of blue velvet, lined with white satin and edged with blue bows. She set it upon her head, adjusted the velvet ribands beneath her chin, and then patted back several glossy curls. "Are you certain you won't come?"

"Don't even suggest such a thing!" Lady Wheatley tossed her hands in the air. "Can't imagine myself sliding about on frozen water anymore than I can picture elephants crossing the Alps. Though history swears it was true. No, I shall stay home by the fire with a warm cup of chocolate and attend to my needlework while you and your friends have a glorious afternoon. Now run along. Your uncle has been waiting this past quarter hour."

Grabbing an enormous rabbit muff, Emma went to join Torquil, who had, indeed, been waiting for the better part of fifteen minutes.

"Ready?" he asked, impatience lacing his question. He was fully dressed for the out-of-doors, a beaver hat upon his head and a high-collared cloak about his shoulders. In one hand he carried two pairs of skates. In the other was a foil-wrapped package. He eyed his niece's new outfit. "Never known you to spend so much time dressing as you do these days," he remarked. Then regarding the harassed lines sprouting upon Emma's brow, he added, "But 'tis well worth it. You look decidedly smart."

Uncle Torquil's remark was not in the least bit appreciated. It was far too perceptive; Emma did not like to be reminded that she had spent two hours readying herself for an engagement with Jeremy Wister. But in spite of her troublesome emotions, Emma could not help laughing as her dear uncle directed a most consolatory gaze upon her. Giggling, she retorted, "And you, sir, have just redeemed yourself from a scathing setdown for being so meddlesome."

Outside, a sleigh was waiting to take them to Summer Cottage. There, Melanie and Jeremy joined them for the ride to the Morris estate, Lemon Hill, where some fifteen other conveyances lined the circular drive.

The skating party was a birthday celebration in honor of the flighty Miss Ann Morris, who was, this week, concentrating her feminine wiles upon Mr. Ethan Breck. As the guests entered the mansion house they deposited their gifts on a walnut console in the entry hall, which was more like a great room than a passageway. Divided into three sections by ornate pilasters, it extended the full length of the first floor. At the front, where pretty packages were mounting up on the console, Mr. and Mrs. Morris received their guests. In the center area, where roaring fires burned in twin paneled hearths, the guests mingled about refreshment tables set with spiced cider, apple tarts, and gingerbread cookies cut in human form and decorated like skaters. And at the rear, several servants waited to assist those guests bold enough to venture out to the pond to put on their skates.

"I should like to skate, my lord." Melanie smiled at Torquil.

"So soon after that chilly ride?" he inquired solicitously.

"If I don't do it now, I shall become too comfortable and not wish to venture out atall," said Melanie, a winsome smile upon her lips.

"Isn't she the most sensible young lady in the whole of Philadelphia?" Torquil asked Jeremy, who was scowling at this interplay between the earl and his sister.

"Only the m-most sensible?" returned Melanie, her flirtatious expression changing to a feigned pout.

Jeremy's scowl blackened to thunderous proportions when Torquil replied teasingly, "Did I forget something?"

Playfully, Melanie's lips pursed. She fixed her fine features into an overly dramatic expression of displeasure.

A hearty chuckle rumbled forth from Torquil. "And, of course, the loveliest," he added.

Gazing into one another's eyes, Torquil and Melanie shared an affectionate laugh as they went to the rear of the hall.

"I should like to skate, too," Jeremy stated abruptly, taking a compelling hold of Emma's arm. "Are you game, Miss Fraser?"

"Yes, I'd love to skate," she said, casting a sideways glance at his anxious expression and wishing that he might sound a bit more enthusiastic.

A manservant laced a pair of skates to Emma's high black boots. A bit awkwardly, she stood and pulled the fur collar of her pelisse about her neck, watching as Melanie and Uncle Torquil hurried outside. In the next instant, Mr. Wister led her out the door and down the snowy path.

At the pond several couples were already gliding about the silvery surface in an orderly circle. A bonfire blazed at the end of the walkway, where two Negro boys, red woolen mufflers about their necks, were playing a rousing version of a popular folk melody on the fife and fiddle.

"Look! There's my aunt and Mr. Rittenhouse," exclaimed Melanie, and she and Emma waved hello. The older couple waved back but did not stop skating. "Hurry. Let's join them." Melanie tugged Torquil's arm, and in the next instant, they were skimming across the ice with the other skaters.

"Ready?" Jeremy asked Emma as he assumed the pose of the other gentlemen holding their partners. Easily, he hooked an arm about her waist, pulling her to his side.

She hesitated, and in a small voice, she said, "I've always wanted to learn to skate."

"Don't tell me you've never skated before, Miss Fraser. Am I to have the pleasure of introducing you to another of the pleasures of our American winters?" He spoke softly, earnestly, in a friendly tone that resonated off that sad hollow spot deep inside Emma. In that instant, he made her feel as if she were the center of the universe.

Oh, why couldn't he be like this all of the time? She sighed and smiled up at his twinkling blue eyes. "I have skated before, but only twice. During the great winter frost when the Thames froze over. I enjoyed it tremendously, but 'twas several years ago, and I fear I may have forgotten what little skill I had."

"Fear not, I shall make certain you don't fall," he replied. His arm tightened about her waist as he linked his other arm in front of them to take hold of her free arm.

"Thank you, sir," was the best she could reply. Yes, it would be heavenly, if Mr. Wister were always this pleasant and kind a gentleman. Then her love would not be an ugly, shameful secret; then it might be a wonder to be shared and nourished and savored.

"Your attention, Miss Fraser," he said, bringing her momentary flight of fantasy to a halt. Carefully, he guided them onto the ice. "The most important thing to remember is relax and bend your knees."

In rigid, little increments Emma bent her knees. "You have been skating for many years?" she asked.

"Yes. Since I was a small boy. My parents loved to skate, and we often had family skating outings. Come now, 'tis easy as one, two, three," he coached as he endeavored to move them into the flow of skaters. "Simply place your weight on one foot, glide, lift, and then repeat with the other foot."

Emma followed his instructions, but the smooth movement he described was more like a series of awkward steps when she tried to copy it.

"Not so quickly, Miss Fraser. Bend your knees and try not to be quite so stiff," he urged. After several more stilted attempts, he added conversationally, "Did you enjoy the dramatic performance, last evening?"

"Yes," she said nearly out of breath. Moving her feet in such jerky motions was exhausting business. "Mr. Sheridan's plays have always been among my favorites."

"Mine as well. You've seen *Scarborough Fair* and *School*

for Scandal?" He held her more securely as he picked up speed, forcing Emma to slide rather then step across the ice.

He made it seem so easy, and as they moved among the pink-cheeked couples, she began to loosen up. "Oh, yes. Each of them more than twice," she replied, quite forgetting that she was on skates and in Mr. Wister's arms. Excitement glimmered in her green eyes, and when she looked up at him, there was a smile of ingenuous delight upon her flushed face.

He grinned back. "Melanie tells me that she and your uncle plan to attend the equestrian performances at the Olympic Theatre, Tuesday next. Would you like to join me then?"

Silently, she nodded her assent. A pang of disappointment pierced her chest, and she looked downward, staring blindly at the silver tips of her skates. Yes, she would like to see the performance, and yes, she would like to attend with Mr. Wister. But as always his invitation was couched in terms of an outing with Melanie and Uncle Torquil, and she could not dismiss the unhappiness this caused. To yearn for this man's love was beyond the bounds of reality; that would never happen, not in a million years. But at the least, it would be nice to have his friendship in a brotherly sort of way.

Deep in thought, Emma's concentration waned, and her knees straightened. She did not see the impending disaster as she set one foot upon the toes of the other. Emitting a tiny cry of surprise, she lurched backward and then forward, but she did not fall. Quickly, Mr. Wister had both arms about her waist, holding her firmly to his chest.

They remained for a moment at the edge of the pond. Emma stood in the circle of Jeremy's arms, her back pressed to his chest, his hands clasped about her middle. She gulped back her fright at having nearly tumbled onto the ice, and she took several deep breaths to still the racing of her heart.

"You're safe," Jeremy whispered, his warm breath fanning her neck where the fur collar had folded back.

Emma shivered and closed her eyes, fighting back the

waves of delight that surged through her with each heartbeat. It was sheer bliss to be held so securely, and Emma wished that this moment might last for eternity.

Slowly, Jeremy turned the trembling girl about to face him. Firm hands remaining at her waist to steady her, he stared into her face.

"There, you see, 'tis nothing to worry about," he said softly, raising a hand to brush back a curl that had escaped the confines of her blue velvet bonnet. Her cat's-eyes were wide as saucers, dabs of high color brushed her cheeks, and delicate clouds of frozen air drifted from between a luscious pair of lips. She was, Jeremy thought, the prettiest sight he had ever seen. Odd, but he had known legions of lovely ladies, yet, at this moment, he was certain not a single one of them could ever be as enchanting as Miss Fraser. It was impossible to deny his attraction to Miss Fraser. She was sweet and enchanting, tempting and thoroughly troublesome, and the physical reactions she aroused within him were vibrant and strong. The memory of those intimate moments in the overturned carriage returned to him. Her lips were the ripest he had ever tasted, her figure the softest, and her response was bittersweet. It seemed as if he had waited an entire lifetime for that delicious and fleeting kiss. Would that he could once again capture so tender a moment with this woman. Impulsively he said:

"Y'know, Miss Fraser, I believe I must be the envy of every man in Philly."

A bewildered little frown puckered her forehead. "Sir?"

The hand that had brushed back the curl lingered by her brow. Gently, he touched her again, allowing his gloved fingers to trail down her cheek to cup her chin. " 'Tis you, Miss Fraser. You are the object of that envy, for I—and no other gentleman—have the honor to hold the most beautiful lady in all of Philadelphia within the circle of my arms."

Oh, but his words were lovely, and those tiny puffs of frozen breath escaping from Emma's parted lips came more rapidly and more frequently. Lovely words, yes, but what was the meaning of them from this man? She wanted to believe him, but a voice inside Emma warned her not to trust him. She turned her head, forcing his hand to fall away.

Unexpectedly, Jeremy experienced a rush of disappointment. "What are you frightened of, Miss Fraser?"

On a brittle laugh, she replied, "Frightened? Nay, Mr. Wister, I'm not frightened, just cautious."

"Cautious of me?" Disbelief colored his words, and if she had been looking, Emma would have seen the elusive flash of injury that crossed his handsome features.

"Why, of course."

The certainty with which she replied stunned Jeremy. Reluctantly, he admitted that she must be afraid of him. It was a dreadful proposition, but one he could not deny. How, he wondered, could this have happened? Granted, she did not approve of his attitude toward her uncle, but that did not account for personal feelings. Could it? And surely 'twas not the kiss, for how could so tender a moment upset one's sensibilities?

"Have I done something to offend you, Miss Fraser?"

"Not precisely, sir," she answered. "Your remarks are exceedingly personal, and I do not think our friendship is of a nature to warrant such intimacy. Although we are often in one another's company, your attention is seldom focused on me. Verily, you never come to call on me alone. Melanie is always with you. With us." She added candidly, "We are merely chaperons. Am I not correct?"

"You're speaking your mind again, Miss Fraser," he said by way of avoiding her question.

Emma lifted her head and stared directly at Jeremy. "Would you seek my company if it weren't for my uncle and your sister?" she inquired, her dulcet tone failing to disguise the skepticism in her singularly straightforward question.

Discomposed, the gentleman glanced across the skating pond. He was willing to admit a strong physical attraction for Miss Fraser, but he was not prepared to consider anything beyond that. "I do not suffer your company, Miss Fraser," he replied, knowing it was not really an answer.

Propelling her toward the edge of the pond, he finished, "Come, let's return to the house for some refreshment."

In the next instant, Miss Morris and her friends crushed about them. Everyone was returning to the mansion house for a round of official birthday toasts and the opening of the gifts. The crowd of young people sang several stanzas of "Afton Water"; Torquil and Melanie, and Lady Cressida and Mr. Rittenhouse appeared; and amid the laughter and merriment, Emma and Jeremy were separated for the remainder of the afternoon.

Two days later, the coastal packet *Carousel* docked at Delaware Avenue carrying a message for Jeremy and Melanie. Their parents were homeward bound from New Orleans, a mere forty-eight hours behind the *Carousel*. Tony and Amelia Wister, their youngest daughter, Augusta, and the lads Willie and Franklin, were traveling on board the brig *Sea Island*, which was scheduled to arrive on Saturday, March 14.

The eldest Wister offspring were thrilled by the imminent homecoming of their family, and preparations for a special dinner commenced posthaste. Lady Cressida, who had not seen her sister Amelia in more than a decade, was elated with the news, and she assisted Melanie with decorations for the great room at Summer Cottage.

Early on Saturday, a procession of carriages entered the city destined for the Delaware Avenue docks. Everyone—save Lady Wheatley, who lectured Emma on the disastrous effects of overexposure to the elements on one's complexion, asserting that a lady should always be vigilant against the sun and the wind, no matter the time of year—had come to meet the returning Wister parents and their youngest offspring. Melanie and Torquil, Jeremy and Emma, and Mr. Rittenhouse and Lady Cressida, who led a cheer when the *Sea Island* entered the harbor, gathered at the end of the windswept wharf. It was a joyous reunion, and even before the crew secured the brig to the dock, Willie and Franklin were shouting out reports of how many turtles and 'gators they had counted in the bayou, while Lady Cressida, in classic prattle-bag style, cupped her hands and delivered a full dispatch of the previous London Season's tattle to her sister.

Once the gangplank was finally lowered, much hugging and kissing took place, and even a few tears were shed, glistening like tiny icicles on wind-chilled cheeks. Introductions were made all around, and with cunning parental instinct, Amelia and Tony Wister were immediately aware of the affection between their daughter and the tall Scotsman. So, too, were they aware of a fully blossomed romance between Tench Rittenhouse and Lady Cressida. It was a blessing to return home and find one's family in good health and fine spirits, remarked Amelia. And it was cause for celebration all around, augmented her husband, who invited Mr. Rittenhouse, Torquil, and Emma to join the welcome-home festivities at Summer Cottage.

The evening was a most jolly occasion. Everyone was lively and talkative and eager to share the events of the recent past and to learn what others had been doing. There was much laughter and good-natured teasing, and for the first time, Emma saw what it was like to be a part of a large and loving family. Tony and Amelia Wister were so different from their eldest son; without hesitation they accepted their new neighbors into the bosom of their family. Just as there had been an instantaneous affinity between Emma and Melanie, so, too, did Emma and young Augusta discover much in common. As for Torquil, his recently awakened interest in business ventures found a common spirit in Tony Wister. The older gentleman was himself a believer in the future greatness of America. Two decades before he had gone against the wishes of his parents; he had been a pioneer in the development of the paddleboat and the opening of commerce along the Mississippi River. He saw much of himself in the earl, and after dinner the two men retired to his private study for cigars.

Oddly, the only one who did not appear to enjoy the evening was Jeremy Wister. Emma was puzzled by this. Although she knew he was a moody man, she also knew he had been looking forward to his parents' return. Yet every time she glanced his way, he was detached from the merriment about him. He brooded the whole of the evening, and by the time she and Uncle Torquil left for River Rest, he was scowling as darkly as an overtaxed judge.

In the morning, Jeremy visited his mother in her sitting room overlooking the Schuylkill. Mrs. Tony Wister, the former Lady Amelia Lytton, was seated on a chaise lounge upholstered in mauve satin, her back propped against a mound of rose-and-sapphire-flowered chintz pillows. She looked as young and beautiful as her likeness in the miniature which Melanie had painted last summer, hardly old enough to be a mother, least of all a grandmother. Her soft hair was swept upward and pinned at the crown of her head, dark curls tumbling about a graceful neck, and her blue eyes shone brightly against a flawless alabaster complexion.

As she regarded her first-born child, Amelia's gentle smile changed subtly to one of maternal concern. Oh, how she loved the tall and handsome gentleman whose high, aristocratic cheekbones and ebony hair were so like her own. And oh, how she worried about his happiness. Of all her babes, it was Jeremy about whom she fretted most. It was ridiculous, she knew, to fuss about a full-grown man, but she could not help herself. Even Melanie with her reclusive ways had never caused Amelia to worry as she did for Jeremy. Even when she had lost her fiancé, Melanie's inner strength had prevailed. Jeremy was another matter altogether. It had always seemed to Amelia that Jeremy, even as a lad, was never quite satisfied, and that he took the business of being the eldest sibling far too seriously.

"I do believe the trip to America has been good for Aunt Cressy," said Jeremy, who was seated on a carved satinwood chair, his long legs stretched out before him. "Of course, she didn't come willingly, and she did sulk for several days. But once she set eyes upon Mr. Rittenhouse, it was a whole new game."

On a little laugh, Amelia remarked, "Poor Jeremy, I can well imagine the hoops my sister had you jumping through!"

"It wasn't that dreadful," Jeremy said, bestowing an affectionate smile upon his pretty mother. With a lopsided grin, he added, "I've encountered worse antics with Augusta, who, by the by, appears to have become quite a young lady during her stay in Louisiana."

"Verily, she went from ragamuffin to ingenue overnight. Never seen such a change come over a young lady with so little parental effort. One moment, she was in the bayou catching frogs with Willie and Franklin, and the next, she was wearing pink crinolines and taking tea with the ladies."

"What happened?"

Again, Amelia laughed. "What else could it have been save love? One look at Henri Gericault, the son of the McKeans' neighbors, and it was nearly impossible to credit that Augusta was the same young lady who had masqueraded as a soldier in last year's Fourth of July celebrations." A faraway look settled upon Amelia's countenance. Her blue eyes misted, and she blinked back tears of melancholy. She sighed. "Oh, how quickly time flies. It is quite a world of changes to which your father and I have returned. Not the least of which is the miracle the earl hath wrought in your sister."

Jeremy's only response was a sullen grunt.

"You don't approve?"

"My idea of a husband for Melanie is not a man who's spent his life chasing lightskirts. Hamilton's a thoroughly improper connection, and I tried my best to thwart it."

His mother straightened on the chaise, eyes flashing with the contrary mixture of indignation and sadness. "And who put you in the position to decide for Melanie? Egad, you sound a worse stickler than your father's great-aunt Augusta!"

Never had his darling mother spoken in such scathing tones. Jeremy was speechless. His own mother was speaking to him as if he were a misguided youth.

"And don't remind me of that pledge you made to Charles Biddle," she continued. "It may have been well-intended, but enough is enough. Melanie's twenty-three, and your father and I shall rejoice in whatever happiness she finds."

Jeremy swallowed hard. "Then Hamilton has spoken to Father?"

"Indeed he has. Last evening after dinner."

"And Father gave his consent?" he inquired on a frown.

"Yes, and I agree wholeheartedly. Never have I seen your sister so radiant, and I don't doubt the earl's devotion and love for her. 'Twas always my dream to see my children as fortunately settled as your father and I, and I believe Melanie shall find such matrimonial bliss with her earl."

Still Jeremy frowned. "The matter is settled, and I suggest you withdraw. It puzzles me, though, how you might be so opposed to the uncle while courting the niece."

Instantly, the frown vanished. Sheer astonishment was reflected in the set of Jeremy's expression. "I'm not courting the niece," he blurted out in denial.

"If not, you've given a pretty good performance to the contrary."

Unsettled, he shifted his weight upon the chair. "You must have misunderstood."

"Misunderstood? Why, Melanie says you haven't left Miss Fraser's side since the Birth Night Ball, and my dear sister Cressy, forever an endless font of knowledge, reports the two of you were acquainted in London."

He ran his hand across his eyes and leaned forward. "'Tis true enough that we were introduced in England. And yes, I've often been in her company. But, Mother, 'twas never my intention to become involved with any member of the Hamilton family. You see, I was merely—"

Comprehension dawned in his mother's expression. "Oh, Jeremy, you haven't done something dreadful in your misguided intent to watch over Melanie, have you?" she asked, already knowing the dreadful truth.

He was silent. His mother knew him too well.

Amelia demanded, 'Have you ill-treated Miss Fraser in some way?"

"Pray, Mother, don't put it so bluntly! I've done nothing to dishonor her."

"That's some small relief. But you may have misled her." Her gentle voice rose an octave, and she sounded like the most rigid of matrons, lecturing a classroom of errant schoolboys. "It appears you've occupied her time. Mayhap deterred the attention of sincere beaux. No gentleman would in good conscience pay as much attention as you've done to Miss Fraser without leaving the distinctly justified impression of matrimonial intentions."

Notably more uncomfortable than before, Jeremy began to shift about in the chair again, uncrossing and recrossing his legs.

His mother would not relent. "Whether you like it or not, the girl's going to be your relation, and I suggest if you've done something you shouldn't have done, you make amends before it's too late," she stated crisply.

"There's no cause to make amends. Miss Fraser hasn't misunderstood anything," he replied in a tone as brusque as his mother's.

"And how, pray tell, do you know she has not?"

He fidgeted with the buttons of his waistcoat. "Well, I just don't think she has."

"That's not good enough, Jeremy. How do you know?"

"Well, she asked me, nay, accused me, of seeking her company merely as a means to chaperon Melanie and her uncle."

"Egad, that's dreadful, Jeremy. And what did you say?"

"I didn't reply," was his quiet and distinctly sheepish response.

"Oh, my dear, my dear," Amelia said with a sad nod. She fell silent to stare at Jeremy. Last evening, she had observed him and Miss Fraser, and she, like Cressida, had realized at a glance that a painful attraction existed between her son and the winsome Highland lass. She knew Jeremy was not perfect and suspected that for some misguided reason he had persuaded himself to deny any interest in the one lady who might give him happiness. Had his youthful folly come back to haunt him? Was her dear boy unable to see Miss Fraser without thinking of that loathsome and scheming Sophie Hingham? If that were the case, Jeremy might never find happiness. She had to do something to help him.

"If Miss Fraser asked again, what would you say? Think honestly before you speak. Have you any interest in the lady beyond using her to keep an eye upon your sister?" Amelia asked gently. "Soon you'll have no excuse to seek her company. And what will you do then? How shall you feel about that?"

Betraying emotions flooded Jeremy's face, and a wealth of submerged thoughts rose to the front of his mind. He had not considered anything beyond the present. A terrible sense of loss washed over him at the thought that Miss Fraser might return to London after Melanie was wed to her uncle. Suddenly, he was stricken with the realization that to lose her would be unbearable.

Amelia Wister watched the panoply of sentiments warring across her son's countenance. "I did not mean to wound, nor discompose you in any way, my dear. I want nothing more than your happiness."

"I know that, Mother. And though painful, your questions have done me a great service." He paused to take a breath before continuing, slowly, deliberately:

"The answer is yes. I have enjoyed Miss Fraser's company for its own sake. And though I did my best to think 'twas nothing more than mere admiration of her comely person, 'tis much more than that. 'Tis an honest respect for her forthright temperament, and her sweet and kindly nature."

Rising from the chaise, Amelia went to stand beside her son. She smiled down at him. There were tears in her eyes as she took his hands in hers. Quietly, she said, "You must tell Miss Fraser what you have just told me. You must answer her question before 'tis too late."

"As always, Mother, you're right. And at the earliest possible chance I shall tell her. I shall say, 'Yes, Miss Fraser, with or without your uncle, I would seek your company above that of all other ladies.'"

And so said, a burden of immense proportions was lifted from Jeremy's soul. He had not spoken of love or marriage, nor had he considered the implication of his words. But for the time being that did not seem important. It mattered only that he could think of Miss Fraser as herself, not someone's niece, and that in doing so he was free to enjoy her company as he liked. He was free to pursue an honorable and unhindered relationship with her... where ever it might proceed.

CHAPTER
ELEVEN

The 1818 Philadelphia social season was drawing to a close when the following announcement appeared in the *Philadelphia Gazette:*

> On Thursday, the 26th of March, a Farewell Ball will be held at the Grand Saloon of Washington Hall, honoring Mr. Quesnet, the retiring chairman of the Philadelphia Assemblies these past twenty-four years.

This final ball of the Season promised to be a spectacular event, and Amelia and Tony Wister decided it would be the perfect evening to announce the engagement of their eldest daughter, Melanie, to Torquil Hamilton, the Earl of Gairloch. Some eighty-five formal invitations, penned in gold italics on ecru-tinted stationery, were sent forth for a gala betrothal dinner to be held after the Farewell Ball for Mr. Quesnet.

No expense was to be spared, and no detail was to be overlooked, Tony Wister instructed his wife. He was immeasurably pleased that his beautiful, delicate daughter was going to marry a man as fine as Torquil Hamilton. The young lovers deserved the finest engagement party Philadelphia's first families had ever attended. Lanterns were to be suspended from the trees lining the drive to Summer Cottage, and torches would blaze at the entrance to the mansion. Inside, garlands of greenhouse flowers would deck the entrance hall, and strolling musicians would ramble between the great room, which was to be arranged for dancing, and the dining room, where banquet tables would offer an array of delicacies from pheasant and roasted venison to pyramids of fruit and marzipan. And there would be new gowns all around, he ordered to the equal delight of Amelia, Lady Cressida, Melanie, and young Augusta.

At River Rest, the excitement was only slightly less fervent. Although Lady Wheatley was secretly disappointed that this Season abroad was not to culminate in wedding plans for Emma, she was delighted by the earl's betrothal to Miss Wister. Any marriage in the household was cause for celebration, and it was a splendid match, even if the young lady was an American.

The bridegroom plunged into arranging a wedding trip for himself and Melanie. Torquil recalled the sights he had seen on the Continent and listened as numerous gentlemen at the bank described their travels to Boston and New York and through the Caribbean. And of a sudden, he was not satisfied with anything; he, too, wanted only the very best for Melanie, and no ordinary trip to Paris or Venice would suffice for his bride. No one knew what the earl was planning, but as time passed, everyone began to suspect it would be unique.

As for Emma, she was beside herself with joy at Melanie and Uncle Torquil's good fortune. She could think of no two people who more deserved the happiness they had found with one another. It was a splendiferous thing. And she marveled at the whims of fate. How odd that Uncle Torquil and Melanie, who were so right for each other, might never have met had it not been for that lamentable duel with Harry Brockton. It was nothing short of a miracle that they had come to Philadelphia and leased the estate on the river adjacent to Summer Cottage.

It was a miracle as well, the changes that had come over Jeremy Wister since the return of his parents. Overnight, the aloof gentleman, who had treated Emma with such disdain, was gone. During the ensuing week, Emma had encountered no one but the friendly and intriguing man she had first met in England. Why, he had actually come to call upon her on several occasions without his sister in tow! Twice he had taken her for a carriage ride with a stop for hot chocolate and pastries at Franklin Garden. And tonight, he was going to escort her to the Farewell Ball and the betrothal dinner at Summer Cottage.

The brotherly friendship he had shown her this past week was not perfect. It had none of the trappings of love or romance; nonetheless Emma derived a small measure of fulfillment each time Jeremy smiled at her with genuine warmth and managed to converse with her without gazing over his shoulder at Melanie and Torquil. That gnawing shame she had suffered for loving a man who did not even like her abated, and her love flourished. She had not lost her heart to a man unworthy of love; Jeremy Wister was, indeed, the kind man who had rescued her in Brickhill and who had chatted so amiably with her at Stanton Hall. And as the conviction of her heart strengthened, a new emotion blossomed within her.

Hope.

Emma had never been a romantic, nor a dreamer. Yet so much had happened since coming to America that she was beginning to think anything was possible. Why, if she and Jeremy Wister could be friends, mayhap, in time, he might come to love her. Thus Emma prepared for the Farewell Ball and betrothal dinner with the highest of hopes. If all went well, this evening would bring her one step closer to showing Jeremy Wister there could be more than friendship between them. For what better setting was there than the celebration of an engagement to bring her one step closer to a total fulfillment of her love?

A dancing frock of figured sarsnet in shimmering gold lay across Emma's bed. She rose from her dressing table and allowed the maid to help her into the exquisite gown. Facing the pier glass, Emma admired the ensemble as the maid fastened the row of tiny buttons that ran up her back. Sprigs of pistache-tinted leaves were embroidered about the narrow skirt and high bodice, and the hem and sleeves were trimmed in ribbons of bright American green cockleshells. The neckline dipped low, but not so low as to be shocking, and against her fair skin Emma wore a magnificent filigreed gold-and-emerald necklace. The thirty-six-button kid gloves were pale gold, and through her curls was threaded a gold-and-green striped ribbon.

The maid handed her a carved ivory fan with a gold wrist tassel. Emma slipped it over her hand and took one final look in the mirror before turning to leave. Feeling quite elegant, she descended the staircase, pausing abruptly on the landing at the sight of Jeremy Wister waiting in the hallway below.

The swish of Emma's crinoline underskirt caught Jeremy's attention. His glance traveled upward. "Good evening, Miss Fraser."

"Good evening, Mr. Wister," she said in a somewhat breathless voice. He was a shockingly handsome sight in a bright blue broadcloth coat edged with white satin and adorned with silver buttons. His midnight black hair and blue eyes were vibrant above a crisp neckcloth arranged in a simple fall, and below his starched white evening shirt, knee breeches of navy satin and white silk stockings accentuated the muscled length of his lean legs. He was compellingly sensual and purely masculine, she thought, restraining a sigh. Her heart skipped a beat, and with monumental effort, she managed to say, "I trust I haven't kept you waiting long."

"No. Not at all," he replied in a voice that sent tiny heat waves rippling through her arms and legs. His ink-blue eyes slowly moved from Emma's halo of soft coppery curls to the green leaves embroidered on the tips of her high-heeled slippers. Emma felt like a doe frozen within a hunter's sight as a light that could be naught but admiration shone from those inky depths. "You're more lovely than ever this evening, Miss Fraser." He hesitated over her name, drawing out the syllables until they sounded like very separate and unrelated entities. With unusual reticence, he inquired "May I call you Emma?"

"Yes," she spoke on a whisper. Her eyes widened. Her cheeks grew warm. Heavens, could it be her imagination? Or were her prayers being answered? This was the Mr. Wister she had longed for; the Mr. Wister to whom she had lost her heart. Truly, this evening was going to be different, and with renewed confidence and rekindled hope, she continued down the stairs. On the last step she paused again. Softly, she repeated, "Yes, you may call me Emma. After all, we're to be family—even Lady Wheatley would approve." This last was said with a touch of levity and the hint of a smile.

"Of that I'm sure." A grin twitched at the corner of his mouth. His eyes twinkled. "And you must call me Jeremy.'"

Intimacy laced his words, and she nodded, swallowing in disbelief at his romantic tone. Her fingers tightened about the ivory fan, and her gaze flitted over the hallway as if searching for something or someone.

Jeremy's right brow rose in counterpoint to his lopsided grin. He had never seen Emma so thoroughly discomposed, and it was impossible to resist teasing her. "What? It can't be! Is the outspoken young lady of Brickhill at a loss for words? Don't tell me you can't say my name?"

Her gaze returned to his. "Of course I can! And I shall call you Jeremy."

"Good. 'Tis how it should be." He moved to the foot of the staircase and extended his hand to her. She accepted and stepped down beside him as he lifted her gloved fingers to his lips. " 'Tis precisely as it should be, Emma." He said her name on a husky whisper, his warm breath seeping through the thin kid glove to caress her skin. Her hand trembled, and he glanced up, his blue eyes flaring and merging with her cloudy green gaze. Mysteriously, he smiled into her flushed face. This was a good beginning for a perfect night, he thought with satisfaction. Soon he was going to answer the question he had avoided at the skating pond. Soon he was going to set matters right as they should have been from the start.

For Emma, the next several hours took on the quality of a dream. Jeremy Wister had never been so attentive nor so romantic. During the Farewell Ball, his hand often strayed to hover by her waist, and there was a distinctly proprietary air about the way he reacted when any other gentlemen asked for a dance. Emma felt very truly courted and special. It was no flight of fantasy to imagine herself the center of this man's attention. It was no girlish dream to imagine it would be possible for Jeremy Wister to fall in love with her.

The Farewell Ball for Mr. Quesnet was an exclusive affair. Many of the city's senior matrons and patriarchs, who had not attended a dancing assembly since its glory days when Philadephia was the nation's capital and Anne Bingham ruled supreme over her stylish saloon, were in attendance, standing solemn sentinel about the perimeter of the ballroom. Utmost formality was the order of the evening. The receiving lines were endless, and nothing more risqué than a Virginia reel was played. Lady Wheatley, who had long bemoaned the recent loosening of high standards by Almack's patronesses, was mightily impressed with the pomp and protocol; in high alt, she proclaimed to a covey of turbaned matrons that Lady Jersey, Lady Sefton, and the Princess Esterhazy would do well to follow the strictures of Philadelphia society. Emma, however, was vastly disappointed that no waltzing was allowed. She thought the evening was downright stuffy. And when the orchestra began another minuet, she could not disguise her chagrin.

"Aren't you enjoying yourself, Emma?" Jeremy inquired as they strolled from the refreshment room toward the grand saloon.

"Oh, I am," she replied with a notable lack of sincerity.

"Then why the gloomy looks?" He paused on the threshold and faced Emma. Two long lean fingers reached out and gently tipped her chin upward. His eyes drank in the sight of her prettily flushed face.

Gazing at Jeremy, Emma swallowed hard. Was this the time to speak her mind? Should she tell him she thought the evening was not as festive as she would have liked it? Or was it better to guard her tongue? Careless speech had gotten her into trouble one too many times before, and Emma did not wish to ruin the evening.

"Well?" he prompted, a single finger moving to the corner of her mouth and stroking as if to draw her expression into a smile. "You're disappointed about something. What is it?"

There was such tenderness in his voice, such gentleness

in his touch that Emma could not dissemble. Her green eyes focused on his intense blue ones. "You see, I had hoped to waltz..." She took a deep breath and added, "*with you.*"

If Emma had made an all out declaration of affection, Jeremy's reaction to this ingenuous statement could not have been more incredulous, nor more delighted. He was enchanted by her breathless confession and beguiled by the shy hopefulness he saw in those lovely green eyes. In boyish elation, his heart beat rapidly against his chest. "And so you shall, Emma. That I promise. As soon as we return to Summer Cottage, I'll insist the orchestra play a waltz just for you. And for me," he finished on a low, intimate pitch.

This was no mere friend talking now, and Emma experienced an intoxicating rush of pleasure. Her chin tingled where his fingers rested against her skin, and she was seized by the incredible desire to feel those fingers all over her body.

Oddsbodikins! That was certainly not the sort of thing one told a gentleman under any circumstances. How could she possibly entertain such brazen notions while surrounded by the highest sticklers of Society Hill? Feeling thoroughly reckless, a giggle escaped her trembling lips as she reached out to pat his upper arm. "Thank you, sir," was all that she said aloud in a clear, gay voice. "I can hardly wait for our waltz."

The Farewell Ball concluded promptly at midnight, and forty minutes later, when the guests entered the great room at Summer Cottage, the orchestra was playing a waltz.

"May I have this dance?" Jeremy bent down and whispered into her ear.

Emma could not control the little shudder that rippled up her spine. "Yes," came her whispered assent.

He swept her into his arms. "Is this what you wanted?" he asked, easily twirling her about the room.

"Oh, yes," she said with a sigh, relishing the sensation of being held in his powerful arms and marveling at the beauty about her. Everything sparkled in silver and white with subtle accents of lilac that coincidentally matched the color of Melanie's satin gown. A fire roared in the marble hearth; the parqueted floor shone brightly beneath crystal chandeliers; the walls were lined with sconces holding flickering white tapers; and at the windows, the green brocade curtains had been replaced by figured white satin draped with garlands of white silk roses intertwined with silk anemones in pale lilac. " 'Tis all so breathtaking," she said. Wonderment laced her undesigning words, and the smile she bestowed on Jeremy was as brilliant as a chest of priceless jewels. An enchanting laugh, light as air and sweet as the tinkling of distant bells, escaped her plum-ripe lips. "Why, it makes me feel like a fairy princess."

Jeremy smiled, warm and deep and satisfied. This was his chance. He had been with her much these past days since the talk with his mother, but never had the moment been right. Now the mood was perfect. Indeed, the great room had been transformed into a dazzling world of romantic enchantment, and there could be no better time to clean the slate and start anew with this lovely lady. It was time to answer Emma's question and tell her that yes, he desired her company regardless of her uncle and Melanie. It was time to tell her that, indeed, he admired her above all other ladies and wished to be with her, know her better, mayhap spend the remainder of his life with her.

Slowly, he allowed his hand to move upward from her waist. It lingered at the nape of her neck, a single lean finger caressing a soft curl. She glanced up at him, startled by this intimate touch, high color sweeping across her cheeks. His expression was warm and sensual, and the twinkle in his blue eyes was positively beguiling. No, it was more than intimate. It was outright seductive, Emma corrected, exhaling a breath and wondering if he had entertained thoughts as shocking as her own. Did he wish to kiss her again as he had in the overturned carriage? And was it as pleasurable to touch her as it was to feel his touch?

"Emma." There was an unfamiliar edge in his voice. It was somewhat vulnerable and definitely anxious.

"Jeremy?"

"There's something I must tell you." Observing her open countenance, he was reminded of their encounter at Stanton

Hall when he had been so affected by her guileless nature. He relaxed, remembering how easy it had been to talk with her, how he had wanted to tell her about his family and share his thoughts with her as he had done with no one else. Again, he felt that she was a unique young lady in whom he could confide, and he was moved to say:

"Do you remember when we were introduced at Sir Nigel's?"

"Yes," she replied, stiffening slightly and putting a small but noticeable distance between them as they continued to circle the parqueted floor. It was an instinctive reaction. She no longer feared Jeremy Wister, nor did she harbor any ill feelings for the way he had treated her. Still, it had been an important moment in her life, filled with joy and discovery and pain. She had grown up much that evening, and every detail was as clear as if it had been only yesterday. Not realizing how much her words disclosed to him, she said:

"Of course, I remember. 'Twas a miserably stormy night, and Lady Stanhope was worried that her party was going to be ruined, and we quite put her in a pother with our ghost stories. Didn't we?" Jeremy nodded, and they laughed together at the memory. Then a faraway look descended Emma's countenance. Staring over Jeremy's shoulder, she continued, "I have a confession to make. Ever since Brickhill, I'd been hoping to meet you. So it was quite a miracle that you were there, and doubly so when you were willing to discuss bonnets to put me at ease. I was greatly impressed by your chivalry and your attention, Jeremy. Truth to say, 'twas my first real evening of flirtation with a handsome gentleman. However could a young lady forget something as important as that?" she concluded candidly.

Suddenly, the sights and sounds about him dimmed. Jeremy's every sense was focused on Emma, and tilting his head to observe her profile, he was reminded of a child who had suffered the loss of faith and innocence in a single moment. She looked brave and resolved and tragically matured. Then it struck him with the force of a deadly physical blow, and all his dreams began to evaporate in that single moment of appalling realization. *He* was the idiotic gentleman who had hurt Miss Fraser, and not only last Season in London, but repeatedly since her arrival in Philadelphia. The enormity of his ineptitude overwhelmed him; perfection had been within reach, yet before his eyes it was splintering into a thousand tiny shards and slipping through his fingers. He sensed a formidable wall rising between himself and Emma. Although he held her in his arms, he felt himself drift away from her, and he knew not what to say or do to stop it from happening.

CHAPTER
TWELVE

Emma scrutinized Jeremy. What had happened? One minute they were waltzing about the room, talking amiably and laughing and sharing reminiscences of a common past. It seemed the world was nearly perfect. But in the next instant, he had withdrawn from her. It was not, however, that callous and disdaining rejection she had experienced before. This time it was different. Verily, he looked positively stricken.

"Jeremy, what's wrong?" she asked, wondering if her cursed unschooled tongue had gotten her into trouble. Had she displeased him in some way?

Her question rang with sincerity, and Jeremy flinched. How could Emma even tolerate his presence? How could she care one jot for his well-being? After what he had done to this artless and unaffected young lady, he did not deserve the faintest smile from her pretty lips. What was he to do? Apologize? That was hardly an adequate solution. There was no way an apology could make up for months of blind cruelty.

The tempo of the music quickened, and unconsciously Jeremy drew Emma closer. The supple curves of her body pressed against his, and a piercing sense of melancholy penetrated every fiber of his being. Again, he knew precisely what Emma meant when she talked about that lonely little spot in one's soul. This beautiful and precious woman was never to be his. This moment was more than he deserved. There was an embarrassing moisture in his eyes, and he pinned his gaze on a portrait on the wall at the far side of the room.

Something horrendous was troubling Jeremy. Emma could not see his expression, but she sensed his pain in the rigid way he held his body. His right hand, as if detached from the rest of him, still stroked the back of her neck, and wanting nothing more than to comfort this man, she allowed her head to rest upon his shoulder. It was a daring, nay, shocking thing to do, but Emma could not help herself. She loved Jeremy Wister, and although she yearned for his love, she wanted his happiness above her own. Mayhap, as it had done in the overturned carriage, physical closeness might help to banish Jeremy's secret sorrow.

The lilting tune quickened again, and across the festive room, Melanie and Torquil waltzed in a perfect harmony of motion. Dressed in a lilac silk ball gown, tiny purple flowers tumbling on ribbons from a crown of black curls and four strands of pristine pearls about her milky white neck, Melanie looked like a fragile porcelain doll beside the tall and intensely masculine gentleman who loomed over her with massive shoulders and a dangerous sweep of golden brown hair.

Watching from the corridor, Lady Wheatley remarked to her cousin that verily, the betrothed couple was an idyllic sight. They seemed to move as one, so swiftly and smoothly that their feet scarcely touched the gleaming floor.

"Oh, to be young and in love! To be so carefree," enthused Mrs. Caroline Shippen, who to the mortification of Lady Wheatley concluded with a teary sniffle.

But all was not bliss, for Melanie and Torquil's thoughts were not perfect ones this evening.

Gazing into his beloved's enormous blue eyes, Torquil said, " 'Tis a shame you can't get them out of your mind.''

"You could tell?"

"Plain as the light of day. I know how much you care for your brother and for Emma, and you've been staring at them so hard you're beginning to scowl. Believe me, that little crease across your pretty brow speaks a thousand words. And if I could kiss it away, I would," he said in a husky voice, his lips moving toward the top of her head.

"Oh, you mustn't! What would my parents say?" She ducked her head and giggled as the frown vanished.

Torquil grinned with satisfaction. "I, too, care about Emma, but this is our night, my dear Mellie. You mustn't let anything or anyone spoil it. And as for your parents. Well, they would be the first to remind you not to forget that."

Emitting a tiny sigh, Melanie smiled. "How can I forget? Look at this room. 'Tis positively extravagant! If I'd known Mother and Father were going to make such a fuss, I'd have suggested we elope."

"Ah, Mellie, how could you have thought they'd ever give you anything less? We would want the same for our daughter, too, I warrant."

"You're right, of course. And 'tis what you would want for Emma as well. Am I right?"

"Yes, 'tis precisely what I'd wish for Emma." He allowed his deep-set eyes to wander across the ballroom and rest upon his niece and Jeremy Wister. They were not talking, were not even looking at one another; verily, they gave the impression of being in two separate worlds.

Observing this, Melanie experienced a renewed sting of remorse. It was not right that she should be so happy while her own brother and her dearest friend were obviously miserable. "Isn't there anything we can do, Torquil? Isn't there something you might say to my brother?"

"Once before, your brother and I had a serious talk of sorts. 'Twas under far different circumstances, but we did come round to Emma, and he's fully aware of my feelings. Don't think there's much else I might say to him, and I certainly don't wish there to be any tension between myself and Jeremy. He knows I wish only for Emma's happiness. There's nothing more I can do."

The music stopped, and couples mingled about the dance floor. Melanie visited a hopeful smile upon Torquil. "Well, then perhaps Jeremy might listen to some sisterly advice from me."

Torquil shook his head. "Mellie dearest, you're a kindhearted and gentle soul, but there are some things each of us must do for himself. Whatever problems Jeremy and Emma face, they can be solved by no one but themselves." He wrapped his arm about Melanie's waist and hugged her close to his side.

Looking up at her Fatal Earl, Melanie raised a slender hand and allowed her fingers to trace the rugged line of his jaw. "You're right, and I promise not to worry anymore. At least not tonight. I shall do naught but enjoy our special evening." Rising up on tiptoe, she whispered, "In fact, that k-kiss might be in order. D-don't you agree?"

In a voice roughened by love and desire, Torquil agreed, "Yes, 'tis in order." Whereupon he pulled her closer, tilting her chin upward to receive an ardent and all too brief kiss.

Moments later they were whisked to the orchestra dais to stand with Melanie's parents. Tony Wister's jubilant voice echoed through the room as he formally announced his daughter's betrothal, and Jeremy joined his family, being the first to lift his champagne glass in a toast to their future.

Emma stood on the fringe of this mirthful gathering and forced herself to smile. It was a horrid, selfish thing, but she felt like crying. Everyone was bubbling with joy, and Emma sincerely wished to celebrate Melanie and Uncle Torquil's good fortune, yet she could not stave off that aching, empty spot within her. Quietly, she turned and slipped into the crowd. Quickly, she fled the great room for the privacy of the ladies' retiring room.

Her departure did not go unnoticed. Jeremy watched her flight and knew that he was the cause. And as swiftly as Emma had departed, he quit the gay assemblage, retreating to the solitude of the veranda. He pulled a cheroot from his vest pocket, lit it, and proceeded to stare across the lawn toward the Schuylkill. He thought of nothing in particular as he listened to the distant gurgling of the river. The winter ice had melted, the water was flowing freely once again, and the muddy scent of thawing earth was heavy on the wind. Spring was nearing, and soon there would be buds on the trees, the rolling hills would turn a lush green, and the air would be sweetened by the fragrance of wildflowers. Jeremy had always harbored a fondness for that time of the year. There would be newly hatched songbirds chirping in their nests and gangly colts in the fields, and the world would go forward in a renewed spirit of exhilaration and hope.

All the world save himself, he thought in disgust. Angrily he threw the cheroot to the ground and crushed its glowing red ember. As the world about him turned into spring, he would stay locked in the cold of winter. And it was his own fault, for being so stupid and stubborn and blind. Jeremy shoved his hands deep in his pockets and hunched his shoulders forward in frustration.

"Nice night for a breath of fresh air," came a voice from behind him.

Spinning around, Jeremy squinted into the darkness.

Torquil stepped forward from the shadows. "I hoped I might find you out here." He was acutely aware of the other man's silent rage, and he paused several moments before he continued, "I hope you know I intend only the finest for your sister. Melanie's the one good and decent thing that's ever come into my life—except for Emma, whom I've no right to hold on to forever. You can be damned sure I'll never do anything to hurt Melanie."

Jeremy nodded his head in understanding, but he did not speak.

"And, though it may be slightly unrealistic of me, I hope we can be friends," Torquil added.

"It's possible," Jeremy said evenly.

"Good." Torquil moved a step closer. "Then as a friend, may I speak my mind?"

With a careless shrug, Jeremy replied, "Go ahead."

"You love my niece."

Following a short laugh of surprise, Jeremy glanced over his shoulder. "Is it so obvious?"

"Only to those who care deeply for the two of you, as do Melanie and I."

At mention of his darling sister, Jeremy's bitterness wavered. If Melanie trusted this gentleman, he was surely a fair-minded and wise man; his offer of friendship was surely genuine. Jeremy desperately needed to confide in someone, and so he began to explain in an exceedingly disordered manner, "I've made a royal botch of my life, and hurt Emma into the bargain as well. Though I think the world of her, I'm not the fellow for your niece. Treated her badly, and no apology will ever do. She deserves better."

"So you say, and I might even agree. But I doubt Emma would."

"What?" He swiveled and faced Torquil.

"She's leagues in love with you," the older gentleman said with certainty.

"Can't be," was Jeremy's incredulous reply.

"Whyever not? No one ever said love was sensible or logical. Plain fact is, the gel's had a soft spot in her heart for you since Brickhill. You were the fellow in Brickhill, weren't you?"

"Yes," Jeremy confirmed.

"Well, do you intend to marry my niece or not?" demanded Torquil.

Running both hands through his hair, Jeremy earnestly replied, "'Tis what I'd like, and never with more conviction than this evening. But despite what you say, I'm not quite as certain of Emma's feelings."

Torquil laughed. "Gad, Wister, there's a lot of things I may have taken you for, but a coward was never one of them. Don't tell me you're going to let a little uncertainty stand in your way."

Unable to help himself, Jeremy grinned. "No, don't suppose I can do that. Though this love business is a strange thing. Could make a coward out of the strongest man."

"Aye, but not you. Not the man my Emma has chosen." And as Jeremy's grin deepened, Torquil added, "Might I suggest you walk home with her tonight. Unchaperoned."

"You would allow that?"

" 'Twould be the perfect time to have a quiet word with her and explain yourself."

"Yes, indeed. It would. A fine opportunity, sir, and you can rest assured I'll do nothing to compromise your niece." He reached out and grasped Torquil's hand, shaking it firmly within his own. "Welcome to the family, Hamilton. And thank you."

Jeremy wasted no time in finding Emma. She was seated in a window embrasure chatting with Augusta, and as he approached she visited a wary look upon him. Reminding himself that he was no coward, Jeremy executed a courtly bow and smiled. Emma nodded, her emotions carefully cloaked beneath an impassive expression. Augusta, sensing with a newly found womanly wisdom that she was *de trop*, excused herself, leaving Jeremy and Emma alone in the window embrasure.

"I hope you'll accept my apologies, Miss Fraser. Emma." He said her name as if for the first time, as if he had no right to do so. "I should not have disappeared after our waltz and left you to fend for yourself."

" 'Twas of no account. Mr. Rittenhouse danced a set with me, and Mr. Breck escorted me to the dining room," she said in a steady voice devoid of any betraying emotion.

"But you're wrong," he rejoined, wishing that she did not seem so implacable. His smile wobbled as he went on, " 'Twas a most ungentlemanly thing to do, and no lady, least of all one as fine as yourself, deserves such shabby treatment."

This statement produced the first crack in her impassive expression. Her eyes widened in pleasant surprise and then narrowed with suspicion. In a less collected voice, she stated, "Your apology is accepted, sir."

Jeremy exhaled an audible sigh of relief. His gaze wandered over the room. " 'Tis getting late. Some of the guests are leaving."

"Yes," she mumbled halfheartedly. Oh, how she loathed such insignificant and purposeless small talk. She fidgeted with the golden cord of her ivory fan. Was this what they had come to? Was there nothing more to be said between her and Jeremy except inane remarks about the passage of time?

He coughed into his fist, and Emma's glance darted upward. He started over, "What I'm really trying to say is that should you wish an escort home, I should be pleased to walk you to River Rest." Emma stopped fidgeting with the fan, and her mouth opened, forming a dainty little *O* when Jeremy amended, "What I mean is: May I see you home?"

Emma hesitated. She would love to walk home with Jeremy. But should she trust him? She did not wish to continually be bounced about like a ball by his erratic behavior. But how could she ever hope for a happy ending, if she did not take risks? Was this apology truly destined to put them on a steadfast course?

If she refused, she would never know the answers to any of those questions, and Emma could think of few worse things than being consumed by regret. It would be horrible to look back on this evening and always wish she had made a different choice. This could be her final opportunity to follow her heart's lead, and what a miserable person she would be, if she did not do everything in her power to make her dreams come true. She had been determined that tonight would bring her nearer to Jeremy Wister, and as she still cherished that wish, there was only one course.

"Yes, Jeremy." She paused only an instant before continuing, "I would like it very much."

He responded with a broad grin and excused himself to retrieve Emma's wrap. Moments later he returned, and without either of them giving a thought to making a proper farewell, they slipped out the door and headed down the wooded path toward River Rest.

It was a beautiful night, and for several minutes neither Jeremy nor Emma said a word as they strolled through the woods. Their way between the trees was illuminated by streaks of moonlight. Silently, they walked upon a bed of pine needles, their footsteps muted by the soft ground cover. The scent of pine clung to the air. And somewhere in a tree high above, an owl sounded its melancholy call.

Emma was the first to speak. "Your American spring shall soon be upon us," was all she said, fearing that anything more personal might shatter the peaceful mood that had settled over them.

"Yes," Jeremy replied, equally uncertain of himself and how to proceed. "In April, the crocus and daffodil will be the first flowers to appear at the edge of the lawn."

"Springtime comes later in the Highlands," she remarked. Her voice drifted away on the wind, and they fell into silence once more.

The mansion house was within sight when Jeremy dared to inquire, "And what are your plans? After the wedding, I mean."

She faltered, "I hadn't really thought that far ahead. Lady Wheatley longs for London, and I'm certain she'll be sailing shortly after Melanie and Uncle Torquil leave on their wedding trip."

Slowing her pace until she came to a halt, Emma paused at the end of the pebbled walk to stare at the stately house. The curtains were closed, and the only light came from twin lanterns flickering on either side of the front door. It looked so empty, so lonely, that of a sudden, Emma was overwhelmed by a sense of foreboding. Soon the house would be empty. Soon she would be the only one at River Rest. Oh, how she would miss her late-night visits with Uncle Torquil. Why, she would even miss her pianoforte lessons with Lady Wheatley. Verily, it would be the first time since her mama and papa had died that Emma would be alone. Involuntarily, she took a tiny step backward. She did not want to go into the house. Not now. She did not want to confront that inevitable loneliness any sooner than was necessary.

"Emma?" Jeremy said her name softly, and her sad eyes met his concerned ones.

Impetuously, she cried, "Please don't go!" In the next instant, she gasped, her right hand flying upward as if to catch those all-revealing and hastily spoken words.

Beside her, Jeremy sensed her sorrow and her mortification as if they were his own. He was certain the prospect of being on her own was frightening, and he was equally certain that that tiny desolate spot was rearing its gloomy head. Gently, he reached out, took hold of her right hand and lowered it, his fingers tightening about hers in an effort to communicate his care and understanding. There was compassion in his fervent gaze. In a somewhat ragged voice, he said: "Don't, Emma. Don't worry, and don't regret a word you've said. Your honesty is a beautiful thing. It is what attracted me to you in the first place. It's what sets you apart, and you should never change," he murmured in a low timbre that was more a caress than a statement.

Heat rose in Emma's cheeks, and her lips parted slightly, trembling with the renewal of hope. His words were as precious as gold. They were all that she could have wished to make this evening perfect, yet a stilted, "Thank you," was the best she could manage. She stared in befuddlement, for Jeremy did not look as encouraging as his words had sounded. His expression was unaccountably grave as he looked from her face to her hand grasped within his own and then to her face once more. Awkwardly, he shifted his weight from one foot to the other, and in response, Emma held her breath. Something momentous was about to transpire, and she could only hope that it would take her another step closer to her dreams.

Jeremy's gaze wandered from Emma's face to roam over the barren garden about them. This was not precisely the setting he would have chosen to make a proposal of marriage, but instinct told him the time was right. There was no better time than the present to set matters between himself and Emma on their proper course. If he did not speak now, he would, indeed, be a coward of the lowest order.

"Emma, you've been plain with me, and now it's my turn to be so with you." His rasped comment broke the silence.

Unable to stave off the tightness in her throat, Emma merely nodded.

"There's no denying that on more than one occasion I've been neither fair nor generous toward you, and I've no excuse for such odious behavior. I was wrong to judge you because of my narrow opinion of your uncle, and I was wrong to think I should meddle in Melanie's affairs. I should have been confident that my sister would choose only a man who would honor her."

Emma opened her mouth as if to reply, but Jeremy raised a finger to her lips. His eyes locked to hers, he continued solemnly, "No, let me finish. I've learned much from you, Emma. Most of all, you've made me reckon with that lonely ache that dwells within each of us. You made me acknowledge that I'm as human as any other man, and you made me reckon with the truth that only you can erase that ache within me."

Abruptly, he fell silent, wondering in desperation if he had said too much. In an effort to determine Emma's reaction, he squinted through the dim light and was rewarded by the sight of a smile turning up at the edges of her mouth. In turn, he smiled a little, and when he began to speak, it was Emma who raised her hand to silence him.

Sweetly, clearly, her soft voice rang through the woods, "And I, sir, have felt the same for you."

"Oh, Emma," Jeremy said on whisper, his heart swelling with joy. "You don't know how happy that makes me." And before she might protest, he slipped an arm about her waist and drew her to him, stopping only when a mere inch separated them.

The heat of Jeremy's body cloaked Emma, and the velvety touch of his breath fanned her forehead. Her heart contracted as it had done that day in Brickhill, and her body began to tingle all over as her cheek had done earlier beneath the touch of his fingers. A strange tremor pulsed through her, and feeling excessively dizzy, she dropped her head backward. It was then that Jeremy's lips touched hers. For an instant, her eyes widened in surprise, then they closed as she lost herself in a storm of unexplored and provocative sensations.

That first tentative kiss fused into another and then

another. Jeremy threaded his hands through Emma's silky curls, cradling her head as his lips tasted and teased and pleased hers. She was swirling in an endless chasm of delight, and she responded to his touch, melting into the hard planes of his chest and thighs. It was positively intoxicating, and at that precise moment when Emma thought that she would do anything for Jeremy Wister their kiss ended.

It was not a harsh ending, merely disappointing. Jeremy simply lifted his mouth from Emma's.

For several moments, he continued to hold her, one hand pushing a coppery curl behind her ear. Emma glanced upward. Moonlight washed the masculine planes of his face revealing unfettered wonderment, and she let out a sigh.

Jeremy drew a shallow breath. "There's only one ending for this, y'know. I cannot allow that empty spot to dwell within your heart any more than I can allow it to plague mine."

"And how, sir, do you propose to accomplish that?"

His hand trembled as he cupped her face and before he lost his courage, he blurted out, "Will you marry me, Emma? Pray, tell me there's nothing to keep us apart."

"I could marry you, Jeremy. But there is one tiny thing that might keep us apart," she replied softly with a touch of merriment mingled with impatience.

A quick frown crossed his brow. He studied her upturned face and seeing naught but affection and bliss reflecting from her green cat's-eyes, he finally understood. And confident of the future, he threw back his head, allowing a full laugh to rumble forth from deep inside his chest. "Oh, forgive me once more. Yes, of course, I love you, my dear Emma. You're a lady of special value, and I love you more than heaven and earth and the stars. Will you be my wife? To love, honor, and cherish all the days of my life?" His lustily proclaimed proposal resounded through the woods.

"Yes," she replied on a laugh of equal delight. "Yes, I'll marry you, for there's nothing more I could wish than to be wife to the man I love."

To Jeremy's surprise and elation, Emma wove her fingers

through the hair at the back of his head, and standing on tiptoe, she brought her lips upward to meet his in a sweetly tentative kiss. Lightly, he returned her kiss, feathering his lips across hers, yet forcing himself to maintain a respectful control over his passions. "Good night, Emma," he rasped on a tender smile. Although he did not wish to leave, he knew that it was long past the time to depart. They had traveled far this evening, and Jeremy did not wish to compromise Emma in any way, nor did he wish to take anything from her that he had no right to enjoy. At least not yet, not until she was his lawfully wedded wife.

He dropped a final kiss to her brow. "Sweet dreams until tomorrow."

Where once only emptiness had reigned, a steadily burning flame of hope had taken root. He had found the one woman who could be his friend and partner and lover, and with a jaunty step, he turned toward Summer Cottage.

"Good night," Emma called after him. A brilliant smile sparkled from the depths of her eyes. It had not been a mistake to follow her heart. Tonight was everything she had dreamed it might be. And much much more. She was going to marry her American. She was going to be Mrs. Jeremy Wister, and together, they would banish that lonely little ache for all time.

L'ENVOI

Christmas Eve, 1818
Emma and Jeremy sat side by side on the plush maroon velvet carriage seat. They were bundled up against the cold, yet each had removed one glove and their bare hands were firmly entwined. Emma's head rested against Jeremy's shoulder as they stared out the window at the passing Pennsylvania countryside.

A new snow had fallen earlier that day, and the Wister carriage was the first vehicle to cut tracks through the drifts north of the metropolis. It was dusk. Light was fading quickly from the December sky, and less stout citizens would not have ventured forth under such conditions. But Mr. and Mrs. Jeremy Wister were determined to reach Summer Cottage by sunset. Following their July wedding at Christ Church, Jeremy had taken his bride to live in the quaint town house on Walnut Street, where his own father had taken his English wife twenty-five years before. They were well used to the ride from Walnut Street to Summer Cottage and River Rest, and they had traveled this same road in all manner of foul weather. Certainly a little bit of snow was not going to stop them.

Unfortunately, they had barely reached the turn for Mr. Morris's Lemon Hill when the carriage jolted to a halt.

"Oh, no!" exclaimed Emma, sitting up. "We can't be stuck. What will your mother say? She's counting on all of us being there."

Everyone was gathering at Summer Cottage. Melanie and Torquil, who had been in residence at River Rest since returning from their wedding trip to Torquil's castle in the Highlands, would, of course, be there; Louisa Catharine, her husband, and their children had come from Washington; and even Lady Cressida, who had triumphed in becoming Mrs. Tench Rittenhouse, would be in attendance with her husband. Amelia had planned a festive dinner to be followed by carols and the exchange of Christmas gifts. Torquil and Willie and Franklin had chopped an enormous evergreen, which the lads asserted touched the ten-foot ceiling in the great room, and tonight, the entire Wister clan would decorate the tree with silver flutes and tin soldiers and bright red apples.

Emma did not want to miss any of this. "Oh, Jeremy," she fretted. "Can't you do something?"

"What seems to be the trouble, Jamieson?" he called out the window to the coachman.

"Deep drift ahead, sir. But not to worry. You and the missus sit tight. I'll shovel a path through in no time." He jumped off the driver's box, his sudden movement making the carriage rock on its springs.

In the dim light, Jeremy turned and bestowed a roguish smile upon his fidgety wife. All too composed, he stretched out his legs and relaxed against the velvet squabs.

"Well, here we are again," he drawled in that low voice Emma so loved.

"Again?"

His smile turned positively sinful. "I seem to remember being stranded with a beautiful woman in the snow once before." He paused and rubbed his chin. A devilish light shone from his blue eyes. "Now as I recall, she knew how to pass the time in a most pleasurable fashion, and she wasn't even my wife."

"Oooh! Yes, she was!" squealed Emma as he turned and leaned toward her with provocative deliberateness. "I mean, she is your wife!" she whispered in the tiny space that separated their lips.

Her next words were lost as Jeremy's mouth brushed across hers. No longer innocent, she knew the pleasures a man and woman could share, and she had discovered, much to her husband's delight, that she possessed a positively wanton nature. Instinctively, she moved closer to Jeremy; she snuggled in the depths of his arms, and tilting her head, she offered her lips to his.

It was a long and passionate kiss that left both Jeremy and Emma breathless and trembling. The interior of the carriage was nearly dark, but not so dark to cloak the high color in Emma's cheeks and the rapid rise and fall of her chest.

"We mustn't," she whispered. "What would Jamieson think?"

Jeremy laughed. "That I love my wife very much, and that I'm a wise man to keep her happy."

"Indeed you do." Looking for all the world like a cat with a bowl of fresh cream, Emma bestowed an utterly beguiling smile upon her husband. "But isn't there another, more proper, way we might spend our time?"

Reluctantly, he replied, "If you insist." Reaching across the narrow aisle, he pulled a brightly wrapped package from the top of a mound of gifts. "Would you like to open this?" he asked, knowing full well that Emma could never say no to such an offer. He had discovered that Emma had a penchant for gifts, and Jeremy delighted in showering her with trinkets at the slightest excuse. On the first-week commemoration of their nuptials, there had been a miniature edition of Lord Byron's works; to celebrate the second week, it was a delicate mother-of-pearl hair comb from China; on the third week, an elegant drawing book of flowers and a press for collecting her own specimens; and so on, for Jeremy never ceased to savor his pretty wife's thrill in these surprises.

As anticipated, Emma straightened bolt upright with excitement as Jeremy sat the large box upon her lap. She lost no time in untying the red ribbons, removing the top, and folding back the layers of tissue paper to reveal a wide-brimmed bonnet of vibrant blue silk. Carefully, Emma pulled the bonnet from the box and once freed, a panache of silver-and-blue Zebra feathers bobbed atop the bonnet.

"You remember!" she said in a hushed voice, tears shimmering in her eyes.

"How could I ever forget the thoroughly enticing sight of you frolicking in Mme de Rigny's shop window?"

Emma blushed. She adored it when her husband spoke of their initial encounters. It made her heart beat with the speed of tiny hummingbird wings to know that he, too, had thought of them as highly romantic.

"Come now," he urged, taking the bonnet from her hands and pushing back her cloak. "You must try it on."

"But what will Uncle Torquil say when he sees me in such a daring bonnet?" she quipped, helping Jeremy to set it atop her curls.

"He'll say that you have a husband who spoils you wickedly," came his reply in a husky, caressing timbre as he dipped his head beneath the brim of the bonnet to kiss his wife.

Neither occupant of the carriage heard Jamieson call, "The way is clear now." Nor were they aware of the rocking of the vehicle as it resumed its journey toward

Summer Cottage. Only when it pulled to a stop and a flood of clamorous Wisters streamed from the mansion did Emma and Jeremy realize they had arrived at their destination.

Exchanging flushed, sheepish looks, they straightened their wraps and turned toward the door as it burst open and Torquil popped his head inside.

"'Gad, Wister," he declared at the sight of Emma, her eyes clouded with passion and the vibrant blue bonnet upon her head, "You're spoiling the girl rotten!"

To which, Emma and Jeremy burst into peals of laughter as they exited the carriage and joined the merry throng in the drive.

"Merry Christmas," yelled one of the lads.

"Merry Christmas," Tony Wister boomed in reply. He stood on the top step, an arm wrapped around his wife's shoulder as they both smiled with pride and affection upon the blessed sight before them. All their babes were happy and healthy, and their dream was a reality; love was the foundation of marriage for their children as it had been for them, and matrimonial bliss was to continue in yet another generation of Philadelphia Wisters.

Regency Romances

IN FOR A PENNY
by Margaret Westhaven
(D34-733, $2.95, U.S.A.) (D34-734, $3.95, Canada)

A tomboy heiress suspects her handsome suitor may be a fortune hunter, until he proves his love is not just for money.

THE MERRY CHASE
by Judith Nelson
(D32-801, $2.50, U.S.A.) (D32-802, $3.25, Canada)

A spirited young woman becomes embroiled in complications with her irascible neighbor and his titled friend.

DIVIDED LOYALTY
by Jean Paxton
(D34-915, $2.95, U.S.A.) (D34-916, $3.95, Canada)

Lady Judith Hallowell arrives in America and is swept up in the social whirl of the area—and into a rocky romance with an unpredictable young man.

Warner Books P.O. Box 690
New York, NY 10019

Please send me the books I have checked. I enclose a check or money order (not cash), plus 95¢ per order and 95¢ per copy to cover postage and handling.* (Allow 4-6 weeks for delivery.)

___Please send me your free mail order catalog. (If ordering only the catalog, include a large self-addressed, stamped envelope.)

Name_____

Address_____

City_____ State_____ Zip_____

*New York and California residents add applicable sales tax.

Regency Romances

___PHILADELPHIA FOLLY
by Nancy Richards-Akers
(D34-893, $2.95, U.S.A.) (D34-894, $3.95, Canada)
A beautiful and titled British aristocrat with a penchant for social pranks finds romance and adventure in Philadelphia.

___TEMPORARY WIFE
by Samantha Holder
(D34-994, $3.95, U.S.A.) (D34-995, $3.95, Canada)
A wealthy and independent-minded young lady and a young lord engage in a marriage of convenience, until it becomes a tangled affair of the heart.

___GENTLEMAN'S TRADE
by Holly Newman
(D34-913, $2.95, U.S.A.) (D34-914, $3.95, Canada)
A sparkling story featuring a New Orleans belle caught up in a contest of wills with a dashing English nobleman.

**Warner Books P.O. Box 690
New York, NY 10019**

Please send me the books I have checked. I enclose a check or money order (not cash), plus 95¢ per order and 95¢ per copy to cover postage and handling.* (Allow 4-6 weeks for delivery.)

___Please send me your free mail order catalog. (If ordering only the catalog, include a large self-addressed, stamped envelope.)

Name _____

Address _____

City _____ State _____ Zip _____

*New York and California residents add applicable sales tax.

DON'T MISS WARNER'S EXCITING REGENCY ROMANCES

__ **A DUET FOR MY LADY** by *Marjorie DeBoer*
(D34-458, $2.95, U.S.A.) (D34-459, $3.95, Canada)
Stephanie Endicott defies convention by insisting on marrying for love and falls hopelessly in love with a dashing journalist, while the wealthy peer her mother favors holds no interest for her.

__ **THE ELUSIVE COUNTESS** by *Elizabeth Barron*
(D34-607, $2.95, U.S.A.) (D34-608, $3.95, Canada)
Lady Rosaline Fleming escapes from her villainous cousin and is rescued by a handsome stranger. But fear of her cousin drives her to join a traveling troupe of actors where she once again encounters her rescuer and discovers that she feels more than gratitude towards him.

__ **LOVE'S GAMBIT** by *Emma Harrington*
(D34-891, $2.95, U.S.A.) (D34-892, $3.95, Canada)
The story of Jessamy Montgomery, a determined English beauty who promises her hand to the one man who can beat her in a game of chess—and finds the finish is a surprise victory for love.

__ **HONOR'S PLAYERS** by *Holly Newman*
(D34-731, $2.95, U.S.A.) (D34-732, $3.95, Canada)
Lady Elizabeth Monweithe has earned herself a "reputation" with her biting tongue and poor manners. But when her fiery spirit is captured and she becomes a reluctant bride, she finds that her spouse has a curious plan to tame her.

**Warner Books P.O. Box 690
New York, NY 10019**

Please send me the books I have checked. I enclose a check or money order (not cash), plus 95¢ per order and 95¢ per copy to cover postage and handling.* (Allow 4-6 weeks for delivery.)

__ Please send me your free mail order catalog. (If ordering only the catalog, include a large self-addressed, stamped envelope.)

Name _____

Address _____

City _____ State _____ Zip _____

*New York and California residents add applicable sales tax.

304